Saratoga

by Brian Macdonald
illustrations by
Brenda Macdonald

Saratoga
Publisher Name/Publisher Logo: Brian Macdonald

Published by Brian Macdonald, Londonderry, NH 03053
Copyright ©2018 Brian Macdonald
All rights reserved.

No part of this publication may be reproduced, stored in a retrieval system, or transmitted in any form or by any means, electronic, mechanical, photocopying, recording, scanning, or otherwise, except as permitted under Section 107 or 108 of the 1976 United States Copyright Act, without the prior written permission of the Publisher. Requests to the Publisher for permission should be addressed to Permissions Department, Brian Macdonald, briankmacdonald09@gmail.com

Limit of Liability/Disclaimer of Warranty: While the publisher and author have used their best efforts in preparing this book, they make no representations or warranties with respect to the accuracy or completeness of the contents of this book and specifically disclaim any implied warranties of merchantability or fitness for a particular purpose. No warranty may be created or extended by sales representatives or written sales materials. The advice and strategies contained herein may not be suitable for your situation. You should consult with a professional where appropriate. Neither the publisher nor author shall be liable for any loss of profit or any other commercial damages, including but not limited to special, incidental, consequential, or other damages.

Names, characters, businesses, places, events and incidents are either the products of the author's imagination or used in a fictitious manner. Any resemblance to actual persons, living or dead, or actual events is purely coincidental.

Book Cover Design: www.DavisCreative.com
Book Layout: Eric V. Van Der Hope | www.EricVanDerHope.com

ISBN: 978-1-7328385-1-2

Library of Congress subject headings:
1. YAF011000 YOUNG ADULT FICTION
2. YAF018000 YOUNG ADULT FICTION

Preface

Although this book is intended to be entertaining, I also wrote it with several objectives in mind. I am very frustrated by events throughout the world, but rather than letting that overwhelm me, I am trying to get people to work together for the common good of all humanity and Mother Nature as well.

We need to begin by truly following the golden rule of treating others the way you would like to be treated yourself. I believe that following the golden rule is laying the groundwork for everyone in the world to learn to live together in peace. However, I know that people looking at the "big picture" of our tumultuous world can get very discouraged. Instead of just giving up on humanity, people should look at following the golden rule as being one small step for a person, one giant leap for humanity.

Another important aspect of the golden rule is to listen to others as well. Take the time to actually listen, and give that person the opportunity to express themselves. We need to do more honest debating in today's world, and less shutting out the voice of the opposition. Following the golden rule in this regard doesn't mean you have to agree with your opponent, just allow them to express their point of view. You can't expect someone to listen to you if you if you won't listen to them. As Max Gropius said, "The human mind is like an umbrella. It functions best when open."

And as French philosopher Joseph Joubert said, "It is better to debate a question without settling it than to settle a question without debating it." And if your ideas and opinion cannot stand up to scrutiny from the other side, then it is time to change your way of thinking on that subject. Truly having an open mind means that you are willing to examine your beliefs from all sides.

Other important principles to live by are stated in the United States Constitution and its Amendments, among them freedom of religion, freedom of the press, due process, and the right to keep and bear arms. All of the principles set forth in our Declaration of Independence and Constitution created an environment that enticed people throughout the world to look up to America, and in many cases, to actually come to America to begin a new life.

Unfortunately, America has not always upheld these principles as well as it should have. There are far too many examples of this, but instead of living in the past, we should all move forward by taking that one small step of truly living by the golden rule. Think of it as a building block for the future. Each individual block, when put together with others, will help build a strong foundation for an America that lives up to its founding principles and leads by example.

And so, as Dr. Martin Luther King, Jr. said back in 1968 "Let us move on in these powerful days, these days of challenge to make America what it ought to be. We have an opportunity to make America a better nation." And, I will add, an opportunity to make the world a better place for everyone. It will be a long and arduous road, but I believe that we can do it.

Dedication

This book is dedicated to the following four people: Robert H. Kendall, my late uncle; Mike Senecal, a very good friend from my teenage years who was taken from us far too soon; Al Friedrich, another good friend taken from us too soon; and Billy Hamilton, the greatest person I have ever had the honor of knowing.

I will start with my late uncle, Robert H. Kendall. Uncle Bob enjoyed climbing Mt. Monadnock and many other mountains. He climbed whenever he could, and on each hike, he picked up the litter left behind by careless hikers who did not "Carry In, Carry Out". He also helped maintain the trails on Mt. Monadnock, and became well known and well-liked by all the Park Rangers there. His love of the outdoors helped inspire my wife and I to enjoy the outdoors and the beauty around us, and I hope this book will inspire a new generation to appreciate and care for the natural world, and humanity as well.

Next is Mike Senecal. He was an easy going, relaxed, friendly guy who knew a lot about cars. He always helped me whenever I had a problem with mine, and never charged me for his time and work. He was just a very nice person who was taken from us much too soon.

Al Friedrich was an amazing person. He was very smart, thoughtful, well spoken, inquisitive, and well prepared for whatever came his way. He enjoyed challenges, and often made his own, such as the time he expanded his barn. Instead of just adding to the barn, he cut off one end completely, moved it out a planned distance, then secured it in place and built the rest of the addition. A conversation with Al was always intriguing because he loved challenging people to be inquisitive of anything and everything.

As I stated previously, Billy Hamilton is the greatest person I have ever had the honor of knowing. He always had a smile and a "how ya doin" for everyone, no matter how bad his day may have been going. He also happened to be black, but to Billy, that was irrelevant. I'm sure that, unfortunately, he did run into prejudice at times, but if it bothered him, he never let it show. He was the epitome of following the golden rule.

On the memorial card from Billy's wake, it states "may he rest in peace". And the church where his wake was held was packed with people, with many, many more standing in line outside waiting to get in. Although I sincerely hope that he is resting in peace, why do we wait until someone passes away to say "rest in peace"? Why can't humanity learn to live together in peace? Consistently living by the golden rule of treating others the way you would like to be treated yourself is one small step in the right direction, and a great way to pay tribute to Billy.

This book is also dedicated to everyone (including my Uncle William Kendall, who was severely wounded on Iwo Jima) who fought throughout the ages for freedom, and those who are continuing the fight today. Hopefully, some day, in the not too distant future, humanity will have learned to live together in peace and freedom, and war will be a thing of the past. In this book, Sara likes to think about many things. And although it is not specifically mentioned in the book, think about this. If everyone in the world lived by the golden rule, we would be well on our way to learning to live together in peace.

So I am asking everyone to not only live by the golden rule, but to conscientiously think about it and keep that thought active in your mind at all times.

Thank you for your time and consideration.

Contents

Preface iii
Dedication v
1. Toga, Toga 9
2. Sara's Baja 23
3. The Birdbath 37
4. Camping 47
5. Pastor Stanley 83
6. Samantha 93
7. The Battle for the Bell 111
8. Mount Monadnock 119
9. The Wolf Whistle 129
10. The Birdhouse 143
11. Deer Hunting 149
12. The Debate 177
13. Shoein' 203
14. The Chickadee Family 213
15. Fried Eggplant 221
Acknowledgments 235

1. Toga, Toga

"Saratoga! You come here right now!"

Uh oh, thought Sara. *Mom doesn't call me that unless she's mad at me.* Saratoga Concord Parmenter was her full name, but everyone called her Sara. Her parents wanted to instill in her the importance of the founding principles of America, so they named her after two of the most important battles in the American Revolution. They were very well versed in the Declaration of Independence, the Constitution and the Bill of Rights, and made sure that Sara was as well.

As she walked through the back yard toward her house, Sara tried to figure out why her mother was mad. *Uh oh*, thought Sara, *maybe Mom found out I was in a fight after school today.* Sara was very proud of her name, but sometimes she got teased about it.

"Toga, Toga," someone had mockingly called her after school, and Sara did not put up with it this time. She was not afraid to fight, and the boy who had bullied her ran away after Sara hit him a few times. She had tried ignoring him, but that did not seem to be working, so Sara had decided to put an end to his bullying once and for all. Maybe he told his mother about the fight and she told Sara's mother.

Sara had been sitting in the tree stand she had built for bird watching when her mother called her. The stand was a very short walk from Sara's back yard, and overlooked a meadow surrounded by woods. A perfect place for bird watching, but Sara also liked to go there to ponder life's mysteries and other things as well. She liked to think about many things and enjoyed debating as well. Debating involves quick thinking, and Sara took pride in her ability to do that. She also liked the challenge of looking at things from a different angle on short notice that a debate provided.

When Sara got back to the house, her mother had come in from the back yard and called Sara upstairs. "You were supposed to do laundry yesterday," said her mother as she pointed to an overflowing laundry basket in Sara's bedroom.

Whew, thought Sara, glad that her mother had not heard about the fight.

"Remember, we have an agreement," said Sara's mother. "I'll buy the clothes you like, but you have to take proper care of them, and that includes doing all of your laundry."

Still thinking about the fight with the bully, Sara paused for a moment, then said, "Sorry that I didn't do laundry yesterday, but I will do it right now."

Sara was in her mid-teens, often a rebellious time for children, but she and her parents maintained good lines of communication that only rarely broke down. Sara knew that she would have to tell her parents about the fight with the bully eventually, but decided to put it off until she could think of a good way to present her side of the story. She knew they would be proud of her for standing up for herself, but disappointed that she had fought with someone.

I should tell Mom today, thought Sara, *before Dad calls tonight*. Sara's father was staying at his parents' house in Florida for a few days helping his father repair some damage from a recent storm. He called every evening just to chat, and Sara decided to make sure she told her mother about the fight before her father called that evening. She did not want to inadvertently mention it to her father without having told her mother.

After she loaded and started the washing machine, Sara went back to her bedroom. She decided to clean it up a little bit before her mother complained about how messy it was. She started by cleaning off her desk. She took everything off except for her computer.

Wow, she thought as she looked at the pile on her bed, *there's a lot of stuff here*. While sorting through everything, Sara noticed a magazine opened to an article about hiking. She made a mental note to call her friend Bob Kendall to ask when he wanted to hike Mt Monadnock. She had met him at a river cleanup recently, and had mentioned that she was interested in hiking. Bob suggested that they hike Mt Monadnock sometime, and Sara was looking forward to doing so.

"Ding-a-ling, ding-a-ling, ding-a-ling." Sara heard her mother ring the supper bell from the bottom of the stairs and said, "I'll be right there." Her mother had a set of bells, one from each state in New England, and liked to use one occasionally, instead of just having them sit on a shelf. When Sara finished putting a few things back on her desk, she went downstairs to the dining room.

"Ooohhh," said Sara, as she sniffed the aroma of sweet potato pie wafting from the kitchen.

"Supper first, young lady," admonished her mother, "and don't vacuum the pie before I have a chance to have some." She knew Sara loved her sweet potato pie, and had made it because Sara had been doing well in school lately.

"I have to stay in shape for hiking, so I'll just have one piece tonight," replied Sara. She was looking forward to hiking Mt Monadnock, and wanted to be in shape for that.

After Sara and her mother said grace, Sara decided to get it over with and tell her mother about the fight. "I have something important to discuss with you," said Sara as she put a piece of chicken on her plate. "I tried hard not to do this," said Sara, "but Erik's poking fun at me has become more than just teasing; he is bullying me and I had to put a stop to it."

"What do you mean, bullying you?" asked Sara's mother.

"Today, he kept saying 'Toga, Toga; why aren't you wearin' your Toga, Toga?" said Sara as she poured a glass of milk. "The third time he said it, I punched him a few times, and he ran away."

Sara's mother said, "I am not happy about this, and your father won't be happy about it either, but I am glad that you told me." Sara's parents had always stressed the importance of her sharing news of events, good or bad, in her life with them. They had earned Sara's trust by listening to her and discussing what had happened before deciding on what, if any, punishment was merited when she had misbehaved. As Sara got older, they even asked her what she thought her punishment should be on those rare occasions that Sara misbehaved.

Sara was not an angel, though; she loved to pull pranks on people. Occasionally, she went overboard, like the time she threw water balloons over the garage during a picnic at her house, and one of them had landed in her mother's potato salad on the picnic table in the back yard. No sweet potato pie for her on that day.

"You need to tell your father about this tonight," said Sara's mother. "What you did is understandable, but not acceptable. It does not follow the golden rule in any way shape or form. Obviously, Erik wasn't doing so either, but we need to find a non-violent way to resolve this issue." Sara's parents had taught her the importance of following the golden rule, encouraging her to ask herself "how would I feel if someone did that to me" at appropriate times.

When Sara finished her supper, she looked at the clock in the kitchen. She thought she might have a few minutes to help clean up after supper before her father called, and she wanted to think about how to tell him about the fight with Erik. Suddenly, the phone rang. Sara looked at the screen as she picked up the phone, and recognized her father's cell phone number.

Well, she thought, *I might as well get it over with*. "Hi Dad," she said.

"What's wrong?" asked her father, sensing the apprehension in her voice. She told him about how Erik had been teasing her for months about her name, and she had finally decided to stop trying to ignore him.

"I only hit him two or three times, and then he ran away," she told her father. "I did not chase after him, I was just glad that he ran away."

"Well, I am glad that you are standing up for yourself, but we have to figure out a better way to resolve problems such as this," said her father. "Let's think about it for a while, and we can discuss it again some time, preferably sooner rather than later." Then Sara and her father talked about her school work and a few other things. When they finished speaking, Sara handed the phone to her mother. She knew that her parents liked to have some private time for phone conversations, so she went up to her bedroom to start working on her homework. She worked on her geometry assignment first, because that was the hardest. She liked to get the hardest homework out of the way first, because everything else seemed easier after that.

When she finished the assignment, she double checked it because she knew it was important to do well in geometry as well as future math classes if she wanted to realize her dream of becoming an environmental engineer. The assignment had taken her a little bit longer than she thought it would, but she was confident that she had done it well. Her English class assignment was to write a one-page paper on one of five subjects that Mrs. Allard had listed on the chalkboard in her classroom. Sara decided to write about one of her family's annual camping trips.

She and her father had gone fishing, and her father had shown her how to prepare the fish they caught for cooking. She was a little bit squeamish about cleaning the fish at first, but then got used to doing it. Before cleaning the fish, they had put potatoes and corn on the cob on the coals at the side of the campfire. Her father had been doing this for years, and was an expert at timing things so everything finished cooking at about the same time. This became one of Sara's favorite meals. She would even cook this at home, in the fire pit they had in the back yard. The tricky part was keeping the flames at the correct level. Too high, the food would burn, too low, it would not cook properly.

When Sara looked at her watch, she was surprised to see that it was after ten o'clock. She had not completed her History class homework assignment, but decided to finish that in study hall the next morning. She wanted to think about how to resolve her problems with Erik before she went to bed. She thought about it for a while and decided to talk to Erik's friend Collin about it. She got along well with Collin, although she did not see him very often other than at school. She sat beside him in a couple of her classes and she sometimes spoke with him before or after class. She wasn't sure what she would say to him, but decided to worry about that later. She was tired, and just wanted to go to sleep.

Jeesh. Time to get up already sighed Sara to herself as she reached over to shut off her alarm clock. *It seems like I just went to bed.* Sara got up and got dressed, then went downstairs to help her mother get breakfast ready. It was a little bit chilly outside, so Sara decided to have a bowl of oatmeal with some maple syrup and raisins mixed in. Her mother had cooked some sausage, so Sara grabbed an apple and sliced it up. She always had an apple with her sausage. She did not know why, but it just seemed like those two foods went well together.

"Don't forget your milk," said Sara's mother.

"Oh yeah; I thought something was missing," said Sara as she grabbed a glass from the cabinet.

After breakfast, Sara checked her backpack to make sure she had everything she needed for school that day. Then she put on her windbreaker, hugged her mother, and went out to wait for the school bus. While riding the bus to school, she thought about what to say to Collin about her problem with Erik.

"Are you going to sit on the bus all day?" asked her friend Brenda as she walked by on her way to get off the bus.

"Oh, I'm lost in thought, as usual," said Sara. She was known as a thoughtful person, not one to rush into things. One of her favorite sayings was "well, if you think about it."

Sara did think about things quite a bit. Her favorite place to do that was at the tree stand she had built in the woods behind her house. Deer hunting with her father had given her the idea to build it. Her father had helped her with it, but Sara did most of the work. She wanted something a little bit more than just a tree stand, but not too fancy. She even built a small roof over it, just big enough to keep her dry in wet weather. It was like a home away from home for her, a place to contemplate the meaning of life and other things. She also loved to read books, and her tree stand gave her the opportunity to do so undisturbed. That was the first place her parents looked if they needed to find her, since she always told them if she was going out away from home.

"Apres vous, mon ami," said her friend Cheri, who had stopped in the bus aisle so that Sara could get out of her seat and get off the bus.

"Merci, etait tres gentil de votre part," said Sara. They were in the same French class in school, and liked to practice together whenever they got the chance. Cheri's family had relatives in Quebec, and Sara wanted to be like her father, who was fluent in several languages. He had taught her a little bit of Spanish, and Sara hoped that Cheri would take that class with her next year. Sara knew that environmental problems and issues can occur throughout the world and felt that being fluent in other languages would help enable her to work on environmental projects anywhere in the world. She planned on learning other languages in college because French and Spanish were the only foreign language classes offered at Lafayette High School.

Sara got off the bus and felt a brisk breeze blowing along the walkway into the school. She quickened her pace, glad that she had worn jeans today instead of a skirt. A sudden burst of wind swirled a bunch of leaves in a corner near the door into a whirlpool, reminding Sara that she had to finish her report on tornadoes before the end of the week. Tornadoes had fascinated her for a long time, ever since she saw one in the movie "The Wizard of Oz". She was glad that they were a very rare occurrence in her home town of Lafayette NH. Her grandfather had told her about one that briefly touched down in Lafayette long before Sara was born, but it had done very little damage and dissipated quickly. Blizzards were more common in New England, which pleased Sara. She liked the good workout that shoveling snow provided and enjoyed snow-shoeing in the fresh snow after a storm.

Later that day, Sara put her books down on her desk in English class, then sat down. She was glad she had a seat near the window. She liked to look out the window at the flower garden planted and maintained by students in the environmental sciences classes. They had planted a wide variety of flowers and a few trees to provide food and shelter for wildlife. Pumpkin plants were also grown, and the pumpkins were raffled off just before Halloween to raise money for the Student Activities Fund.

Every year, on the first Monday in December, the Senior Class decorated a Christmas tree that the local Lions club donated. The tree was put up at the edge of the school garden, and was left there after the decorations were taken off in January to provide additional shelter for wildlife. Sara's class had planted a new variety of blueberries her freshman year, and Sara was thinking about the blueberry pie her mother was making that day. Her daydreaming was suddenly interrupted when Mrs. Allard asked, "Sara, are you with us today?"

"Oh, yes, I'm here," said Sara sheepishly while she turned to look at the teacher. She liked Mrs. Allard, and was disappointed that she had not been paying attention in class. That was the disadvantage of sitting near the window, and Sara made a mental note to try to not let that happen again. She knew the importance of having good grades in school when it came time to apply to colleges. Mrs. Allard was not a strict disciplinarian, but Sara knew that she needed to improve her writing skills, and daydreaming about a blueberry pie would not help.

"Well, I'm glad that you are with us, Sara, and now, it's time for the hat," said Mrs. Allard.

"Oh no," groaned just about everyone in the room.

Sometimes, on the day after an essay assignment, Mrs. Allard would put everyone's name in a hat, and pull out a name. That student had to stand up in front of the class and read their essay. Generally, the students in her classes did not like to get up in front of class to read their essay, but some students, including Sara, did not mind. Because she was in the debating club, Sara was used to speaking in front of people.

After everyone had written their name on a slip of paper, Mrs. Allard collected the slips, and put them in the hat. Then she pulled one out of the hat and looked at it to see who would go first. "This one is blank," laughed Mrs. Allard, "but I know who it is." She walked over to Henri's desk and said "Nice try, wise guy." Henri had a reputation for pulling pranks, and Mrs. Allard had figured that it must have been Henri that put the blank slip of paper in the hat.

"It wasn't me. Check the hat, my name is in there," Henri protested to no avail.

"Well, either way, you're out of luck today, Henri," said Mrs. Allard as she walked to the back of the room. She always sat in the back of the room to listen to the presentations so she could make sure the student reading their paper spoke loud enough. Henri picked up his paper, and walked to the front of the room.

"The subject that I wrote about is planting a tree," said Henri. He proceeded to give a clear and concise report on how to properly plant a tree. Mrs. Allard was pleasantly surprised. She knew Henri had a reputation as the class clown, but he had done a really good job writing his paper and presenting it.

"Well done," said Mrs. Allard, making a mental note to try to think of a way to encourage Henri to do better at school. She thought he was smarter than he showed, and hated to see someone not doing as well as she thought they could.

"Ok, who's next?" said Mrs. Allard as she reached into the hat to pick out another name. "Enrique Gonzales, you're next," she announced. Enrique was an exchange student from Mexico. He was staying with the Gerhardt family, about two miles down the road from Sara's house. The Gerhardts had emigrated from Germany to America ten years ago, and wanted to give a foreign student the opportunity to experience the America that they had grown to love.

Enrique struggled a bit with his English at times, but Mrs. Allard walked a fine line between giving him special treatment because of his circumstances and treating him like any other student. Enrique got up and walked to the front of the room. This was his first time speaking in front of the class, and he was a little bit nervous. Mrs. Allard sensed this and said, "Relax, Enrique, you'll be fine."

Enrique smiled and said, "My report is on Pico de Orizaba, the highest mountain in Mexico." He went on to note that the mountain was important in pre-Hispanic cultures, such as the Aztecs and the Totonacs. During the 1600's, the Spanish had built several important roads circumventing the volcano, one of which became the main road between Mexico City and Vera Cruz, which is on the Gulf Coast. Also, there were many battles fought near the volcano throughout Mexico's struggle for independence. Enrique concluded his report by noting that the Mexican government had made the volcano and surrounding area a National Park in 1937.

When he finished reading, Enrique tentatively looked at Mrs. Allard, and she said, "That's fine Enrique, you may sit down now." He gave a short sigh of relief and went back to his seat.

Saratoga

Mrs. Allard pulled another name out of the hat and said, "Rebecca, you're up," knowing that Rebecca, or Rebby, as she was called by her friends, was a star player on the Lafayette High School softball team. She was one of the best pitchers in the state, and was getting interest from a few Division One colleges. Several college coaches had come to see her pitch, and they were very rarely disappointed with her performance. Rebby got up, walked to the front of the room, and said, "My report is on how to make lasagna."

In the back of the room, Erik leaned over toward his friend Marcus and said in a stage whisper "Figures; a fattie talkin' about food." Major mistake. Erik had forgotten that Mrs. Allard was within hearing distance of his comment. He caught the glare of her eyes as she quickly and sternly but quietly told him to "See me after class."

Mrs. Allard did not want to make a scene, so she immediately looked at Rebby, and said, "Ooh. Lasagna, one of my favorites. Let's hear it." Rebby knew that something had happened in the back of the room, but her training as a softball pitcher did not allow the distraction to bother her. She had pitched quite a few important games in front of large crowds, and was used to people trying to distract her. She read her essay and returned to her seat. Several other students got up and read their essays, then Mrs. Allard said, "All right, that's all we have time for today," as she got up and walked to the front of the class room. Then she added, "Please pass your essays to the front of each row." Mrs. Allard collected the essays and put them in a pile on her desk.

Rrrrrriiiinnnnggg!!! The bell signaled the end of class, and Erik thought about trying to hide in the crowd of students flowing out the door into the hallway, but Mrs. Allard had already spotted him. Her raised eyebrows were all he needed to see to convince him that any attempt at escape was futile. He walked over to her desk, and she said, "Come and see me after school today."

"I will," said Erik, then he walked out to the hallway to go to his next class.

After school that day, Erik returned to Mrs. Allard's room, and found her standing near the door waiting for him. He came in and she had him sit down while she shut the door. Then she sat down at her desk and said, "You know that what you said about Rebecca today was not very nice. There is no place for that in my class room. I can't control what you do and say outside of this room, but I want you to think about what you said. Remember this when someone says something mean to you."

Erik shifted nervously in his seat and said, "I was just teasing her."

"No, that is not teasing. That is bullying, and you know it," said Mrs. Allard. Then she looked at Erik without saying anything for a few moments, trying to make him think about what he had done. When Erik remained silent, Mrs. Allard said, "I am not going to give you a detention for what you said today, but only on the condition that you write a one page essay on the difference between teasing and bullying. I will give you until the end of next week to complete this assignment. If the essay is well written, you will not receive a detention. Understood?"

"Yes Mrs. Allard," said Erik.

"Alright. You may leave," said Mrs. Allard.

Mrs. Allard was surprised when Erik came up to her after class two days earlier than when his essay was due. "I just wanted to get this done and out of the way," he said as he handed her his essay.

"I will read this later on, decide what to do, and let you know tomorrow," said Mrs. Allard as she set the paper on her desk.

"Ok" said Erik as he walked away.

Mrs. Allard was going to put the essay away and read it later, then thought, *I might as well read it now and get it out of the way.* She was still upset with Erik about the incident, but vowed to read his essay with an open mind. She hoped that he had understood that what he had done was wrong, and would not do something like that again. Mrs. Allard had been fortunate enough to not have been bullied when she was a child, but one of her junior high school classmates had been bullied. She thought about this occasionally, and regretted that she had not done more to help her classmate at the time.

She read the essay and was pleasantly surprised. She did not know Erik very well, but in her opinion, he did not put as much effort as he could in to his schoolwork. He got passing grades, but she felt that he, like a few of her other students, could do better with a little bit more effort. Therefore, she was surprised by the fact that he had thoroughly researched the subject of bullying for his essay. She had some grammatical issues with the paper, but at least he had thought it out. Mrs. Allard decided to not give him a detention, but keep an eye on his actions in the future, hoping that he really did learn from this.

The following day, as he walked into his English class, Erik looked at Mrs. Allard. She quickly and quietly told him "See me after class."

Erik nodded and went to his seat. After the class was over, he pretended to be fumbling with his backpack and waited until all of the students had left the room. Then he walked up to Mrs. Allard and somewhat timidly said, "Yes or no?"

"I'm presuming you're asking about a detention, and the answer is no detention," said Mrs. Allard.

"Thank you," said Erik. "And I have no excuses for what I said that day, but writing the essay for you made me realize why I have bullied people in the past. I never really thought about it, it was just the way I was. Ironically, it made me feel better about myself and unfortunately, it gave me more social recognition than being Mr. Nice Guy. I think those are the two biggest reasons why I used to do what I did, but as my essay mentioned, there are many aspects of bullying that are only beginning to be understood."

"Sad but true in that regard," said Mrs. Allard, "but hopefully, society is coming to realize just how much of a problem bullying really is." Then Mrs. Allard added, "And speaking of problems, to prevent you from having one in your next class, I'll write you a note."

After school that day, Sara was unlocking her bicycle when Erik walked up behind her. "Hi Sara" said Erik. "Do you have a few minutes? I'd like to speak with you about something." Sara did not recognize Erik's voice and was surprised when she turned around and saw who was speaking to her.

"Sure," said Sara as she put her bike lock in her backpack.

"This is difficult for me, but I'll just have to do it," said Erik. "I'm sorry that I bullied you in the past and hope that you can forgive me for having done so. I don't want to go into the reasons but..."

Then Sara cut him off by saying, "Apology accepted Erik, and you don't need to explain anything to me. I just hope that you really have learned from this and won't bully others in the future."

"Yes, I have learned," said Erik. "Mrs. Allard recently caught me saying something mean about Rebby in English class, and I had to write an essay about bullying. Writing that essay made me realize how much of a jerk I had been to you and others. I feel really bad about it, and would like to make it up to you somehow."

"Well, as far as I'm concerned," said Sara, "if you have truly learned your lesson, then we're fine."

"Ok," said Erik, "but how about ridin' our bikes to Pete's Pizza Parlor for a couple slices of their "loaded with everything"? My treat, of course."

"Sounds good," said Sara. "I have to mow the lawn at my house today, so I'll work off a couple of slices in no time. Let's go."

They got on their bikes and rode to Pete's Pizza Parlor. "No need to lock our bikes here," said Sara. "We can just keep an eye on them from inside."

"Fine with me," said Erik as they walked in to order their pizza. "Two slices for you?" asked Erik as he looked at Sara.

"Yes, please," said Sara. "And an apple juice, if that won't break the bank."

Erik laughed and said, "It just might….no, only kidding. That'll be fine." Then he turned to clerk and said, "Four slices loaded to the gills, and an apple juice and a root beer."

A few minutes later, their order was ready. They took their food and sat down at a table where they could keep an eye on their bikes. After they sat down, Sara said, "Can you excuse me for a moment? I would like to say grace."

"Oh, sure," said Erik. "But I'd like to add something when you're done."

"Ok," said Sara. After she said grace, she paused before saying 'amen'.

During her pause, Erik added, "And please forgive me for bullying people in the past." Then they both said, "Amen."

"I am so glad to get that off my shoulders," said Erik. "I wasn't real happy doing what I used to do, but I guess you could say that I didn't know any better. In a way, that incident in Mrs. Allard's class was the best thing that ever happened to me."

"Strange how things like that happen," said Sara, "but in the meantime, my pizza's gettin' cold. Time to chow down."

"Yes ma'am," said Erik as he picked up a slice of pizza. A few minutes later, Erik said, "Hey! Somebody's tryin' to steal your bike." When Sara turned around to look out the window, Erik took her plate and started sliding it over to his side of the table.

Then Sara turned back around and said, "Wise guy. I ought to smack you around again."

Erik just laughed and said, "Please, once is enough," while he slid Sara's plate back to her.

When they finished eating their pizza, Sara said, "Well, thank you for the pizza, but I've got to get going. I promised my parents that I would mow the lawn today, and the grass ain't gettin' any shorter."

"No it's not," laughed Erik as they walked out the door. "But you're welcome for the pizza, and maybe we could do this again some time."

"Sure," said Sara as she got on her bike and started riding home.

2. Sara's Baja

FOR SALE BY THIEF
2004 Subaru Baja

That was all that Sara could read on the sign in the car window as she rode by with her friend Mike. She had gotten her driver's license a few weeks ago, and had been saving money, with help from her parents, for a long time to buy her own car. Her mother did not go out very often, so most of the time, Sara could take her mother's car if she needed to go somewhere, but Sara, like many teenagers, wanted her own car. Her first bicycle had amplified her love of independence, and owning a car would give her even greater freedom. She loved her parents, and got along well with them for the most part, but took pride in their confidence in her decision making. Her parents trusted her, and put very few restrictions on her activities.

"Did you see that sign on the Baja beside the road?" asked Sara.

"No," said Mike. "I didn't happen to notice it."

"It said for sale by thief," laughed Sara.

"Really?" asked Mike. "Creative way of getting attention, that's for sure."

"You know, a Baja could be a good car for me," said Sara. She had been researching different cars, trying to decide what kind of car she would like to buy. She had narrowed it down to about four different cars, and the Baja was near the top of the list.

"Well, we'll check it out on the way back," said Mike as he pulled into the parking lot of the parts store. He needed some spark plugs and other things for a car he was working on, and Sara had gone along for the ride. She enjoyed talking with Mike about cars and other things. He had been working on cars for years, and amazed Sara with his knowledge of everything about cars.

Sara was not really interested in working on her own car, but she did want to learn how to take care of it, especially with regard to

Saratoga

preventative maintenance. Mike had an easy going way about him, and enjoyed talking about cars with just about anyone. Sara enjoyed being with Mike, but did not realize he was growing fonder of her every time he saw her. He thought she was very pretty, even though she hardly ever wore makeup or got dressed up. He was seriously thinking about asking her out, but had not been able to muster the courage to do so.

"That will be seventy nine ninety five, please," said the clerk at the counter. Mike took his wallet out and paid the bill but had a quizzical look on his face.

"Dang," said Mike. "There was something else I was thinking of getting while I was here, but I can't remember what it is."

"That happens to me sometimes too," said Sara as she tried to remember if Mike had mentioned anything on the way to the parts store.

"Well, I practically live here, so I'll just have to get it the next time I'm here," said Mike.

"I guess we're ready then," said Sara. Then they walked out to Mike's car and headed back to his house.

"Oh yeah. Don't forget to stop at the thief's house," said Sara. "I'd like to check out that Baja." Sara liked to be different, and the Baja was definitely not a typical car. It had a sporty sedan front with a pickup truck rear. She was initially attracted by its quirky looks, but having all-wheel drive was huge for Sara. Her mother's car only had front wheel drive, and Sara preferred the extra sense of control that all-wheel drive gave her. Her father's pickup truck was a standard, and learning how to drive a standard was on Sara's to-do list.

"I wonder if anyone's home," said Mike as he pulled into the driveway where the Baja was parked.

"Well, if nobody's there, we can still take a look at the car and call them later, assuming there's a phone number on the sign," replied Sara. Mike parked his car, and they got out and started to look at the Baja. "Good" said Sara "it's an automatic."

From behind her, Sara heard "It's a great little car, but my damn arthritis won't let me drive it any more." Sara turned around and saw an elderly man with a cane coming out of the front door of the house next to the driveway. "My name's Joe, by the way," he said while gingerly walking out to the Baja.

"I'm Mike, and my friend Sara here is interested in buying your Baja," said Mike. Then he added with a smile, "Unless it's really stolen."

"Oh that," laughed Joe. "Just tryin' to get people's attention. Seems to have worked today."

Joe slowly eased himself into the driver's seat and started to pull the lever that released the hood latch. "Damn arthritis," he said as he took his fingers off of the lever and rubbed them.

"I'll get it," said Mike as he reached in and pulled the lever.

"Thanks," said Joe.

Then Mike lifted the hood up and put the prop rod in place. "Looks fairly clean here," said Mike as he gazed under the hood.

"Oh yeah," said Joe. "I figured if I took good care of her, she would take good care of me, and she did. I'd be keepin' her if it wasn't for this damn arthritis."

Mike got down and slid on his back under the front of the car and looked around. Then he got out from under the car, stood up and said, "Front looks good underneath."

"I'll start it up, and you can take a listen to it," said Joe as he turned the key in the ignition. "By the way," he added, "she's only got a hundred and ten thousand miles on her. Not bad for a 2004."

The car started and Mike was listening to the engine when Sara said, "While it's running, let's check the lights."

Mike stepped back from the front of the car and said to Sara, "I'll check the front, and you can get the rear."

Sara went to the back of the car and said, "Lights, camera, action."

Joe smiled and yelled, "Hang on; I'm slammin' on the brakes," as he stepped on the brake pedal.

"No biggie, but," said Sara, "it needs a new bulb on the right side."

The rest of the lights worked, and Joe shut the car off. When Sara started looking at the tires, Joe said, "Relatively new brakes, front and rear. I've got the paperwork from Smitty's Garage. I woulda done it myself if it wasn't for this damn arthritis."

"Tires look good," said Sara, "but does it have a spare?"

"Yep. Under the bed if you want to check it," replied Joe. "There's an access panel for it in the bed. I'll show you now so we don't forget about it." Joe eased himself out of the driver's seat and hobbled to the back of the car. They checked out the spare tire, and it was fine. "You can check the car out some more if you have the time," said Joe, "but I gotta get in the house. Must be gonna rain soon. My damn arthritis gets worse just before it rains."

Sara looked up and saw that it was starting to get very cloudy. Mike looked up at the sky too and said, "I think we can get this done before it rains, so let's go. I know Smitty, and he does a good job, so we won't have to check the brakes."

Then Mike checked the exhaust system while Sara checked the interior. "Not perfect down there," said Mike after he got out from under the car, "but it should last another two, maybe three years."

Sara finished checking the interior, and got out of the car saying, "Looks good; a little bit worn here and there, but nothing real bad."

"Ok," said Mike. "Let's take a look at the oil and other fluids." Mike showed Sara how to check the oil, transmission fluid and brake fluid, and mentioned that the color of the fluid was an important indicator of the condition of that particular system in the car. "Fluids are clean, and everything else looks pretty good," said Mike as he closed the hood. "He doesn't have a price on the sign in the window, so let's go see what he says."

They walked up to the house and knocked on the door. "What do you want now? Can't you see I'm busy sleeping," said Joe as he opened the door with a nasty look on his face that quickly changed to a sly smile. "So waddya think; ain't she a beauty?" asked Joe.

"You mean the car or Sara," countered Mike. *Oh crap*, Mike thought as he looked at Sara to get her reaction. Mike really liked Sara a lot, and did not want to mess things up in their relationship.

Sara just smiled at him, and he smiled back, then turned to Joe and said, "Pretty decent car. How much you want for it?"

Joe thought for a bit, then said, "Since it's hot and I gotta get rid of it before the cops come, I'll let it go for......No, gettin' serious now, I think nine thousand nine hundred dollars is a damn good price for a beauty like that."

Sara pulled her checkbook out of her pocketbook and said, "I'll give you an autographed basketball for it right now." Joe gave her a puzzled look and Sara said, "If I write a check for that kind of money, it'll bounce from here to the moon."

Joe winked at Mike and said, "My kinda girl."

Damn, thought Mike *she definitely is my kinda girl, but I'm too chicken to ask her out.*

Sara put her checkbook away, looked at Joe, and said, "I might be interested in giving you a deposit for the Baja, but I need to speak with Mike first."

"Help yourself," replied Joe. "I'll park this bag o' bones on the porch here, and you two can have a seat on the bench over there and hash it out." Joe pointed over to a wooden bench he had built near the edge of a meadow. He liked to sit out there and drink his morning coffee and watch the birds if his arthritis wasn't acting up.

"Ok," said Sara. "We'll be back in a few minutes." Sara and Mike walked over to the bench and sat down. "I really like the car," said Sara, "but what do you think?"

Mike thought for a minute, then replied, "Well, it seems to be in fairly good shape, nothing major wrong with it that I can see. Price seems a little bit high, but that's up to you."

"Hhmmm," sighed Sara. "I've done some research online about Bajas, and I think you're right about his asking price."

Mike stood up and said, "Well, use your debating skills and whittle down the price."

"Good point," said Sara. "I never thought of it that way, but negotiating a price is basically debating. Thanks for the tip."

Mike and Sara walked back up to the porch where Joe was waiting for them. Sara decided to just make a much lower offer, and see what Joe thought. "I'll give you seven thousand dollars for it, and not a penny more," declared Sara in a determined voice.

"Oh come on," said Joe. "This beauty is worth a lot more than that. She's in great shape, and not a lotta miles on her either."

Sara countered with "Yeah, but it's going to need an exhaust system, the interior's a bit worn, and the tires."

Joe cut her off with "Alright, alright, how about nine thousand dollars?"

Back and forth they went for about fifteen minutes before Joe said, "Ok, Ok, you wore me out. You're stealin' her from me at that price, but I'm too worn out to argue any more."

"Great," said Sara as she took her checkbook back out of her pocketbook. "I'll give you a deposit right now, and the rest of the money within two weeks."

"Oh, that's ok, you don't need to do that," said Joe. "I'll take the sign down, and if you don't come back by then, I'll just put the sign back up."

"Works for me," said Sara, and Mike nodded in agreement while making a mental note to congratulate Sara on her negotiating skills.

Joe gave Sara his phone number, and said, "Give me a call when you're ready, and I'll write up the paperwork for you."

"Thank you," said Sara as she reached out to shake Joe's hand.

"My pleasure," replied Joe as they shook hands.

"See you in two weeks," said Sara as she and Mike turned to walk back to his car.

"See you then," replied Joe as he wistfully watched them walk to Mike's car. *Oh, to be young again, and in love* thought Joe. He did not know them very well, but thought they just belonged together naturally.

After they got in his car, Mike said, "Well, I think you got a pretty good deal." Then he thought *pretty good deal for a very pretty girl.*

"Good. I was just about to ask you about that," replied Sara.

"Yes, you did very well," said Mike. "Negotiating the price of a car can be tricky, and like I said, I think you did very well."

Sara thanked him for the compliment then added, "Now I just have to talk to my parents about it. They've helped me to save for a car, but I'm just a little bit under what I need for this one."

Mike thought for a moment, then said, "Well, I can speak with them about the car, and explain that it's a great price for a very decent car if that will help you."

"Great," said Sara. "I'll let you know if I need to have you do that. Thank you very much."

"My pleasure," replied Mike.

Mike pulled into his driveway and parked next to Sara's bicycle. When they got out of his car, Mike looked up at the sky and said, "Uh oh. Looks like it's gonna rain soon. Do you want me to see if I can finagle your bike into the trunk of my car and give you a ride home?"

Sara looked at the sky and said, "Nah. Thanks for asking, but I think I can make it home ok. I better get going now though." Sara stuck out her hand to shake Mike's hand and said, "Thanks for helping me get a good deal today."

Mike shook Sara's hand and said, "My pleasure", then impulsively kissed the back of her hand before he let go.

Sara smiled at him, then got on her bike. "Au revoir," she said as she rode away.

"See ya later," replied Mike. His heart was racing as he thought about what he had just done, and Sara's reaction to it.

Interesting, thought Sara. *I've never been kissed like that before.* She mostly hung out with her friends at places like Pete's Pizza Parlor, the town athletic fields and the swimming hole at the river, but she had been on a few dates where it was just a guy and her. Only one guy had tried to kiss her on the lips, but she managed to wiggle her way out of that without too much fuss. Suddenly, a dog's loud barking brought Sara back to reality. She took a quick look in the direction of the barking and saw that the dog was in a fenced in yard. Then she felt a few rain drops, looked up at the threatening sky, and started peddling faster.

By the time Sara got home, she was a little bit wet, but not soaked. She parked her bike in the garage, and went into the house. "Just in time," said her mother. Sara looked out the window and saw that it was raining much harder now.

"Hmmm. Maybe I'll take a shower outside," said Sara. "I'll change into my bikini, grab some soap, and go out in the back yard."

"Go right ahead," dared her mother.

Sara gave it a thought and said, "Maybe next time." Then she added, "I need to speak with you about something after I take a shower."

"OK, I'll be in the living room," replied her mother.

While she was in the shower, Sara thought about what she wanted to say to her mother. She appreciated that her mother let her use her car often, but Sara really wanted a car of her own. She decided to just speak her mind, and let the chips fall where they may. She was confident that she could make a good case for purchasing the Baja, and Mike had said he would speak to her parents if need be. She finished her shower, dried off, and got dressed. *Well, here goes,* she thought as she went downstairs to the living room.

"I know that Dad needs to be in on this decision, but I just wanted to run this by you for now," said Sara.

"Hmmm. Sounds like a major decision," replied her mother as she sat up on the couch. She had been laying down, reading a book when Sara came into the room. She put the book down on the coffee table and said, "Ready when you are."

Sara sat down on a chair near the couch, and took out her cell phone. She had taken a few pictures of the Baja, hoping they would help with her sales pitch to her parents. "I found a car that I would like to buy. I have a few pictures of it, and I'll show them to you in a minute," she said as she put her cell phone down on the table.

"What kind of car is it?" asked her mother.

"It's a 2004 Subaru Baja," said Sara.

"Baja?" replied her mother with a quizzical look on her face.

"Yes. It's a great little car; sort of like a car and a pickup truck combined. It has room for four passengers, and the back compartment is set up with all kinds of options for storing my camping gear and whatever else I want to put in there." Sara opened the photo gallery on her phone, and showed her mother the pictures of the Baja.

"Well, it is a unique looking little car for a unique little girl," said her mother.

"Oh mother," replied Sara with a bit of exasperation in her voice. "I know that you want me to always be your little girl, but I am growing up. I will always, always be here for you, but I need my independence as well." *Uh oh* thought Sara, *this is not going well*.

Her mother sensed Sara's apprehension, and said, "Yes, I know dear, but it seems like you were just born yesterday, and now you're ready to fly away."

"Oh good. I think Dad's home," said Sara as she got up and looked out the window toward the driveway. "I'd like to talk to him about this as well, if he has time right now."

Her father had arrived, and soon walked into the house. Sara greeted him and let him take his coat off before she said, "Dad, Mom and I have something we need to discuss with you."

"Uh oh, what did I do now," joked her father.

"It's what you didn't do," laughed Sara. "Seriously, I just spoke with Mom about this, but if you have time right now, I'd like to add you to the mix."

"Stirred or shaken, either way, what's up?" asked her father.

"Well, I think I've found a car that I would like to buy," said Sara as she sat back down.

"Ok. Maserati, or Lamborghini?" asked her father.

"Oh. You payin' for it?" asked Sara with raised eyebrows and a smile.

"Ok, what did you really find?" replied her father.

"It's a 2004 Subaru Baja, and I have a few pictures of it to show you," said Sara while she retrieved the pictures in her cell phone.

"Looks nice," said her father.

"It is. My friend Mike and I checked it out pretty good, and he said he thinks I negotiated a very good price for it," said Sara.

"Mike Bergeron?" replied her father with a quizzical look on his face.

"No, no. Mike Bergeron doesn't know beans about cars," said Sara. "Computers, yes, cars, definitely not. My friend Mike Senecal knows all about cars. You could blindfold him, and he could still take apart and put back together any car engine in no time."

Her father looked at her mother and said, "Well, what do you think?"

"It sounds good, but how much does he want for the car?" asked her mother.

This is the part Sara was worried about. She was a little bit short of what she needed just to buy the car, and would have to figure out how to pay for the registration and insurance. New Hampshire does not require automobile insurance, but Sara did not want to take that kind of chance.

"I talked him down about three thousand dollars...well, maybe not that much, but I did get the price down quite a bit," said Sara apprehensively. Then she added, "We agreed on eight thousand dollars. I'm about a hundred dollars short of that, plus I would need to pay the registration fee and insurance."

"Did you give the guy a deposit?" asked her mother.

"No, but I told him I'll be back in two weeks to buy the car," said Sara. "He said he'll hold it for me for that long, and if I don't come back, he'll just put the "for sale" sign back up."

"Good. That gives us a little bit of time, and I think we can work something out for you," said her father as he looked at her mother.

"Yes, we can do that," replied her mother. Then she looked at Sara and said, "I'll call the insurance company Monday morning to see how much it will be to add you to our policy, and we'll go from there."

"Great!!" said Sara. "Thank you both very much."

"You're welcome," replied her parents.

Sara went up to her bedroom to call Mike and give him the news. Then she posted some pictures of the car, including one of the "For Sale by Thief" sign, on her Facebook page. Sara checked her Facebook page maybe three or four times a week, but was more interested in outdoor activities than electronic devices. She knew that her dream of becoming an environmental engineer necessitated using computers quite often, but she just did not feel the need to spend much time on social media. Mike was glad to hear the news about the Baja, and told Sara that if she had any problems with the car after she bought it, he would be glad to help her resolve them.

Monday afternoon when Sara got home from school, her mother was waiting for her in the living room. "Good news," her mother said as Sara came in the house. "It won't break the bank to add you to our insurance policy."

"Excellent," replied Sara. Then she thought for a moment and said, "I'll have to call Joe and ask him how he wants me to pay for the car. I don't want to carry that much cash, but I don't think he'll want a personal check either." Sara called Joe, and found out that he was a member of the same credit union as Sara and her parents.

She mentioned this to her mother, and her mother said, "Might as well take care of this now, if that's ok with Joe." Sara asked Joe, and he said his neighbor could drop him off at the credit union in half an hour if someone could give him a ride home. Sara asked her mother about giving Joe a ride home, and she said, "Sure, that'll give me a chance to see your new wheels."

"I miss her already, and she hasn't even left me," said Joe as he hobbled into the credit union where Sara and her mother were waiting for him. Then he added, "But I'm sure you'll take good care of her."

"I will," promised Sara. "I'll bring her to the car wash once a month, maybe more often in winter." Mike had told her that New England winters could be rough on cars, especially the salt used on the roads to melt snow and ice. He recommended washing and waxing the car once a

Saratoga

month, and making sure that the car wash facility did an undercarriage wash as well.

When the money for the car had been deposited in Joe's account, he signed the paperwork and handed it to Sara, along with the keys to the car. "Oh yeah, almost forgot this," he said as he pulled an envelope out of his back pocket. He handed Sara the envelope and said, "Sorry that it's a little bit smushed, but that's the maintenance record I kept on my little beauty. Damn this arthritis, I really don't want to sell her, but I don't have any choice."

Sara took the envelope and said, "I promise I'll take very good care of her for you, and bring her back to visit every once in a while."

Joe's face lit up with a big smile, and he said, "Please do that. No need to call, just stop in any time."

After they walked out of the building, Sara's mother brought her car to the front of the credit union so Joe wouldn't have to walk across the parking lot. Sara and Joe got in the car, and Joe told Sara's mother how to get to his house.

"There she is, your new little beauty," said Joe as Sara's mother pulled into his driveway.

"It does look nice," said Sara's mother. They got out of the car, and walked over to the Baja. Sara's mother got in, sat in the driver's seat and said, "A lot more bells and whistles than on my first car. Lots more. I was lucky to have an AM-FM radio."

"Lucky indeed," said Joe. "My first car didn't even have a radio, but I sure had a blast with it."

Sara's mother got out of the Baja and said, "Well, it was nice to meet you Joe, but we have to get going. I've got to get supper started, and Miss Procrastinator here needs to tackle Mt Laundry."

Sara rolled her eyes but smiled and said, "Thanks for airing my dirty laundry in public Mom." Doing laundry was one of the few things that Sara's mother had to nag her about. Sara didn't know why, but she just hated doing laundry.

Joe looked at Sara's mother and said, "Nice to meet you as well." Then he turned to Sara and wistfully said, "You can pick her up any time you want. I took all of my stuff out of her, and she's ready to go. You just need your plates and registration."

Sara sensed Joe's feeling of loneliness, and made a mental note to make sure she visited him occasionally. The next day after school, Mike brought her over to the Lafayette town hall and she got her car registration and license plates. Then they went to Joe's so Sara could pick up her new wheels.

Joe was sitting on his porch when Mike pulled into his driveway and parked behind the Baja. When they got out of Mike's car, Joe said, "I'd get up, but this damn arthritis has got me stuck in this chair for another hour or so. I forgot to take my medication this morning, so I took it a little while ago, and it hasn't kicked in yet."

Then Mike and Sara went up to the porch and talked to Joe for a little while. Joe had been a mechanic earlier in his life, and he enjoyed talking with someone like Mike who knew all about cars. Sara listened for the most part, trying to pick up tips she could use for taking care of her Baja. Then Joe said, "Well, you might as well put the plates on and take her away. I'm gettin' too sentimental sittin' here lookin' at her while we're talkin' shop."

Sara and Mike shook hands with Joe, and promised to come back and visit occasionally. Then they walked over to the Baja. Mike got a screwdriver out of the trunk of his car and started putting the plates on Sara's new wheels. "All set," said Mike as he stood up after attaching the front plate. Sara took the registration out of her pocket and put it in the glove box of her new wheels.

Then she gave Mike a quick hug and said, "Thanks. You've been a real sweetheart, helping me out with this."

"My pleasure," replied Mike. For a fleeting moment, Mike thought about telling Sara right then and there how he felt about her, but he decided this was not the best time or place to do so. *Some other time*, he thought, *but it better be soon, or someone else will beat me to it.*

"Get that piece of junk out of my way," said Sara to Mike with a laugh. "I've got places to go and things to do in my new wheels."

"Yes ma'am," said Mike as he put his screwdriver away. Then he waved to Joe, got in his car and drove away.

Sara walked up to the porch and said, "Thanks again, Joe, and we'll come back to see you soon."

"My pleasure," replied Joe, "and I'm lookin' forward to seein' both of you again."

Then Sara walked over to her new wheels. She got in and drove away, but kept thinking about what Joe had said about looking forward to seeing both of them again. She thought that Mike might ask her out, but she wasn't sure if he would. She had even been thinking about asking him out, but felt it would happen either way if it was meant to be. She just knew that she liked being around him, and believed that he felt the same about her.

3. The Birdbath

"Yuck! How can they drink that water?" said Sara. She was looking out the front window of her living room when she noticed some birds drinking water from a muddy puddle at the end of her driveway.

"Well, they must be very thirsty," replied her father.

Hhmmm, thought Sara, *I wonder if I could build a birdbath. I know I could buy one, but I'd rather make my own.*

Sara had a pensive look on her face, and her father couldn't resist. "Lost in thought, Miss Einstein?" he asked.

Sara smiled and said, "Yes, Miss Mitchell is thinking about how to build a birdbath."

"Ok, I'll bite," replied her father. "Who was Miss Mitchell?"

"Maria Mitchell may not have built any birdbaths, but she did discover a comet, and thanks to her work in astronomy, there is a crater on the moon named for her," said Sara.

Whenever Sara's father saw her with a pensive look on her face and asked, "Lost in thought, Miss Einstein?", Sara always replaced "Einstein" with the name of a female scientist in her reply. She knew her father was only teasing her by calling her Einstein, and he was always interested in hearing about another female scientist that his daughter had read about. Sara was a very determined girl growing into a woman and was annoyed that women scientists throughout history often did not receive the credit they deserved. Just thinking about it gave her extra motivation to become an excellent environmental engineer.

"A birdbath; that sounds like a fun project to work on," said her father. "The first thing we need to do is figure out the best place to put it."

Sara thought for a moment, then replied "Probably near the bird feeders, but not underneath them." Sara had loved nature and the outdoors ever since she was old enough to walk. When Sara was a toddler, her mother had to watch her like a hawk, or Sara was out the door, roaming around in the woods and fields behind her house.

Sara's parents had always had bird feeders in the back yard. One was filled with sunflower and safflower seeds, and another had thistle seeds. They also had an old onion mesh bag filled with suet hanging next to the other feeders. Occasionally, Sara or her father would make a special treat for the birds by carefully melting suet in a pan on the stove, then pouring the melted fat through a strainer into a meat loaf pan. While the fat was still warm, they would mix in some raisins, unsalted chopped peanuts, and shelled sunflower seeds. Then they would freeze it in the pan. When they wanted to put it out in the mesh bag for the birds, a little bit of hot water from the kitchen faucet would loosen the contents of the pan enough for it to slide out.

Sara and her father went to the back of the living room and looked out the window. "If we put it just to the right of the feeders, we can probably still see it from the kitchen as well as here," said her father.

"I'll check it and see," said Sara as she walked into the kitchen. "Perfect," said Sara as she walked back into the living room. "Mom will be happy, because she likes to watch the birds too. You've got her slavin' in the kitchen all day and…" She looked at her father and smiled, and he knew that she was just kidding around.

"Hmmm. What do we do in the winter, though," said her father.

Sara thought for a moment, then said, "Oh! My friend Nandee has to heat the water buckets for her horses to keep the water from freezing in winter. I'll ask her how she does it." She called her friend, and Nandee told her that she used a heater designed for water buckets, but it should work fine in a birdbath, as long as the water was deep enough. "We'll just make the birdbath deep in one end, and have it slope up to the other end" said Sara. "That way, smaller birds can use the shallow part, and bigger birds can go deep."

"Good idea," replied her father. "Maybe we can even get some ducks to go for a swim. Seriously, though, I think that will be fine. Different birds need different depths of water for splish splashin' around."

Sara thought for a moment, then said, "Just tryin' to figure out what to build it with. I think cement would work, but how do we get it into the shape we need?"

"Let's go down to Moison's Hardware and ask Mr. Hamilton. He'll know what to use," replied her father. Sara and her father went to the hardware store and spoke with Mr. Hamilton.

He told them that cement would be fine for a birdbath, then said, "I've got what you need to keep the water in the bath right over here," as he walked over to a stack of plastic tubs. He picked one up and said, "These actually are for mixing relatively small amounts of cement or concrete, but I'm sure it will work just fine as a birdbath. And you'll need sealer for the cement as well."

"Sealer?" asked Sara.

"Yes," replied Mr. Hamilton. "Cement is actually very porous. Sealing it will help your birdbath last a lot longer." He picked up a gallon can of sealer and said, "I recommend this one. You just brush it on with a paint brush. It actually soaks into the cement and fills all the pores within the cement substrate."

"Sold," said Sara and her father.

"By the way," Mr. Hamilton added, "you have to let the cement cure for one week before you seal it." As they walked over to the cash register, Mr. Hamilton said, "Do you have anything to mix the cement with?"

Sara looked pensively at her father, who thought for a moment then asked, "Can we use a garden hoe?"

"Sure," replied Mr. Hamilton. "Just make sure you rinse it off afterwards. If the cement dries on it, you'll never get it off. You can mix the cement in a wheel barrow, but again, make sure you rinse it out when you're done." He was just about to ring up the merchandise when he thought of one more thing. "Do you have any gloves for this?" he asked. "I recommend wearing a pair of rubber dish gloves when you smooth out the cement in the tub. You don't have to use them, but if you don't, just make sure you rinse your hands off right away."

Saratoga

Sara's father looked at Sara and said, "Ok, we'll probably just "borrow" some dish gloves from your mother."

Sara paid for the merchandise, then Mr. Hamilton said, "Ok, you can drive around to the back of the store to pick up the cement. One of the boys back there will put it in the car for you." Sara and her father took the tub and the sealer and put them in their car, then drove to the back of the hardware store.

After the cement was loaded in their car, Sara and her father headed for home. "Mr. Hamilton sure knows his stuff," said Sara.

"He certainly does, and he's a very nice person as well," replied her father. Then he added, "Unfortunately, some people are not very nice to him only because he happens to be black. As your mother and I have taught you, the color of a person's skin is not important; it is the content of their character that matters."

"Absolutely," replied Sara. She was glad that her parents believed this and had taught her accordingly. And she felt bad for anyone who was prejudiced, such as her friend Samantha. Sara had only been to Samantha's house two or three times, and it seemed clear to her that Samantha had been taught her prejudices by her father. Sara did not lecture Samantha about this, but tried to gently nudge her in a better direction whenever possible.

When they got home, Sara brought the wheel barrow and hoe over to the car. Her father helped her put the bag of cement into the wheel barrow, then said, "We'll put the sealer in the garage for now, near the paint." Sara handed the can of sealer to her father and he put the can on the garage shelf next to the paint. Then he took a new paint brush off the shelf.

"Perfect," he said. "Just what we need for our little project." He put the paint brush on top of the can of sealant and said, "Remember, Mr. Hamilton said to wait one week before we put this on the cement."

"Ok. Will do," replied Sara.

Then she put the hoe in the wheel barrow beside the cement and pushed the wheel barrow into the back yard. She put it near where they had decided to put the birdbath. Her father brought the tub out to the back yard and said, "I think we should raise the birdbath up off the ground a little bit. I'll bring out some cinder blocks. We'll put them on their side, and put the bath on top of them."

"Ok," said Sara. "While you're doing that, I'll get the water for mixing the cement." Sara read the instructions on the bag of cement, and filled a watering can with the correct amount of water. She brought the can out and set it down next to the wheel barrow. Her father brought four cinder blocks out in the gardening wagon, and Sara helped him unload them and put them in place. Then Sara put the plastic tub on top of the cinder blocks.

"Time to slice and dice," said Sara's father as he sliced open the bag of cement and dumped it into the wheel barrow. Then he said, "You pour the water and I'll mix the cement." Sara remembered that Mr. Hamilton had advised them to not add all of the water at once. More water could be added if need be, but as Mr. Hamilton said, "You can't take water out once you put it in."

Sara poured about three quarters of the water from the watering can into the wheel barrow as her father mixed the cement. "It seems a little bit dry," said Sara.

"Yep. Pour the rest of the water in, please," replied her father. Sara dumped the water in and her father kept mixing. A few minutes later, he said, "Looks good to me."

"Great," said Sara, then "Oh shoot, we forgot the shovel." Sara went to the garage to get the shovel to move the cement from the wheel barrow to the tub that would become her birdbath.

"Ready?" asked Sara when she came back with the shovel.

"Shovel away, mate," replied her father. Sara shoveled the cement into the tub and then held the tub in place while her father spread the cement around with the hoe.

Then Sara began to smooth the cement with her hands. "No gloves?" asked her father.

"Nah. This won't take long, and I'll just rinse my hands off when we rinse the tools off," replied Sara. She finished smoothing the cement, then pressed one hand in a little bit. "Just want to leave my mark," she said, then added, "How about you?"

Her father said, "Sure, why not. I helped make this, I might as well leave my mark too." He made an imprint next to Sara's, then said "Ok, let's get the tools, and our hands, rinsed off." They rinsed off the tools and their hands, then went back to the birdbath to admire their work.

"Almost done for now," said Sara's father.

Sara thought for a moment, then said, "That's right. Mr. Hamilton said we needed to cover this with a piece of plywood while it cured." Sara found a piece of plywood leaning up against the garage. It was a little bit too big, but good enough to do the job. She put a piece of two by four at one end of the birdbath before she put the plywood on to allow air to get at the cement.

After she put the plywood in place, she put a couple of good sized rocks on top of it to hold it there. One week later, she uncovered her birdbath, sealed the cement as instructed and put the plywood back in place. A few days later, after the sealant had dried, Sara said, "I think we're ready for a test drive," as she looked out the kitchen window toward her birdbath.

"Fill her up," replied her mother. "Then we'll put some fish in it, and maybe we can get a bald eagle or two to show up."

Sara rolled her eyes and said, "You've been around Dad too much. His sense of humor is rubbing off on you." Sara went out to the birdbath and took the rocks off the plywood and put them at the back edge of the yard. Then she removed the plywood and piece of two by four before she filled the birdbath with water.

"Looks great. I hope to see some visitors soon," said Sara as she walked back into the house.

"Probably a few days before we see any birds there. I remember when your father and I first put the bird feeders up here, it took three or four days before they started making reservations," replied Sara's mother. Then Sara sat down at the kitchen table with a book she had been reading, and her mother went back to washing dishes.

A few days later, Sara's father walked into the living room and said, "You've got your first visitor." Sara set her book down and went to look out the window.

"Wise guy," laughed Sara as she looked at her father.

"Couldn't resist," he replied. He had taken one of his old duck hunting decoys and put it in the birdbath.

"Oh good, that's Naomi," said Sara as she took her cell phone out of her pocket. "What's up, girlfriend? I haven't talked to you in a while," said Sara.

"Just wonderin what you're up to," replied Naomi.

"Not much. How 'bout ridin' your bike over here and checkin' out my new pool," said Sara.

"New pool? I'm on my way," said Naomi.

"See ya in a bit," said Sara.

"Pool?" said her mother incredulously.

"Couldn't resist," replied Sara.

"Oh yeah; your birdbath," said her mother with a laugh. Sara went up to her bedroom and put her new bikini on, just to completely fool her friend when she came to the door at Sara's house. Sara had made it recently along with several others that she had sewn for her mother, who had her own small sewing business. When orders started to pile up for Sara's mother, Sara helped with sewing, and was able to earn enough money to forego looking for a part time job after school.

About twenty minutes later, Naomi rang the doorbell at Sara's house. Sara opened the door and said, "Check this out," as she led Naomi out to the back yard.

"Where's the pool?" asked Naomi.

"Well, it is a wee bit small; it's over there," Sara said, pointing to her birdbath.

Naomi laughed and said, "I ought to smack you one, girl. You had me thinkin' you really did have a pool." They walked over to the birdbath, and Sara described how she and her father had built it themselves.

"Impressive, girl. Especially the hand prints. Those are really cool," said Naomi.

"Naomi, are you staying for lunch?" asked Sara's mother as she came out to the back yard from the kitchen.

"Sure," said Naomi. She knew that any meal prepared by Sara's mother was bound to be good, and she had only eaten a candy bar for breakfast that day.

Sara was feeling hungry now and asked, "What's for lunch, Mom?"

"My own secret recipe chicken salad, homemade applesauce and homemade biscuits. Unfortunately, the butter for the biscuits is not homemade, but you can't have everything," replied her mother.

"Sounds scrumptious to me," said Naomi.

"We'll be chompin' at the bit waitin' for the bell," said Sara. Then Sara and Naomi threw a Frisbee around while they waited for lunch. Soon the meal bell rang, and Sara and Naomi went in the house and sat down at the dining room table. The chicken salad and applesauce were already on the table, and Sara's mother came out to join them. Her father had gone to help his brother cut some fire wood, so it would only be the three of them.

After they said grace, Sara's mother stood up and said, "I left the biscuits in the oven to keep them warm. I'll bring them out now." When she got out to the kitchen, she said, "Sara, can you get the beverages please?"

Sara stood up and asked Naomi, "Juice, soda, or milk?"

"Cranberry juice, if you have any. If not, milk is fine," replied Naomi.

"Cranberry for you as well, Mom?" asked Sara as she went out to the kitchen.

"I think I'll have milk today," replied her mother. Sara brought out the beverages, and filled each glass accordingly.

After they finished eating, Naomi said, "Awesome as usual," as she contentedly patted her belly.

"But wait," said Sara's mother. "We're not done yet. We have sweet potato pie for desert."

"Ooohh. Sweet potato pie. I'll **have** to make room for that," said Naomi. "Even if I have to spend an extra hour at the gym."

"Or a few extra laps in my new pool," smirked Sara.

"More like a thousand laps in that pool, girl," joked Naomi with a smile.

Sara's mother brought out the pie, looked at Sara and said, "Let me save a slice for your father first. We'll be sleepin' in the swamp if we don't."

"Yes indeed. We must save some pie," said Sara. She remembered the time she had finished off one of her mother's pies without realizing that her father had not had any. He didn't get angry, but did take every opportunity to humorously remind Sara of her transgression for quite some time.

When Naomi finished her pie, she said, "Well, girlfriend, it was nice to see you again, but I have to go to the gym now. I haven't been for a couple of weeks, and really need get back on schedule." Then she got up, turned to Sara's mother and said, "Thank you again for the great meal, even though it'll cost me an extra hour at the gym."

"You're welcome, Naomi. It was nice to see you again as well," replied Sara's mother. Then she added, "If you want to skip the gym, our lawn needs mowing, and we only have a push mower. I'm certain that will give you plenty of exercise."

Sara laughed and said, "Is that a hint, Mom, for me to mow the lawn?"

Mowing the lawn was one of the responsibilities Sara's parents had given her in exchange for their financial support. Sara had been taught from an early age the importance of saving money. When Sara was old enough to begin helping with household chores, her parents had set up a savings account at the Lafayette Credit Union. Every week, they gave her a small amount of cash in exchange for her doing household chores, and deposited a similar amount in her savings account. Sara could spend the cash if she wanted to, but she usually put at least some of it in the piggy bank she had in her bedroom. Occasionally, she would splurge on a special treat, such as taking one of her friends out for an ice cream cone at Johnson's Restaurant and Dairy Bar on their birthday. Sometimes, the piggy bank got completely filled, and Sara would deposit most of the money in her savings account. Then she would buy something special for her parents.

"I'll leave the mowing for Sara," replied Naomi with a smile. "She told me she loves the smell of fresh cut grass, and it can't get any fresher than being behind the mower."

"I'll try to get the lawn mowed after church tomorrow, weather permitting," said Sara as she walked to the front door with Naomi.

"Sounds good," said her mother.

When they got to the door, Sara said, "Thanks again for stoppin' by to see my new pool."

Naomi hugged Sara and said, "You know, I really was lookin' forward to goin' for a swim, girlfriend, but that's ok, cause I got a great meal out of the deal." Then she walked out the door, got on her bike and rode away. Sara watched her for a moment, glad to have seen a good friend again, and made a mental note to spend more time with Naomi. Then she shut the door, and went up to her bedroom to get changed. It was a warm day, but not warm enough to stay in the bikini that she had put on to fool her friend.

4. Camping

"Ooohh. I almost forgot the squirms," said Sara as she went back to the garden. She had filled a large coffee can with worms from their compost heap, but she had left it near the garden when she put the garden fork away. Sara came back with the can of worms and said, "This is my final answer; we're ready to go." Sara and her parents were headed north, on their annual June camping trip. Sara was out of school for the summer, and the temperatures in June were still generally favorable for midafternoon to early evening fishing, one of Sara and her father's favorite pastimes.

Sara put the can of worms in the back of her father's pickup truck and got in, sitting behind her father's seat. Sara's father opened the door for her mother, and she got in the truck. He had always opened doors for her, ever since their first date. After Sara's father took one last look in the back of the truck, he got in the truck and said, "Let's buckle up, and we're on our way."

"Let's see," said Sara's mother as she unfolded the directions she had written down.

"I'm presuming we're going north on the highway," said her father.

"Correct," replied her mother. A friend of hers had recommended a campground on the Samoset River, and they had decided to give it a try. There were many nearby places to go fishing, and plenty of other activities available in the area.

"Alrighty," said Sara's father. "I know it will be a while, but what exit should I be looking for?" "Twenty-six," replied her mother.

"Ninety-nine bottles of beer in a wall, ninety-nine bottles of beer," sang Sara's father.

"Oh puuhlleese," grimaced Sara and her mother.

"I guess nobody wants to sing, or at least not that song," said Sara's father.

Saratoga

Then Sara's mother got the campground brochure out and said, "This is the perfect time to discuss what we want to do this week. I know that you two want to do some fishing, but there are plenty of other things to do here as well."

"I'd like to go tubing down the river," said Sara.

"Yeah. That sounds like fun," said her father.

"Great," replied her mother. "Listen to this," she said as she read from the brochure, "Rent a tube from River Raft Rentals and enjoy a relaxing day floating down the crystal clear waters of the Samoset River, which averages three feet deep with some small rapids and sandy beaches. There are even some rope swings for the more adventurous."

"Cool," said Sara. "I love rope swings."

"Not for me," said her mother. "I'll probably just find a spot to sit by the river while you two swing away."

Suddenly, Sara's father broke in singing, "I'm swinging in the rain, what a glorious feeling, just swinging in the rain." Before Sara and her mother could say stifle it, he stopped singing and said, "Just couldn't resist the play on words to that old classic 'Singing in the Rain', but I do hope we get at least a few days of good weather for our vaca."

"I'll check the weather right now," said Sara as she took out her cell phone. She checked the weather forecast and said, "Supposed to be nice today and tomorrow, maybe showers later in the week."

"Great," said her father. "We can get camp set up today, see what the campground is like tomorrow morning, and go fishing in the afternoon."

"Yes! Horseshoes. We'll have to check that out for sure," said Sara's mother as she looked through the campground brochure.

"Uh oh, Dad," said Sara. "I think Mom wants to kick your butt in horseshoes again."

"No way Jose," replied her father. "I've been practicing at the horseshoe pit behind the fire station, and I'm ready and rarin' to go. Bring it on, woman!" Sara's father was a volunteer firefighter, and had been

48

practicing throwing horseshoes at the fire station with some of his fellow volunteers.

Sara's mother just smiled and said, "I've heard that tune many times before, and I still kick your butt every time."

"Speaking of kicking butt, Ol' Bessy'll be kickin' my butt if we don't stop and get gas soon," said Sara's father. He had always called whatever vehicle he owned at the time 'Ol Bessy'. There were several theories in the family as to how that came to be, but no one could get the true story. Whenever anyone asked about it, Sara's father would just make up another story. Sara was so amused by some of his stories that she would slyly encourage people to ask him about it just to hear him make up another story.

"Might as well take a bathroom break while we're at it," said Sara.

"Perfect timing," said Sara's mother. "We just went by a "gas next exit" sign."

Sara's father took the next exit off the highway and saw that the gas station was just up the road. A couple minutes later, he pulled up to the pumps and said, "I'll fill Ol' Bessy up while you two find the bathrooms. I'll park next to that old tractor over there after Bessy gets her fill." Sara and her mother got out of the truck and walked into the gas station to ask about bathrooms while her father pumped the gas.

When Bessy was filled, Sara's father parked near the old tractor and got out to look for the bathroom. He saw Sara and her mother walking back to the truck and said, "If you're done seein' that man about a horse, it's my turn."

"Around the corner, and ya don't need a key," said Sara as she pointed to a corner of the gas station.

Sara and her mother were looking at the old tractor when her father came back to the truck. "I'm guessin' this one's before my time," said Sara.

"Yep," replied her father. "Your grandpappy had one like it when I was a little boy. It's a 1961 John Deere, a real beauty. They built 'em to last back then. We had that one for over thirty years, and it still ran well when my father sold it. He's probably still kicking himself to this day for selling it too. Some slick salesman talked him in to buying a brand new tractor, and it just weren't the same."

"I remember the last parade he drove that old tractor in," said Sara's mother. "Fourth of July, 1992, and he was pulling the Grange float."

"I remember that parade," said Sara's father. "You were on the Girl Scout float, helping set up the tent. I thought that was a great idea, setting up the tent and the rest of the campsite while the float was riding in the parade." *Strange how that works* he thought *I remember seeing her on that float, but I had no idea that I would end up falling in love with her and marrying her.*

"Ok, let's get back to the future here, and back on the road, or we'll be setting up camp in the dark," said Sara.

"Yes ma'am. On the double," replied her father as they got back in the truck.

Soon they were back on the highway, headed north. A while later, Sara's father said, "I know you told me, but what exit are we lookin' for?"

"Twenty six. Then take a right off the exit ramp," said Sara's mother.

Suddenly, Sara said, "Wow! Did you see that?"

"See what?" replied her parents.

"A hawk just grabbed a rabbit in that field over there on the left," said Sara.

"Aww," said Sara's mother.

"Well, you know, a hawk's gotta eat too," said her father. Then he added, "Speaking of eatin', it's just about lunch time."

"Oh yeah, Joanie told me there's a small picnic area on the side of the road shortly after you get off of the highway. We could stop there for lunch," said Sara's mother.

"Sounds good," said Sara.

"Ok," said Sara's father.

A few minutes later, Sara's father said, "Exit twenty-six, coming up," as he put on the turn signal in his truck.

"Great. My stomach has been runnin' on empty for a while now," said Sara. "I hope that picnic area isn't too far from here."

"Joanie said it was on the right, about a mile from the exit," said Sara's mother.

"Uh oh, I think that was it," said Sara.

"Yep, it was," added her mother.

"Looks like a lot of everybody missed it," said Sara's father as he pulled off the side of the road where other cars had done so to turn around. Sara just smiled. Her father liked to twist expressions around, just to see if people were paying attention. Sara's father turned the truck around and drove back to the picnic area. He parked the truck and everyone got out and stretched their legs.

Then Sara's mother looked at the picnic table and said, "Glad I brought a table cloth."

Her father looked at the table and said, "Oh come on now, it's not that bad. A little bit of bird poop won't hurt you."

"Eeewww, Dad, that's gross," said Sara. "And if you think about it, you'd realize you can get very sick from that. Do you want to take a chance on that during vaca?"

"Well, ok, we'll clean it off," said Sara's father as he took a stick and knocked the bird poop off the table. Then her mother covered the table with the picnic cloth, and put the cooler on the table.

"Better check the seats too," she said.

Sara looked both benches over and said, "Clean and green. Time to chow down."

Sara's father opened the cooler and helped her mother spread lunch out on the picnic table. Then they sat down, said grace, and started eating.

"Scrumptious as usual," said Sara's father as he finished the last bite of his piece of pie a little while later.

"Yes, very good indeed, Mom. Thanks," added Sara.

"You're both very welcome," replied Sara's mother.

"Since Ma made lunch for us, we'll clear the table and put stuff away," said Sara's father as he started clearing off the picnic table.

"Yep, will do," said Sara.

Soon they were back on the road. "Are we there yet? Are we there yet?" joked Sara's father.

"Where's the duct tape when you need it?" moaned Sara.

"Now children," admonished Sara's mother. She looked at the map and said, "Probably another hour or so."

"Sara, quick, look to the left," said her father. "There's somebody fly fishin' downstream a ways."

"Why would anyone want to go fishin' for flies?" joked Sara's mother.

"Oh no, it's contagious," said Sara. "Mom's been around you too long now, Dad, and your humor has taken over her mind. She's doomed."

"Help, help. Sign me up for therapy, quick," joked her mother.

"Surrounded by assassins," sighed Sara's father.

A while later, Sara's father said, "Chimney sweepers, Ma, you did it again," as he turned into the campground parking lot. "You said about an hour to get to the campground, and it's been fifty nine minutes. Close enough for me."

Sara sniffed the air a couple times and said, "I swear I can smell the fish fryin' already." She was really looking forward to going fishing. She hadn't been able to go for a while, and missed the serenity and yet excitement of going fishing. The serenity of being one with nature, and the excitement of fighting a fish on her line.

"Ok, we need to check in at the General Store," said Sara's mother. Her father parked in front of the store, and they got out and went in.

Then her father said, "I'll check us in, and you two can walk around just to see what they have here. I think we've got everything we need except ice and firewood, and I'll come back and get that later." After they checked in, they got back in the truck and Sara's father drove to their camp site. They had chosen a lean-to site at one end of the camp ground. Sara didn't mind roughing it, but her parents preferred having a lean-to. They liked knowing that they had a dry place to sit in case it rained.

The first thing Sara and her father unloaded was the garden wagon they had brought. "A bit cumbersome, but it does come in handy," said Sara's father.

"Yes indeed, especially for hauling firewood," replied Sara. While Sara's parents set up their tent, Sara finished unloading the truck.

"Uh oh, did we bring the screen house?" asked Sara's mother.

"Oh yeah, that was the first thing I put in the truck," replied Sara's father. "I knew I'd be sleepin' in the swamp if I forgot that."

"Yep, there it is," said Sara. "I don't think we'll need it at this time of year, but it's nice to have it just in case."

Sara and her father could tolerate a few skeeters, black flies or other bugs, but as Sara's mother said, "I can't stand bugs buggin' me when I'm knittin'." She loved to knit, and bugs buzzing around her while she was knitting just drove her crazy.

"Hmmm," said Sara, with a quizzical look on her face.

"Uh oh, I smell brain cells burnin'. I hope you have some extras there," joked her father.

"Smells serious from here," added Sara's mother.

"Thanks a bunch you two. You took the best spot for your tent and now I have to find a space to squeeze mine in," said Sara.

"You snoze, we chose," said her father.

Sara just rolled her eyes and said, "I think I can fit my tent in over there, between those maple trees." Sara grabbed her tent, and spread it out between the trees. "Yeah, I think this will be fine," she said. Then she put up her tent, and put her suitcase, sleeping bag and pillow in the tent.

"Ok, wood an' ice. We need anything else?" asked Sara's father.

Sara was tempted to say "wooden ice; how's that gonna keep anything cold?", but she let it slide.

"I'm all set; how about you, Mom?" asked Sara.

"All set," replied her mother.

"Be back in a bit," said her father as he took the wagon and walked toward the general store. While her father was gone, Sara and her mother continued to set up camp. They put up a folding table at the end of the picnic table, and set the "kitchen box" on it. The kitchen box was a set of various sized drawers that Sara's father had built to hold kitchen gear for camping. He had put a paper towel holder on one side, and some pot holder hooks on the other.

"Time to tackle the grill," said Sara's mother.

"Sure," said Sara as she climbed into the back of the truck. Her father had secured the grill with bungee cords to hooks on one side of the back of the truck. Sara undid the cords and rolled the grill to the tailgate of the truck. Her mother held the grill in place while Sara jumped down out of the truck. Then they took the grill off of the truck and put it down. Sara rolled it to the other end of the picnic table and set it in place.

Just then, her father came back with the wood and ice. "Mom, can you distribute the ice while Dad and I unload the propane?" asked Sara.

"Will do," said Sara's mother as she picked up a bag of ice cubes from the garden wagon. Sara climbed up into the back of the truck and unbuckled the clamp holding the propane tank in place. She picked up the tank and brought it to the end of the truck.

"Just one of those quirky things in life," she said. "This is only a gas, but it sure is heavy." Sara handed the tank to her father, then jumped off the back of the truck.

Sara's father attached the propane tank to the grill, then said, "Settin' up the grill's makin' me hungry. What's for supper tonight?"

"Baked beans and chili dogs," said Sara's mother.

"My mouth's waterin' already," said Sara. "Especially if it's your chili and Grammy's baked beans."

"Of course. Only the best when we're on vaca," replied Sara's mother.

"Hmmm," said Sara's father. "The beans and chili will probably take a while to heat up, seein' as how we don't wanna burn 'em."

"Ok, I'll start them now," said Sara's mother. Then she added, "Sara can get the buns ready, and Dad can fire up the grill in a few minutes."

"Yes ma'am, that's a plan," said Sara and her father.

Sara walked over to the kitchen box and took out a plastic plate to put the hot dog buns on and said, "Bun count."

"Two for me," said her father.

"Just one for me," said her mother.

Tempted to take two for me thought Sara *but no, I'll just have one hot dog. There's plenty of beans and chili too*. Then she took the buns out of the bag, set them on the plate and took the butter spread out of the cooler. She put a thin layer of butter on each side of each bun and set them back on the plate. *Thanks Claude*, she thought. Last summer, her friend Claude had a cookout and introduced Sara to buttered then toasted hot dog buns. It was kind of a fuss to make them that way, but Sara and her parents wouldn't go back to just plain buns. They all agreed that for whatever reason, hot dogs just weren't the same without buttered toasted buns.

"Beans and chili are warming up," said Sara's mother as she took a bite of beans from the pot.

"Firin' up the grill as I speak," said Sara's father.

"Claude's buns are ready to roast," joked Sara. Then she put the butter spread back in the cooler and took the package of hot dogs out.

"Grill's ready to rock," said Sara's father. Sara gave him four hot dogs, closed the package and put it back in the cooler. Sara's father put the hot dogs on the grill, leaving room for Sara to put the buns on.

"Might as well put the buns on now," said Sara. "If they're done before the dogs, no big deal."

"No, no," said her father. "They must all be done at precisely the same time."

"Says who," laughed Sara. "Out the way, you," she said as she nudged her father over enough so she could put the buns on the grill.

A little while later, Sara and her father heard "ding-a-ling, ding-a-ling." They looked over to see her mother ringing the dinner bell.

"Well, the beans an' chili are ready. How about the dogs?" asked Sara's mother.

"Couple more flips for the dogs," said Sara's father.

"Buns are ready," said Sara as she grabbed the plate and took the buns off the grill. Sara and her mother set the table while Sara's father finished cooking the hot dogs. Then they all sat down at the picnic table, said grace, and ate supper.

Soon after supper, Sara's father said, "Bugs are gettin' hungry, time to start the camp fire."

"Sara and I will clear the table and clean up while you start the fire," said Sara's mother.

"Well, we vacuumed the beans as usual," said Sara as she put the empty pot into the dish pan.

"Yep. Grammy's beans don't last long," replied her mother.

"A little bit of chili left; any room for it Dad?" asked Sara.

"Nope, I'm all set for now," replied her father. "But I will have it with breakfast tomorrow. I don't care if it's cold; sorta like eatin' cold pizza." Then he got the camp fire started while Sara and her mother washed the supper dishes.

"Nice fire Dad," said Sara as she set up her camp chair.

"Nice and cozy," added her mother. She put her camp chair next to Sara's and sat down.

"Since I'll be tendin' the fire, I'll just park at the picnic table," said Sara's father. "No sense gettin' nice and comfy in my camp chair only to have to get up and tend to the fire."

"Yes, Mr. Fussbudget," teased Sara's mother. Sara's father always poked the fire more than was really needed to keep the fire going, but that's just the way he was.

"Hey, we didn't have any dessert," said Sara.

"We could make some popcorn," replied her mother.

"Jiffy Pop on the camp stove?" asked her father.

"Jiffy Pop," laughed Sara. "Dad, that's ancient history. We've got something much more modern here."

"More modern?" queried her father.

"Check this out," said Sara as she took a bag out from behind her mother's seat in the truck. She walked over to the picnic table and pulled an old popcorn popper out of the bag.

"Oh my God; our old popcorn popper!" exclaimed her father. "I haven't seen that in eons!"

"Yep, we found it in the garage, behind those boxes of magazines that you keep claimin' you'll recycle one of these days," said Sara's mother with a smile.

"Another one of those Dadwasgonnas," joked Sara. She couldn't resist needling her father, but knew he would return fire as soon as he found some good ammo.

"Well, I'd put a reminder note in my smart phone, but this is a device free week while we're on vaca," said her father with a wry smile.

"Nice try," said her mother, "but the next time you check the weather, which is allowed, we give you permission to add the memo, right Sara?"

"Permission granted," replied Sara.

A while later, Sara's father said, "Ok, coals are just about perfect for the popcorn."

"Yes they are," said her mother. "I'll melt some butter while you get the popper set up."

"Ok," said her father. He opened the popper, and set it back down on the picnic table. Then he poured in a little bit of oil, added some popcorn, and gently shook the popper from side to side to mix the popcorn into the oil.

"Can I pop it?" asked Sara.

"Sure," replied her father. "Just hold the popper over the coals, but not too close. Shake it side to side and/or back and forth so the popcorn doesn't burn. When it stops popping, take it away from the coals. Then take a pot holder and slide open the lid. Put the popcorn in the bowl, and pour some butter on it as you stir it up."

Then her mother added, "But beware the vacuum cleaner standing next to you." Sara's father loved popcorn, and Sara and her mother always razzed him about vacuuming it before they had a chance to get any of it.

Sara took the popcorn popper and held it over the camp fire. Her father said, "You can let it warm up a little bit first before you start shaking it." Sara waited a minute or so, then started shaking the popper like her father said. It took a little while, but eventually, the popcorn started to pop. One or two at a time, then three or four, until it was one right after the other. That lasted about a minute, then the popping slowed down.

When the popping had mostly stopped, Sara took the popper away from the coals, grabbed a pot holder and opened the lid. She dumped the popcorn into a bowl her father had put on the picnic table. Her father held the bowl while her mother stirred in the melted butter.

Sara's father looked at her mother and said, "Wow! This takes me waaaaayyyy back to the days when I was a courtin' you and we went campin' at Eagle Lake."

"Yep. Great memories there," replied her mother. "And I remember my mother insisting that we sleep in separate tents."

"Jeeesh," said her father. "The way she was carryin' on, I thought she might insist on chaperoning us for the weekend."

After her father put some more wood on the camp fire, they sat down to enjoy the popcorn. "I still can't believe that you hid my engagement ring in the popcorn," said Sara's mother. Sara's eyes popped wide open and she looked at her father.

"It was a great place to hide it," he said. "I didn't want to do the traditional 'get down on one knee' thing. I wanted to do something different."

"You're something different all right," joked Sara, "but I love you just the same."

"I remember pouring the popcorn into the popper, seeing the ring and saying "What! Oh my God." I could not believe that you had done that, but I'm very glad that you did," said Sara's mother.

"Me too," said her father. "A moment that I will treasure forever."

When they finished the popcorn, Sara's mother said, "Gettin' a bit of a chill here. I'll put some more wood on the fire."

"It is a bit chilly," said Sara as she got up from the picnic table and sat in her camp chair near the fire.

Her father joined her there and said, "Awesome. I love sitting around the camp fire with my family."

Sara looked at her father, smiled, and said, "Yes, awesome it is."

Her mother put some wood on the fire and said, "I'll third that motion." Then she gave her husband a kiss on top of his head, pulled her camp chair next to his and sat down. They sat around the camp fire for a while, feeding it occasionally to ward off the chill. It was a beautiful June night, perfect for sitting around the fire.

Later on, Sara's father sighed and said "I love sittin' around the fire, but it's gettin' kinda late. I think I'll hit the sack soon."

"Me too," said Sara's mother. "Gotta rest up so I can smoke you in horseshoes tomorrow morning."

"Good luck gettin' any sleep tonight," said Sara. "You know what happens when Dad has baked beans."

"I'm prepared," said Sara's mother. "I brought a can of air freshener."

"Jeeesh. Surrounded by assassins," sighed Sara's father.

Then Sara got up and said, "I think I'll put on a sweatshirt and go swing in the hammock for a while. Maybe I'll see some shooting stars." She had set up a hammock at the back edge of the camp site, and had a good view of the sky from there.

A while later, Sara woke up to the sound of "Who cooks for you? Who cooks for you?" It was the sound of a barred owl calling. She lay in the hammock and wondered who the first person was that thought the owl's call sounded like that. She loved listening to the sounds of nature. It was one of the reasons she wanted to become an environmental engineer. Sara was tempted to try to stay awake in the hammock and watch for more shooting stars but decided to go to bed instead. *Plenty of time for more star gazing later on this week* she thought.

"Up an' at em. Come on, lazy bones," said Sara's father as he poked his head into Sara's tent the next morning.

"Does the princess expect breakfast in bed?" asked her mother from the picnic table. She was getting breakfast ready while Sara's father was collecting firewood. The camp ground allowed wood gathering from near the camp sites, but only downed wood. Sara's father had to go a little way into the woods but found some good wood and brought it back to their site. He didn't take a lot; he wanted to leave some for other campers as well.

"Yes, the princess will have poached eggs, French toast, and perfectly crispy bacon, posthaste," joked Sara from her sleeping bag. "And a glass of freshly squeezed orange juice."

"Yes, your majesty," replied her father. "In the meantime, Cinderella needs to get out here and help with breakfast."

Sara stretched her legs and arms, then got out of her sleeping bag. She got dressed, went out to the picnic table to help her mother and said, "What can I help with?"

"Set the table please," replied her mother. "And keep an eye on the apples."

"Yay. Fried apples," said Sara. Her mother had cored two apples, then cut the apples into cubes and mixed the cubes in a bowl with some sugar and cinnamon. Then she heated up a frying pan, melted some butter in it and stirred in the apple cubes. She had just turned the heat down low when Sara took over and finished cooking them.

"Ding-a-ling, ding-a-ling." Sara rang the bell to let her father know that breakfast was ready. He was cutting some of the wood he had gotten earlier that morning.

"Be right there," he said as he put down the saw.

Sara was about to sit down at the picnic table when her mother said, "Can you get the juice, please."

Her father added, "Get my chili, too, please."

"Sure," said Sara as she walked over to the cooler. "Orange, or apple?" asked Sara.

"Both," replied her father. "Since we don't have pineapple orange, I'll have apple orange."

"Sounds interesting," said Sara's mother. "Maybe I'll try it myself."

"No mix and match for me," said Sara. "Just plain OJ is fine for me."

After breakfast, they walked down to the campground store. They checked the bulletin board for activities, and Sara's mother noticed that the horseshoe pit was available the next morning. "I'm signin' you up for a butt kickin'," she said as she filled out a spot on the sign-up sheet.

"Yeah, well we'll see who's kickin' whose butt tomorrow morning woman," replied Sara's father.

"Now children," said Sara with a smile. Then she added, "Cool. Volleyball is starting in twenty minutes. Let's go see if they need any more players."

"Sure," said Sara's father.

"I'm game. Haven't played volleyball in eons, but yeah, let's go," said Sara's mother.

They walked over to the volleyball court and got in line to put their names on a slip of paper that would be drawn out of a hat when enough players were there. A few minutes later, a camp employee started drawing names out of the hat. Sara and her father ended up on one team, and Sara said, "Sorry Mom, but you guys are toast."

"You think so huh," replied her mother. "Well, we're toastin' hot and you guys are in for a beatin'."

It was a spirited game, with some great volleys, but Sara's team came out on top. Sara was ready to play another game, but her parents were bushed.

"Let's go for a swim in the river and cool off," said Sara's mother.

"Sounds good," said her father. Sara was tempted to stay for another game, but decided to go swimming with her parents. They went

Saratoga

back to their camp site, got changed and went swimming. Then they went back to their camp site and ate lunch.

After lunch, in the early afternoon, Sara sniffed the air and said, "I smell rain in the near future."

Her father looked up at the sky and said, "Yep. It is getting a bit cloudy. Perfect weather for fishin'." Then Sara took their fishing backpack from the lean-to and made sure everything on the checklist was there. Sara was glad that her father had taught her to be prepared, and having an index card check list for the backpack worked well.

"All set here," said Sara as she closed up the backpack. "We've got rain gear, bug spray, flashlight, towel, first aid kit and a whistle here. Hope we don't need the bug spray, but it's good to have it just in case."

Sara's father looked at her feet and said, "Flip flops for fishin'?"

"Oh yeah, I knew there was something else I needed to do before we left," replied Sara.

"Boots please," said Sara's father. "The campground owner told me about a great spot to go fishin', but it's a bit of a hike to get there. That's why not many people go there."

"Boots it is," said Sara as she went to change her footwear. Sara's father put the fishing gear and fish cooler in the back of the pickup truck while Sara put her boots on. Soon, they were buckled up in the truck and ready to go. Before they left, Sara's mother got up from the picnic table and walked over to the truck.

Sara's father put the window down, leaned out of the truck and gave Sara's mother a kiss, then said, "We'll be back before dark."

"Ok," said Sara's mother. "If you come back empty handed, we'll just have corned beef hash. I brought a couple cans of it. Put that in the fryin' pan, add some of my salsa, heat it up and voila, supper is ready."

Sara's father looked at Sara and said, "Works for us, right?"

"Sounds good to me," replied Sara.

"Ok, see you in a while," said Sara's mother as she walked back to the picnic table to resume her knitting.

"We're off to fish the Samoset, the wonderful Samoset River," sang Sara's father to the tune of 'We're Off to See the Wizard'.

"Uh, Dad, we're not in Kansas anymore," said Sara, playing along with her father. They both loved the Wizard of Oz movie, and worked references to it into their banter quite often.

"Ok, back to reality then," said her father. "The owner said take a right coming out of the campground, go about three miles, and look for a large rock on the side of the road. Pull over just past the rock, and you can park there. You'll see a path into the woods, and that will take you to the best kept secret fishin' spot on the Samoset."

They left the campground and had driven for a few minutes when Sara said, "Thar she blows."

"Huh. The rock does sorta look like a whale indeed," said her father. He pulled in past the rock and parked the truck. They got out of the truck, went to the back of it and started taking out their gear.

"I'll carry the tackle box and fishing poles if you'll wear the backpack and carry the fish cooler," said Sara's father.

"Deal," said Sara as she put the backpack on. Soon, they were walking along the path to the river.

"Jeesh. It's like we climbed Mt Everest," said Sara's father when they got to the top of a somewhat steep hill.

"Yeah, and no view from the top, either," said Sara. They walked along the path to the bottom of the hill, and came to a small creek.

Sara looked up the creek a ways and saw that it led to a beaver pond. She looked closer and quietly said, "Dad, look. A great blue heron."

Sara's father looked over and said, "You're right," just as the heron stabbed it's beak into the water and pulled out a frog. One gulp and the frog was gone.

"There goes another one of your mother's relatives," joked Sara's father. Sara's mother was French Canadian, having immigrated to America with her parents when she was a young child. Sara knew her father was only teasing, but wasn't sure why French people were sometimes called frogs. Another one of those "one of these years I'll

Saratoga

google it" things on her to-do list. Maybe it had something to do with the French love of eating frog's legs. Sara would sometimes tease her cousins or French Canadian friends about their heritage, but only in a friendly way. Sara firmly believed in the golden rule, and did her best to treat people the way that she would like them to treat her.

After they carefully crossed the creek, they walked for a while, then Sara's father stopped and said, "Listen. Do you hear that?"

Sara stopped and listened. "Sounds like rapids," said Sara. "We must be close to the river." They continued walking, and soon came to the river.

"Wow," said Sara. "This is a great spot for fishing."

"Certainly looks that way, and we'll find out soon," replied her father. After they set their gear down, they got ready to start fishing.

"Squirm or lure?" queried Sara's father.

"I'm gonna start with a squirm," said Sara.

"Ok. I'll try a daredevil. Those always seem to work well for me," said Sara's father.

"Sorry dude, but I need food," said Sara as she took a worm from the can and put it on the hook. She respected all forms of life, but understood that the natural food chain meant the sacrifice of some for the gain of others. Catching and killing a fish for food for herself was no different than that same fish being caught by a great blue heron and swallowed alive in one gulp. After she put the worm on the hook, she picked up her pole and looked for a good spot to fish from.

"I think I'll try that little pool over there," she said to her father. She had seen a log sticking out into the river, creating a good sized pool next to the log on the downriver side. She knew that trout liked to hide there, waiting for food that got pushed downriver by the current.

"I'm going to go upriver just a little bit. There's some bigger pools up there," said Sara's father.

A few minutes later, Sara's father said, "Got one. It's a good sized one too." Sara looked upriver and watched as her father reeled in a brook trout. He scooped it into his net, then set down his fishing pole. He took the fish out of the net and removed the hook from the fish's mouth. After he put the fish on the stringer, he secured the stringer to a small log and put the stringered fish in the water.

"At least ten inches," said Sara's father.

"I'll just have to catch this twelve incher here," replied Sara. "She's got two of my squirms already, and that's enough." She had seen the fish for a split second once, and knew she had to catch it soon or move on to another spot.

A little while later, Sara said, "That's the last squirm you're stealin' from me you little brat," and moved to another spot. Her father had caught another fish, and Sara was determined to not be shut out. She decided to try the rapids a little bit downriver from where the trail came out to the river. If she didn't catch anything in the rapids, there was a shaded pool at the end of those rapids, just after the river started curving.

"I'm goin' downriver a bit, maybe past the curve," said Sara.

"Ok, I'll work my way down in that direction too," said Sara's father. "But don't get too far ahead of me. Gotta keep each other in sight."

"Will do," said Sara. Then she added, "Uh oh, sprinklin' a bit. Hope it doesn't last too long."

"Well, we've got our rain gear if need be," replied Sara's father. He looked up at the sky and said, "Clouds aren't too dark, so I think we'll be fine."

Sara looked up at the sky and said, "Yeah, I think you're right." Then she took the can of worms and walked a little way downriver. She found a spot she wanted to try, put a worm on the hook and cast into the river. Soon she felt a little tug on the line, and tried to set the hook but the line went limp. She reeled her line in enough to see that the worm was still there, and decided to just let it ride the rapids. Then she felt another tug, and this time was able to set the hook in the fish's mouth.

"Got one?" asked her father. He had been walking down the riverbank and saw that Sara's pole was bent, and she was reeling in her line.

Saratoga

"Finally," said Sara. "But I should keep my big mouth shut until the fish is in the net."

"Yep. I know how that works," said her father.

The fish put up a good fight, but Sara reeled it in, carefully netted it and said, "Yesss. Bout time I caught one today."

"Wow. That's a good sized fish," said Sara's father as he took the fish stringer out of the water and opened a spot on it for Sara's fish.

"Yes indeed, the queen of fishing has bested you again," joked Sara as she took the fish off the hook.

"Well, I'm still ahead, two to one," replied her father with a smile.

"Still a bit of time left," said Sara. "But the sun is getting a bit low."

"We do have the flashlight, but I'd rather not have to use it to get back to the truck," said Sara's father.

They had fished for a little while longer when Sara's father said, "My line just snapped. I guess that's a hint that it's time to go."

"Ok," sighed Sara. "Guess I'm only gettin' one today, unless," she paused as she reeled her line in, then said, "Nope. That's it," after she reeled the line in with only a worm on the hook. She took the worm of the hook, tossed it in the river and said, "Sorry dude, but you're a tasty snack for some lucky fish."

They gathered their gear and were about to leave when Sara said, "Brain cramp. What did we almost forget?"

Sara's father said, "Hmmm", then laughed and said, "Only the most important part of our trip: supper." He went back to the river and took the stringer out of the water.

"I'll get the cooler ready for you," said Sara as she picked up the cooler. She opened the cover just enough to drain out the water from the melted ice. Then she opened the cooler all the way and her father took the fish off the stringer and put them in the cooler.

"Maybe move some of the ice around so it's on top of the fish," said Sara's father.

"Yep. Good idea," said Sara. "It's a bit of a walk back to the truck and we want to keep these guys fresh."

Soon they were on their way back to the truck. A few minutes later, Sara's father said, "Are we still on the right path?"

Sara looked around and said, "Yes. I remember that big tree with the woodpecker holes in it."

Sara's father looked at the tree and said, "Wow! Those holes are as big as my fist. Musta been a pileated woodpecker that made those holes."

"Probably," replied Sara.

They walked along a ways, then Sara's father said, "Here trucky, trucky, trucky."

"Oh puuleeease," said Sara. "We're almost there. I remember seeing that log across the trail shortly after we started walking in."

"Good. I'm gettin' hungry," said Sara's father.

"Me too. I can almost taste the fish already," replied Sara.

When they got back to their campsite, Sara's mother said, "Any luck today?"

"It's not luck, its skill, woman," said Sara's father as he smiled and opened up the cooler to show off their catch. Then he added, "But I am lucky to have the skill to be able to do well fishing."

"You fish in a well, Dad?" asked Sara. "Good luck catching anything there."

"Touché," said Sara's mother. "But in the meantime, we should get supper started. The corn and potatoes are ready to go, so I'll put those on the coals and you two can do your thing with the fish." Sara started cleaning the fish while her father put their fishing gear away and got out his fileting knife.

"The patients are ready for surgery," said Sara as she put the last fish to be cleaned on the plate with the others.

"Doctor Filet is ready to operate," replied her father. Sara watched in amazement as her father quickly fileted the fish.

When he finished, she picked up one of the fish remains by the tail, looked at it closely and said, "Perfect again; only the bones are left. One of these years I'm going to get the hang of this and be able to do it as well as you."

"Eight years of medical school to learn how to filet fish," laughed her father. Then he added, "Seriously, it does take a while to get the hang of it, but I'm sure you will."

"Mom, should I fire up the grill for the fish?" asked Sara.

"Not quite yet," replied her mother. "Let the corn and spuds cook a little bit more first."

"Ok," said Sara. A few minutes later, she fired up the grill while her father put the fish in the griller.

"Yep. Another one of those "why didn't I think of this" things," said Sara's father as he put the fish on the grill.

"Although it was designed for shish kebab, it does work very well for fish," said Sara. "Much easier than tryin' to flip the fish over with a spatula. Just flip the griller and voila."

A little while later, Sara's father said, "Time for the dingaling, if the corn and spuds are ready."

Sara's mother laughed, looked at her watch and said, "Yep. They're ready." Sara's father shut off the grill, flipped the fish one more time and set the griller back down on the grill.

Sara picked up the dinner bell, rang it and said, "I know we know supper's ready, but I just like the sound of a dinner bell."

Sara's mother walked over to the cooler and took out the butter spread. As she brought it over to the table, she said, "Sara, can you get the beverages, please. I'll have cider."

"Sure" said Sara as she walked over to the cooler.

"I'll have a Red Stripe, please," said Sara's father.

"Ooohh. That sounds good. I think I'll have one of those instead of cider," said Sara's mother. Neither of Sara's parents drank much alcohol, but they were fond of Red Stripe Ale. They had tried it once when they went to Jamaica on vacation and liked it very much. However, they both felt strongly that moderation was the key to drinking responsibly, and limited their drinking accordingly.

"Two Stripes on their way," said Sara. She brought the beverages over to the picnic table and set them down. She joined her parents at the table and they said grace.

Then Sara's father looked at her and said, "Wench, where's the lemon? You know I always have lemon with my fish."

Sara looked at her mother and said, "Did you hear anything? I thought I just heard some mindless gibberish, but perhaps it was the nearby babbling brook."

"Yes, that must be what it was, the babbling brook. I would ignore it completely," replied Sara's mother.

"Jeeesh. A man's work is never done," said Sara's father as he got up from the table. Then he said, "Do we need anything else while I'm up?"

"I'm all set," said Sara's mother.

Sara thought for a moment, then said, "I'll have some cinnamon apple sauce please. I think I'll try that with the fish." Sara's father got the lemon and apple sauce, brought them to the table and sat down again. Sara cut off a piece of her fish, put just a smidgeon of apple sauce on it and ate it.

"Wow! That's good," said Sara as she put a thin layer of apple sauce on the rest of her fish. Then she said, "Well, I know lemonhead Dad won't try it, but how about you, Mom?"

"Nah, I'll stick with my plain fish; it's just the way I like it. All natural, nothing added," replied her mother.

A little while later, Sara's father said, "There's a little bit of fish left. Any takers?"

"Not me," said Sara. "I'm stuffed to the gills of the fish I just ate."

Sara's mother looked at the plate with the fish on it and said, "That's a little bit all right. Not even worth fightin' over."

"Yeah, I know," replied Sara's father. "But if I just ate it without askin', I'd never hear the end of it."

Saratoga

"Yes indeed," said Sara with a smile.

Then her mother added, "I would never", but Sara's father jokingly cut her off with "Yeah, right."

"Well, now that we're all too stuffed to move, I'll call the maid and have her clear the table and wash the dishes," said Sara's mother.

"Works for me," said Sara.

"Somehow, I get the feeling that you misplaced the number for the maid, and you two are really just sittin' there waitin' for me to clean up," said Sara's father.

"Sounds like a volunteer to me," said Sara's mother.

"Sure does. Thanks Dad," added Sara with a sly smile.

"You're welcome," said Sara's father as he got up and started clearing the table.

"Gettin' a little bit chilly here," said Sara.

"Yes, it is," replied her mother. "I'll get the fire goin' again if you'll go get some more kindling."

"Will do," said Sara as she got up from the picnic table. Sara went out to collect some dead wood that could be easily broken up and used to supplement the larger pieces of firewood that they bought at the camp store. While Sara was collecting the wood, her mother got the fire going again.

"Uh oh, is that a sprinkle I feel?" said Sara's mother just after she fed the fire. She looked up at the sky and said, "Cloudy, but not dark gray. We'll see what happens."

"Yeah, if it starts raining too hard, we'll just sit in the lean-to and play cards," said Sara's father.

"Or Yahtzee," added Sara as she put the wood she had gathered next to the lean-to.

Sara's father finished washing the dishes, and joined Sara and her mother around the campfire. An occasional sprinkle did not put a damper on their enjoyment of sitting by the campfire together. After a while, Sara's mother said, "I hate to say it, but it's gettin' a bit late. Maybe we should let the fire die down now. Don't want to be sleepin' the day away tomorrow cause we stayed up too late tonight."

"You're right, as usual," said Sara's father as he leaned over and kissed Sara's mother on the cheek.

"Flattery will get you everywhere," said Sara's mother with a smile.

"Silly lovebirds," said Sara as she got up and poked the fire a little bit.

When the fire was down to a bed of coals with no flames, Sara's father looked at her mother and said, "Time to go count sheep. You joinin' me?"

"I'm right behind you," replied her mother.

Sara poked at the coals a little bit and said, "In a few more minutes I'll soak the fire, then hit the sack."

"We'll see you in the morning then," said Sara's mother as she got up from her chair. Sara's father joined her and said, "Good night, sleep tight."

"Night all," replied Sara. A few minutes later, she put the fire out and went to bed.

After breakfast the next day, Sara and her mother were about to start washing the dishes when Sara's father said, "Relax; I'll take care of this."

"Great. Thanks," said Sara and her mother. They sat down in their camp chairs while Sara's father washed the dishes.

When he finished, Sara's mother said, "Ready to get your butt kicked in shoes?"

"I'm ready, but I'm the one who's gonna be kickin' butt," replied Sara's father.

"Come on, Dad. She owns you," said Sara with smile. "You haven't beaten her in years."

She loved to get her father 'wound up', and horseshoes was the perfect vehicle. Her father did not like to lose, especially at horseshoes against his wife. He did well against the rest of the firefighters that he worked with, but for some reason just could not throw the shoes well against Sara's mother.

"This time, it's gonna be different," said Sara's father defiantly.

Sara and her mother looked at each other and said, "Same old song and dance."

"Not this time woman. Let's go," replied Sara's father.

"Alrighty then. Let's go," said Sara's mother as she and Sara got up from their chairs. Sara's father joined them, and they walked over to the horseshoe pit near the general store.

When they got there, some other campers were using the pit, but one of them said, "We're almost done here."

"Ok. Thanks," said Sara. She and her parents went over and sat on the bench near the horseshoe pit and watched the rest of the match.

When the other group finished, Sara's mother said, "Ready when you are."

"After you, milady," replied Sara's father.

"A true sportsman being led to slaughter," joked Sara as they walked over to the pit.

"We need an official, unbiased judge for this here whippin'," said Sara's mother as she got ready to throw her first shoe.

"Yep, that's me," chimed in Sara. "I've got my judgin' ruler ready to go."

"Unbiased? You're about as unbiased as Roger Goodell," said Sara's father as he reached down to pick up his shoes from against the post.

"The only thing that's gonna be deflated here is your ego," said Sara's mother. "Now quit stallin', get out the way, and let me throw my shoes." Sara's father walked away from the post, and Sara's mother threw her first shoe.

"I'll be the ringside announcer too," said Sara as she walked over toward the other post. Her mother threw her second shoe, and Sara announced, "One ringer, and maybe another point."

"We'll see how long that lasts," said Sara's father as he got ready to throw his first shoe.

"Close, but no cigar," said Sara after her father threw his first shoe. He threw his second one and Sara said, "He stole your point, Mom, but not your ringer. You're up three to one."

Her parents walked over to the post to examine the results and take their shoes. Sara took the ruler, and made sure her mother's ringer was legit. On their next throws, Sara's mother got nothing, and her father got a ringer and a leaner. When he saw that, he looked at Sara's mother and said, "Just try and stay out of my way. Just try! I'll get you, my pretty, and your little girl, too!"

Her parents battled back and forth, but in the end, Sara's mother prevailed. "Once again," started Sara's mother.

Her father cut her off with "Once again, a few lucky throws, and Roger Goodell as judge, jury and executioner. I never stood a chance."

"Come on Dad, she beat you fair and square," said Sara.

"I still say that was a ringer that I threw that woulda won it for me," said her father.

"No, we checked it and the ruler touched the post," said Sara.

"Yeah, it touched the post cause you leaned it that way Roger," said Sara's father. "I want to take a look at that ruler and make sure it's not warped."

"Now children," said Sara's mother.

"Next time," sighed Sara's father as they leaned the shoes against the post and walked back to their campsite.

The next morning, Sara's father came back from the camp store and said, "The weather's supposed to be perfect for tubing today." He had gone to the store to get ice, and checked the weather while he was there. After breakfast, they got ready to go tubing.

"No water shoes Dad?" asked Sara after she saw her father put his stuff in the back of the truck.

"Good catch," replied her father as he went to get his water shoes.

Saratoga

"Mine are right here," said Sara's mother as she put them in the back of the truck. Then she said, "Sunscreen." After she put her sunscreen on, Sara and her father came over and put theirs on as well. Then they got in the truck, buckled their seatbelts and went over to River Raft Rentals on the Samoset River.

After renting their tubes, they walked to the river. Then Sara's father said, "Hmmm. Yes, I did, just before I clipped my keys to my shorts with a carabiner."

"Yes, you did what?" asked Sara's mother.

"I stashed our wallets and other 'don't want this getting wet' stuff in the truck and then I locked the truck," replied Sara's father.

"We're all set to float away then," said Sara as she waded into the water and then got in her tube. Her parents got in their tubes and they all started floating down the river.

"Awesome. I love this," said Sara. "Floatin' down the river on a beautiful day."

"Yep. Great way to spend time with my family," said Sara's father.

"Amen to that," said Sara's mother. After a while, they came to a small beach. There were a few people there, but there was room enough for Sara and her parents to sit or lie down near the water. Sara and her mother sat with their legs crossed while Sara's father lay down on the sand and watched the few clouds that were in the sky.

"I can hear the gears whirling now," said Sara as she looked at her father. She knew he liked to get creative with the shapes of the clouds and see how many different objects he could conjure in the sky.

Sara's mother looked up at the sky and said, "I just hope those cumulus clouds don't start cumulatin', cause that could bring some rain."

"Look! There's a dog chasin' a cat. And over there, a big fish about to grab a small one," said Sara's father.

Sara looked up and said, "Just a wee bit of a stretch, and I could maybe see a dog and a cat, but the fish just aren't there."

"Maybe I need to get my imagination checked, but I don't see any of those things up there," said Sara's mother.

A little while later, Sara said "gettin' a bit crowded here. I think it's time we floated on."

"Agreed. I'm startin' to feel like a sardine," said Sara's father. "So it's time to tube on." Then they all took their tubes and started floating down the river again.

"I hope we didn't miss the rope swings," said Sara.

"Yeah, I've been lookin' for one, but I haven't seen any yet," said Sara's father. They floated on for a bit, then he said, "Thar she swings."

Just as Sara said, "where", she heard a splash in the river and saw some people on the river bank watching as a girl popped up out of the water.

"Yes," said Sara. "I'm totally there." Sara and her father paddled over to the riverbank just upstream from the rope swing and got out of their tubes. They left the tubes on shore and went to get in line for the rope swing.

Sara's mother said, "Have fun, but I'm watchin', not swingin'." Then she paddled to the shore, got out of her tube and found a place to sit and watch the show.

"Cannonball," yelled Sara's father as he swung out over the river and dropped in.

"Where's my cell phone when I need it?" laughed Sara. "That would have made a great video." Then it was Sara's turn. She took the rope and swung out over the river, but she let go just a little bit too early and ended up doing a belly flop into the river.

"You ok?" asked Sara's father when she got back to shore.

"Yeah, just embarrassed, that's all," replied Sara. They each swung out a few more times, and Sara was glad she did not belly flop again.

Then Sara's father said, "That's enough entertainment for your mother, so let's float on down."

"Sounds good," said Sara as she and her father rejoined her mother and they started floating down the river again.

As they floated away down the river, Sara heard someone yell "Geronimo" as they swung out on the rope. It reminded Sara of one of the few things that she and her parents did not like about America. Her parents had instilled in her the importance of the founding principles of America, and the treatment of the Indians by Americans did not live up to those principles. Slavery and women's rights were on that list as well, but Sara and her parents did not dwell on the past. They recognized that America was not perfect, and did their best to try to make sure that America, and the world, would be a better place to live for generations yet to come. That was one of the reasons Sara wanted to become an environmental engineer.

"Jeeesh. Seems like we just started our journey, but we're done. There's the sign for the River Raft Rentals shuttle," said Sara's father as he floated around a bend in the river.

"Yes indeed," said Sara. "Time certainly does fly when you're having fun, and I had a blast."

"Me too," said Sara's mother. "And now I need to recharge my gastronomical batteries. I can feel them complaining now."

"Mine are gettin' a bit low too," said Sara's father.

"I saw a clam shack on the way over here. Let's go check that out," said Sara.

"I want the clam, the whole clam and nothin' but the whole clam," said Sara's father. "If they only have clam strips, I'll get something else."

"A lobster roll sounds good to me," said Sara.

"Maybe scallops for me," said Sara's mother.

After they took the shuttle back to their truck, they went to the clam shack. "Great. They have the clam, the whole clam and nothin' but the clam," said Sara's father.

Sara got a lobster roll, and her mother opted for grilled tuna instead of scallops. They took their food and found a table overlooking the river behind the clam shack. They sat down, said grace, and started eating.

"What's that over there?" said Sara's father to her mother.

"Oh no you don't. You're not stealin' any of my tuna with that trick. You got me a few times when we started dating, but not anymore, wise guy."

Then Sara stole a clam from her father's plate, and her mother said, "Touche to the payback."

Sara put the clam in her lobster roll, took a bite and said, "Good combo; clam and lobster."

A few minutes later, Sara's mother noticed the faraway look on Sara's face and said, "Uh oh, what's the mad scientist scheming about now?"

Sara smiled and said, "The mad scientist is on vacation, but I just can't help thinkin' about Geronimo and the Declaration of Independence."

"Geronimo and the Declaration of Independence?" asked Sara's mother. "How are those two tied together?"

Sara's father said, "The Declaration states that all men are created equal, yet look what we did to the Native Americans."

"Sad but true," said Sara's mother.

Then Sara said, "And as I've said many times before, it should be 'all **people** are created equal', not just men."

"Yes, you're absolutely correct," said Sara's father. "But it was a different world back then. Thankfully, we've made a lot of progress, but we're not done yet."

"Yes," said Sara's mother. "And conversely, here's hoping we never get to the point where our government no longer has the consent of the governed, and the people feel compelled to alter or abolish it, and to institute a new government, as the Declaration gives us the right to do."

"Amen to that," said Sara's father. "But can you pass me the tartar sauce? I'm runnin' a little low here."

Sara picked up the jar of tartar sauce and said, "I'll trade you some tartar sauce for some butter for my corn on the cob."

"Deal," said Sara's father as they swapped items.

When they finished eating, Sara's mother said, "Time to walk off some of this food before it settles in permanently."

"Good idea," said Sara's father. "In fact, there's a rail trail near the campground."

"Great," said Sara and her mother. They walked back out to the truck, and Sara's father drove over to the rail trail. They walked for about half an hour, then turned around and walked back to the truck.

When they got back to their camp site, Sara said, "That walk made me hungry. I'm ready for supper." Then she added, "Just kidding. I think I'll swing in my hammock and read for a while."

Sara's father said, "I think I'll just park at the picnic table and read."

Sara's mother went over to the lean-to and got her knitting bag. Then she sat down at the picnic table and said, "I think I'll work on some socks for Christmas." Every year, Sara's mother knitted an assortment of socks, mittens and hats that she donated to the Salvation Army in early December.

Later on, they had a light supper of chicken salad, pickled beets and banana bread. When they finished eating, Sara said, "Another delicioso homemade meal; Dad's pickled beets, Mom's chicken salad and my banana bread." While Sara and her mother cleaned up after supper, Sara's father walked down to the camp store to get some wood and ice.

When he came back, he said, "Supposed to rain tomorrow. Maybe we'll go check out some covered bridges, or do some souvenir shopping."

"Well, I'd like to check out the bridges, rain or shine," said Sara. "Historical things like that are very interesting to me."

"Me too," said Sara's mother. "But I'd like to stop somewhere and get some postcards. We can write them when we get back to camp, and mail them from the camp store."

"That's right. We haven't done that yet, and we usually do send cards to family and friends while we're on vaca. Just a nice little touch, I think," said Sara's father.

When they got up the next morning, it was raining lightly. "Uh oh. Did we bring an umbrella?" asked Sara's mother.

"Oh, come on Mom. You're very sweet, but you won't melt that fast in this rain," joked Sara.

Sara's father looked at her mother and said, "Actually, I did pack an umbrella, 'cause I know you like to take pictures with your digital camera, and you don't want it to get wet."

"Well, thank you sweetheart," said Sara's mother.

"You're welcome, milady," replied Sara's father as he took his wife's hand and kissed the back of it.

"Silly lovebirds" said Sara with a smile. She smiled inside as well, thinking of the time that Mike Senecal had kissed her on the back of her hand.

After breakfast, they put on their rain gear, got in the truck and went to check out covered bridges. They started at the Samoset River Bridge, built in 1890. When they got out of the truck, Sara said, "Wow. This is cool. I love looking at old stuff like this. I can just imagine working on something like this back then. No machines, no power equipment, all done by hand and real horse power." They checked out some other bridges in the area, and at their last stop, the covered bridge had a gift shop inside.

"Fantastic," said Sara's mother. "A gift shop in a covered bridge. How cool is that?"

They walked into the gift shop and Sara said, "Yes, it's a great idea, and it looks like they have a lot of interesting stuff here too."

"Uh oh," said Sara's father. "I can see the money flying away already."

"Oh come on, Mr. Skinflint," said Sara's mother.

"Besides," said Sara. "We can do some early Christmas shopping. Never too early for that."

"Good idea," said Sara's father. "I'll bet they have real maple syrup here, and you know Grammy loves that."

They did some shopping, then headed back to camp. When they got back to camp, Sara's mother said, "Not too late. We've got time to

Saratoga

write a few postcards before supper." They each wrote out a few postcards, sometimes adding a line or two to someone else's.

When they finished the cards, Sara said, "I'll bring these down to the mailbox at the camp store. I'll bring the wagon and get some ice too."

"Great. That'll save me a trip. My legs are gettin' beat," joked Sara's father.

"Well, you can help me with supper, then," said Sara's mother as she put away the pens they had used to write the postcards.

"Ok," said her father.

After supper, they sat around the campfire and reminisced about previous camping trips. "Well, another good camping trip is about to come to an end," said Sara's father.

"I know," said Sara sadly. "The time just went by way too quickly."

"I can't believe it. One more full day here, then time to close up shop and head for home," said Sara's mother. Then she added, "You two want to get in one more afternoon of fishin' tomorrow? I can stay here and knit or read. That's fine with me. Nice to be able to just sit around and relax."

Sara's father said, "I'm game for that."

"Me too," said Sara.

After breakfast the next morning, they went for another walk along the rail trail. When they got back to camp, they reluctantly packed up a few things in anticipation of leaving the next day. Then they had lunch. When they finished eating, Sara's mother said, "I'll clean up here. You two go ahead and go fishin'."

"Ok. Thanks Mom," said Sara.

"Ditto," added her father. They got their gear ready, got in the truck and went back to spot they had fished from before.

When they got back to camp, Sara's father got out of the truck and said, "We only caught one, and it was this big." He held out only one hand, palm facing sideways.

"The fish around the world, eh," said Sara's mother with a smile.

"Yeah, we caught goose eggs today," said Sara. "But we didn't come back empty handed. We stopped at a pizza place on the way back and got supper."

"Works for me," said Sara's mother. "Let's eat." They sat down at the picnic table, said grace, and ate supper.

"Time out," said Sara as she got out of her tent the next morning. "I should have said this earlier in the week, but I was having too much fun to think of it."

"Time out?" asked Sara's mother.

"Just tryin' to slow down time. It always flies when we're on vaca," replied Sara.

"Indeed it does. Seems like we just got here, and now it's time to load up the truck and head home," said Sara's father.

"Yes, we should get started doing that right after breakfast," said Sara's mother. Then she added, "No time for cooking this morning, so we'll just have fruit, cereal, and juice or milk."

"Sounds good. I'll set the table," said Sara. Sara's mother got the fruit, cereal and beverages out while Sara's father started packing things up.

When they finished breakfast, Sara said, "I'll do the dishes, then I want to swing in the hammock for just a few minutes before I take it down."

Sara's father checked the large cooler and said, "All set here. What little we have that needs to be kept cold can fit in the small cooler, and there's enough ice left for that." While he took care of the coolers, Sara's mother emptied out the tents, then swept them out.

Sara finished washing the dishes and went over to the hammock. "I love this," said Sara as she swung gently in the hammock. "So peaceful and relaxing."

A few minutes later, Sara got out of the hammock, sighed, and said, "Back to reality." Then she helped her parents finish packing the truck.

Soon they were heading home. "Well, another great vacation in the books," said Sara's father.

"Yes, and some great pictures for the vaca album as well," said Sara's mother.

Sara sighed and said, "Good-bye vacation, we'll see you next year."

5. Pastor Stanley

Sara woke up to the smell of pancakes and fried apples. *Interesting*, thought Sara *I usually don't smell breakfast until I'm downstairs*. Then she realized she had slept through the night on the couch in the living room. She had been on an all-day bike ride Saturday with her friend Brenda, and after a late supper, she had started watching a movie with her parents. She fell asleep halfway through the movie, and her parents left her on the couch to spend the night when the movie was over.

"Breakfast is served, princess," said Sara's mother as she came out to the living room and rang the bell.

"Vermont?" asked Sara.

"Correct," replied her mother. "You know my bells very well."

"Interesting. They all sound the same to me," said Sara's father.

"Not sure what the difference is, but each one sounds just a wee bit different," said Sara as she sat down at the kitchen table. Her parents joined her, they said grace, and then ate breakfast.

When they finished breakfast, Sara's mother said, "Are you going to church with us today?"

Sara stood up and stretched her arms and legs, then said, "Yes, I will. I am in need of recharging my spiritual batteries, so I'll run upstairs and get changed and be right with you."

Her parents had always brought Sara with them to church on Sunday when Sara was younger, but when she turned ten years old, they had allowed her to decide whether to go or not. Sara liked Pastor Stanley, and enjoyed listening to his sermons. He was not a "fire and brimstone" preacher, yet he stressed the importance of following God's Word and living by the golden rule.

Sara understood the importance of the golden rule, but did not always see eye to eye with Pastor Stanley regarding his sermons. However, her parents had taught her the importance of listening to others and examining issues from different perspectives. After each Sunday service, Pastor Stanley always had hot coffee and fresh pastries available in the sanctuary of the church for those who wished to stay and chat with him or socialize with other members of the church. Sara and her parents usually stayed after the service for this social hour, as it was called. They enjoyed socializing with Pastor Stanley and other church members, and visitors were welcome as well. Sara was not afraid to speak her mind, but made sure that she listened to other points of view as well.

Sara enjoyed the challenge of trying to convert someone whose opinion on a given subject did not match hers, but she was willing to be converted herself if her "opponent" put forth convincing facts. Verbal sparring was one of her favorite pastimes.

Although Sara was not sure if she believed in God the way that her parents did, she did believe in what she felt was a power far stronger than that which any human being possessed. Her parents did not impose their religion upon Sara, but did stress the importance of following the golden rule and the fact that there is no right way to do the wrong thing. From a young age, Sara's parents had encouraged her to think about, and question, anything and everything. One issue that Sara did have with religion in general was the treatment of "non-believers" in the past as well as in current time. She just could not understand how a benevolent God could sanction sinful actions against those who did not believe in a particular religion.

And she often *thought why do we wait until someone passes away to say "may she rest in peace"? Why can't everyone in the world learn to live together in peace? If everyone would always, always treat others the way they would like to be treated themselves, the world would be a much better place.*

Sara was looking through her closet for something to wear to church when her father, at the bottom of the stairs, said, "The bus is leaving in thirty seconds."

"Ok, ok," said Sara, and she quickly threw on a blue skirt and a light green blouse. *No time for heels today*, she thought, so she put on a pair of black penny loafers.

When she got in the car, her father said, "Jeesh, I thought you were sewing something new to wear."

Then Sara said, "Not much to choose from; I really need....uhhh." Sara paused for a moment, but knew she was sunk.

Before she could say another word, her mother said, "You really need to tackle mount laundry."

"I know," sighed Sara. "But I don't know why I hate doing laundry. Just one of those things I guess. I'll try to remember to do laundry when we get home from church today."

A few minutes later, as she was pulling into the church parking lot, Sara's mother said, "Well, miracle of miracles, we made it on time, no thanks to last minute laundry lady." Then she quickly added, "Just kidding sweetie pie. I'm glad you came with us today."

"Speaking of pies and miracles, it's a miracle I didn't vacuum this pie on the way over here," said Sara's father. He was holding a sweet potato pie that Sara's mother had made for the social hour after church.

"Oh! I'm so tempted," said Sara. "Even just a teeny tiny slice would be heaven, but…".

Sara's mother cut her off with "Well, thank you both for the compliments, but please leave the pie for others at the social. I'll make another one soon, just for the three of us."

After Sara's mother parked the car, they got out and walked into church just as the service was about to begin. "Good. We didn't miss anything," whispered Sara's father as they sat down. Then the music started, and everyone stood up for the hymn. After Pastor Stanley said a special prayer for the day, everyone sat down for the reading from the Old Testament. Sara took a quick look at the church pamphlet and saw that the subject for that day's service would be the love of money. *Good subject* thought Sara *but I should be paying attention to the words at hand*. Then she noticed her mother fidgeting a little bit just before she sneezed a stifled sneeze.

"God bless you," whispered Sara and her father.

"Thank you both," whispered her mother. Pastor Stanley may have heard Sara's mother sneeze, but he didn't miss a beat and kept going with the service.

After the service, Sara's father went out to their car and got the sweet potato pie while Sara and her mother went to the church sanctuary. Sara's father brought the pie in to the sanctuary and said to Pastor Stanley, "Although I have been led into temptation, I was delivered from evil, and thus have the entire pie to give to you."

Pastor Stanley smiled and said, "Thank you for delivering the pie and resisting the evil of temptation. You can put the pie on the table over there and I'll get a pie knife for it." Sara's father put the pie on the table while Pastor Stanley went to the sanctuary kitchen and got a pie knife.

After Pastor Stanley put the knife on the table, Sara walked over to him and said, "That was a very good sermon today. The love of money, and the power that large sums of money can bring, continues to be a problem in the world today, just as it has been in the past."

"Thank you for the compliment," said Pastor Stanley. "And I'm glad that you understand that it is the love of money, not just money, which is the root of much evil in the world today. Many people mistakenly leave out the "love of" part of the quote, and that changes it completely. Money, when understood and handled properly, is a good and necessary thing."

Then Pastor Stanley added, "Speaking of good and necessary things, a piece of very good sweet potato pie is necessary for me right now. I had no time for breakfast today, and although pie is not really a breakfast food, I'm certain my stomach will forgive me for this dietary transgression."

Sara smiled and said, "Thank you for complimenting my mother's pie, and I'm certain that your stomach will forgive you."

Pastor Stanley cut a piece of Sara's mothers' pie and said, "May I cut a piece for you?"

"Thank you but no," replied Sara. "We brought the pie for others to have. My mother promised my father and I that she'll make another one for us soon. But I will take a piece of that tasty looking pastry over there and be right back." Sara went over to another table and took a piece of pastry, then returned to continue her conversation with Pastor Stanley.

When the subject of music happened to come up, Sara sighed and said, "Although I know that modern dance music most likely isn't on your playlist, I do happen to like quite a bit of it. But getting back to our "love of money" discussion, I **don't** like the fact that female singers, especially the younger ones, feel compelled to use sex to sell their merchandise. I don't mean that literally, but look at the CD cover of just about any **female** singer, and you'll see a scantily clad girl. Yet how many scantily clad **male** singers do you see on their CD covers? Not very many, that's for sure."

"Yes, that's another unfortunate aspect of the love of money," said Pastor Stanley.

"And one of the biggest reasons that sex sells," said Sara, "is because Hollywood and Madison Avenue push it so hard. And the harder they push it, the more money they make."

"Oh, it is indeed a very vicious cycle," said Pastor Stanley.

"Well, that's enough discouraging conversation for such a beautiful day," said Sara. "Do you have any plans for this afternoon?"

"Actually, yes" replied Pastor Stanley. "I'm officiating at an outdoor wedding ceremony at the Shady Maple Farm and Museum in Wilmington." The Shady Maple Farm and Museum was a working farm that housed a museum in the old farmhouse.

"That's great," said Sara. "I know Roy MacGregor and he's done a nice job of keeping the farm going and having a museum at the same time."

"Yes, he has," said Pastor Stanley. "And he's getting married today to a girl named Nancy Bond."

"Awesome," said Sara. "And although I have no plans to get married yet, that would be a great place to have a wedding."

Then Sara thought with a smile, *Sara Senecal....it does have a nice "ring" to it*. She had just started to think about the time Mike had kissed the back of her hand when her father said, "Earth to Miss Einstein, come in please."

"Miss Einstein?" queried Pastor Stanley.

Sara laughed and said to Pastor Stanley, "My Dad's just teasing me. He calls me that whenever he wants to speak to me and sees me in a pensive mood." Then she turned to her father and said, "And what plans do you have for the mad scientist here?"

Sara's father smiled mischievously and said, "In our garage, there's a wheeled, bladed object with a long handle that needs to be put in motion for an hour or two to prevent it from becoming rusted and immovable."

Pastor Stanley laughed and said, "I'm not a rocket scientist, but it sounds like a lawn is in need of mowing and the mad scientist has been volunteered for the operation."

"You have deduced correctly, mi amigo," said Sara. "And I do need to burn off those pastries I ate here this morning, so I must reluctantly say "adios" for now."

"Adios, mi amiga," replied Pastor Stanley. Then he turned to Sara's mother, handed her the empty pie pan and said, "Thank you very much for the excellent as usual sweet potato pie."

"You're welcome, Pastor Stanley," replied Sara's mother. "And we'll see you next week."

"Yes, see you next week," said Sara's father as he shook hands with Pastor Stanley. Then Sara and her parents walked out to their car and headed for home.

When they got home, Sara's mother said, "Well, I had enough to eat at the church social, so I'm skipping lunch today."

"Me too," said Sara's father.

"I think I will too, but I might snack on something after I mow the lawn," said Sara. Then her parents went in the house and Sara started mowing the lawn. She started in the back yard, because that was the biggest and Sara wanted to get that done and out of the way first. By the time she got to the front yard, she noticed that the sky was getting very cloudy, and it looked like it might rain soon. *Better hurry up before the deluge* thought Sara. She quickened her pace and was almost done when it started to rain lightly. She managed to finish mowing before she got too wet, and put the lawn mower back in the garage.

Then the deluge came just as Sara went in the house and into the kitchen. She took an apple from the bowl of fruit on the kitchen table and started washing it. Her father came into the kitchen and said, "You know, you could save some water by opening the window, sticking the apple out and washing it in the rain."

"What about the screen on the window?" asked Sara.

"Oh, I can't be bothered with minor technical details," said her father. Sara just rolled her eyes and finished washing her apple. After she ate her apple, she went up to her bedroom and started working on her homework. About an hour later, she had finished her homework and decided to do some more research on colleges. She was looking for a college that had a strong environmental engineering program and participated in the Reserve Officer Training Corp, more commonly known as ROTC. Sara felt that by serving her country as an environmental engineer, she could also help show the importance of living up to the ideals of the founding principles of America.

Sara loved her country, but felt that America could have done more to ensure that every government truly was a government of the people, by the people for the people. As President Jefferson once said, "America's role in the world is to preserve and to spread, by example and by action, the "sacred fire of liberty"." She was frustrated at times by the thought of how vast a project that would be, but she was also determined to do her part, however minor that may be in the overall scheme of things.

Whispering Pines. That's an interesting name for a college, and it's close to home, thought Sara as she looked at the home page of the college's web site. When she discovered that it had a very reputable environmental engineering program and participated in ROTC, she added it to her list of colleges to apply to. She was about to resume researching other colleges when she heard the supper bell ringing. "I'll be right down," said Sara.

After Sara shut off her computer, she went downstairs and when she got to the dining room, her parents were sitting at the table waiting for her. After Sara sat down, they said grace and started eating supper. "That was a very interesting sermon today," said Sara's father.

"Yes, and very appropriate in today's world," said Sara's mother.

"It is a very important subject," said Sara. "And Pastor Stanley's sermon got me thinking, as usual."

"Uh oh. Where's my "mad scientist at work" sign," joked Sara's father.

"Seriously, Dad," said Sara. "Pastor Stanley spoke of the love of money and greed, but I also believe that the power that large sums of money can bring is a major problem in the world today as well."

"Yes indeed," said Sara's mother. "Far too many people are too self-centered and don't follow the golden rule."

"Confession time," said Sara's father.

"Ok Dad, what did you do now?" asked Sara.

"Well, on my way home from work one day last week, somebody cut me off in traffic," said Sara's father. "I'd had a rough day at work and wasn't in the best of moods, and I gave the other driver the one fingered salute and sent a few choice words in his direction."

"Not good," said Sara's mother.

"I know," said her father. "But I can't rewind and edit the tape of life, so I'll just have to do my best to not do it again."

"The tape of life: a very fascinating subject indeed," said Sara. "Where, when and how did it all originate? As an environmental engineer, I won't deal directly with that question, but in a way, the two subjects are related. Research on helping the environment today may lead to more information regarding the origin of life here on earth."

"Interesting thought," said Sara's father. "But in the here and now, I need some more chicken and corn. Anybody else?"

"More corn please," said Sara. "And that'll do it for me."

"Ok, I'll take the last biscuit then," said Sara's mother.

After Sara put some more corn on her plate, she took one kernel of corn and held it between her thumb and forefinger. "Just another fascinating aspect of life," said Sara. "That the "parent" of this kernel in a sense "knew" what to do to become a corn plant and produce more offspring to continue the cycle."

"And that knowledge came from our Creator," said Sara's mother. "Because information originates in minds, not chemicals. The knowledge needed for the evolution of life could only have come from our Creator."

"And the most fascinating and mysterious aspect to me is the question; where did it all come from?" said Sara's father. "Basically, according to the big bang theory, everything was all very compressed and then something set off the "big bang" and created the universe. But where did that compressed material come from? And where did our Creator come from?"

"Well, I don't know about the big bang," said Sara's mother. "But our Creator did not "come" from anywhere. Our Creator has always existed and always will exist. That's a difficult concept for humans to understand, because we think everything has to have a beginning and an end."

"That is a difficult concept for me to understand," said Sara. "But I do believe in following the golden rule, and in being thankful to our Creator." Then she added, "Sometimes I wonder, though, if maybe the Earth, and the universe as we know it, is just a laboratory experiment for some other intelligent life form in another dimension."

"Very interesting," said Sara's father. "But all this thinkin' is too much thinkin' for me. As far as I'm concerned, it is what it isn't, but that isn't what it is."

"OK. Whatever you say Dad," laughed Sara.

"Yep. Your father's been thinkin' too much again," said Sara's mother. "And his brain's gettin' all fogged up." Then she added, "But I'm thinkin' that clearin' the table and loading the dishwasher will clear that fog right out."

"Yes, yes, just what the doctor ordered," said Sara.

"Jeesh. A man's work is never done," said Sara's father as he got up and started clearing the table.

6. Samantha

Interesting thought Sara as she walked along the trail in the Lafayette Town Forest on a Sunday afternoon. *That looks like Samantha sitting on the bench up ahead, but why would she be here by herself?* Sara liked to occasionally walk by herself along the trails just to get some fresh air, but knew that Samantha was almost always hanging around with her friends. Sara was not real close friends with Samantha, but occasionally, she would hang out with Samantha and her friends in town, especially at Pete's Pizza Parlor.

They had a pool table there, and Samantha was a very good pool player. Sara liked to play pool, but she was not at Samantha's level. However, Sara did not go over to Samantha's house very often at all, because Samantha's father made Sara feel uncomfortable. He was very domineering, and often severely criticized Samantha, her sisters and their mother in front of whoever happened to be there at the time.

Sara continued walking toward the bench, and as she got closer, she heard Samantha softly crying. *Uh oh. That's not good*, thought Sara. *I wonder what's wrong*. When Sara got to the bench, Samantha was still crying, and Sara softly said, "What's the matter Samantha?"

Samantha did not respond, and began to cry harder. Sara sat down next to her, put her arm around Samantha and said, "What is it? I want to help you, but I need to know what the problem is."

Between sobs, Samantha managed to blurt out "I'm pregnant."

Sara was at a loss for words, but knew she had to say something. The best she could come up with was, "Are you sure?" Samantha just continued to sob, and Sara knew that her friend was indeed pregnant.

"Well, sitting here sobbing isn't going to help you or change anything," said Sara. "So let's go for a walk."

Samantha sighed and said, "All right."

They got up and walked along the trail and Sara said, "Do your parents know?"

"No, they don't, but I'm too afraid to tell them," said Samantha. "I just don't know how...." Samantha's voice trailed off and she started sobbing again.

"Well, we have to figure out a way to do that soon. How far along are you?" said Sara. "Do you think your mother may have an inkling?"

"I don't know how far along I am," said Samantha. "All I know is I took a pregnancy test and it came back positive. My mother..... I don't know. I haven't had my period for a while now, but she hasn't said anything."

Then Sara said, "Have you told the child's father yet?"

Samantha started sobbing again for a moment, then controlled herself and said, "I don't even know who he is. I was at a party at Hampton Beach last summer, and the one time I didn't use protection...."

Her voice trailed off again and Sara said, "Well, there's nothing we can do about that, so let's talk about what you need to do **now**." Then Sara said, "It probably would be best to talk to your mother first, when your father is not home, but have you thought about what you want to do, and what your options may be?"

"I haven't thought about anything except how mad my father's going to be," sobbed Samantha.

"Well, you have to think about your options, and think about them **now**," said Sara. "You don't have much time."

"I know," said Samantha. "And I think you're right about telling my mother first."

"If you need me to be there when you speak with your mother, let me know," said Sara.

Samantha sighed and said, "Thank you for the offer, but I think it would be better if I spoke with my mother alone."

"All right," said Sara, "but call me if you need me." Then she added, "In the meantime, you need to think about what you want to do. Basically, you have three options; keep the baby, give the baby up for adoption, or have an abortion. I am opposed to abortion, but it is not my decision to make. Whatever your decision is, I will support you one hundred percent."

"Thank you very much," said Samantha. "I'm so glad that you came out here today and stopped to talk to me. A few other people walked by while I was sitting here crying, but no one stopped. Of course, I probably couldn't have told them anything, but it has been a huge relief to have someone to talk to."

"You're welcome," said Sara. "And I'll do whatever I can to help you. As soon as I get home today, I will start checking out all three options for you. Probably would not be a good idea for you to do that until after you speak to your parents."

"That's true," said Samantha. "My parents don't spy on me, but sometimes my Mom comes into my room to talk to me while I'm on my computer, and it definitely would not be good for her to see me researching pregnancy help."

Then Sara tried to take Samantha's mind off of her situation by talking about other things while they continued to walk along the trail. A few minutes later, they had completed the loop around the pond, and were back at the bench where Sara had first seen Samantha. "Well, we're back to where we began, just like the cycle of life," said Sara. "And I know that things may look difficult now, but you are a strong girl, and I'm sure you'll work your way through this."

Samantha smiled a small smile, gave Sara a big hug and said, "Thanks very much, I really appreciate your help." Then she looked at her cell phone and said, "Gotta get goin'. My Mom needs her car to go shopping, but do you need a ride home?"

"I'm all set," said Sara. "I rode my bike here and locked it in the bike rack at the entrance. I'll ride home in a while, and talk to you about this after school tomorrow. I'll drive my car to school, and we can go to the mall and sit in the parking lot to talk."

"Thank you. That sounds good," said Samantha. "I can just tell my mother I'm going shopping with you after school." Then she gave Sara a long hug, walked out to her mother's car and drove home.

Saratoga

After Samantha left, Sara walked around the forest for a while, but could not get her mind off of Samantha's problem. She decided to ride home and start doing the research that she had promised Samantha she would do. She walked over to the bike rack, unlocked her bike, put on her helmet and started riding home. Sara was a little bit less than halfway home when it started to rain. *Wow*, thought Sara, *I didn't even notice that it was getting cloudy. Better hurry up here before I get soaked.*

She started peddling faster, and managed to get home before she got too wet. It was still raining when she walked in her house, and her father said, "Taking a shower outdoors to save water, just like a future environmental engineer should do. I'm impressed."

Sara just smiled and said, "Maybe on a hot summer day I would, but it's a bit too chilly for that today, so I'll just take a plain old indoor shower."

After Sara took a shower and got dressed, she went to her bedroom and turned on her computer. She googled "teen pregnancy help" and sorted through the multitude of results for her search. She found information regarding each option that Samantha had, and made notes about each one. Although Sara was personally opposed to abortion, she knew that it was not her decision to make. Samantha was in a very difficult position, and Sara felt that just being there for Samantha right now was the most important thing. Discussing all of Samantha's options with her in the very near future would give Sara the best opportunity to persuade Samantha to not have an abortion, but in the end, the final decision would be Samantha's alone to make.

Well, that's all I can do right now, thought Sara as she took the index cards she had written her notes on and put them in her backpack. Then she went back to her desk, sat down and finished her homework.

When Sara got to school Monday morning, Samantha was waiting for her just inside the door. Sara wanted to try to help Samantha maintain a positive attitude, so she said, "I did quite a bit of research yesterday and found out a lot about all of your options."

Samantha managed a slight smile and said, "Good. Thank you very much."

"You're welcome," said Sara. "And I'll meet you here after school today, and we can go for a spin in my Baja."

"Ok. I'll see you then," said Samantha as she turned to walk down the hall to her homeroom. Sara watched her for a moment, then headed down the other hallway to her homeroom.

Finally, thought Samantha as the bell ending the school day rang. All day, she had been anxiously awaiting her meeting with Sara. She hurriedly went to her locker, put her books away, and got her backpack ready to take home. Then she headed down the hall to meet Sara.

When she got to the school door, Sara was waiting for her and tried to lighten things up a bit by saying, "Jeesh. I thought you forgot about me."

Samantha managed a weak smile and said, "Oh, I didn't forget. Not with something like this, that's for sure."

"I know," said Sara. "I'm sorry, I was just trying to lighten things up a little bit."

Samantha sighed and said, "Thanks for trying. Now, shall we hit the road? I'm anxious to hear what you found out."

"Yes, Ma'am. We're on our way," said Sara as she opened the door.

As they walked out to Sara's car, they chatted a little bit about the school day, but waited until they got into Sara's car before they began their serious conversation. "I've got quite a few notes here in my backpack," said Sara, "but I can give you a brief background of what I found out while I drive to the mall."

"Good," said Samantha. "What have you got?"

Sara chose her words carefully, as she did not want to have to deal with a distraught passenger while driving. She briefly touched on all three options Samantha had, and was glad that the ride to the mall went smoothly. When they got to the mall, Sara drove to the far end of the parking lot and said, "We can hide here. Plenty of other cars around, and nobody will notice us."

"Perfect," said Samantha.

Saratoga

After she parked her car, Sara undid her seatbelt, reached over to the backseat and grabbed her backpack. She took her notes out and returned the backpack to the back seat. Then she said "As I said before, you're a strong girl, and I'm sure you'll work your way through this difficult time. So, let's get started."

"I'm ready," said Samantha.

Sara had paper clipped the notes for each option separately, and had a pencil ready to take notes if need be. "We'll start with abortion," said Sara. "Although I am opposed to abortion, this is not my decision to make and I feel that you need to be thoroughly informed about **all** of your options in order to make the best decision for yourself." Then Sara unclipped her notes about abortion and said, "The first thing we need to discuss is parental notification."

"No way would my parents let me get an abortion," said Samantha. Then she started sobbing and said through her tears, "I'm not ready to be a mother but I don't want....oh, I just don't know what to do."

"Well, we're here today to try to figure that out," said Sara. "Now, regarding parental notification, New Hampshire law does require it. However, that can be bypassed by obtaining court approval."

"Court approval?" asked Samantha.

"You need to go in front of a judge," said Sara, "and explain that your safety and/or family situation precludes informing your parents before you get an abortion."

Samantha sighed and said, "Well, I really don't want to think about that, but if it came down to it, I'd rather bite the bullet and tell my parents, but maybe not. I just don't know."

"Now comes the hard part for me," said Sara. "But there's no getting around it. You need to know how various types of abortion are performed and how it may affect you. From what you told me, you are still in your first trimester. There are basically two types of abortion for that time frame; nonsurgical and surgical. Nonsurgical abortions use either a pill, a liquid or an injection to induce a miscarriage. However, this treatment must begin within seven weeks of your last period, so I would say this is not an option for you."

"Nope" said Samantha. "It's definitely been at least eight weeks."

"Ok," said Sara. "Then your only option would be surgical. There are two types, the most common being vacuum aspiration, but suction curettage is also an option."

Samantha started sobbing again and said, "I don't like the sound of either one, but I just ....."

Samantha's voice trailed off and Sara said, "It's not pretty, but you need to know this in order to make the best decision for yourself. You're a strong girl, and I'm certain that no matter what you decide to do, you'll be able to get through this and get on with your life. You're not the first person in this situation, and you won't be the last, but we can discuss support groups and things like that later on."

Sara paused for a moment and said, "As I said before, abortion isn't pretty, but it may be the best option for you. I'm not trying to affect your decision, but I truly believe that you need as much information as possible to help you make this decision. If you decide to have an abortion, understanding what you will be going through during the procedure will help you to recover, both physically and mentally, after the procedure. Now, getting back to the surgical procedures available to you, they both entail removal of the fetus from your uterus, either by suction or curettage."

"What is curettage?" asked Samantha.

"The doctor basically reaches into your womb," said Sara, "and pulls the fetus out piece by piece."

Samantha started sobbing again and Sara said, "I'm sorry to put it that way, but that's what happens."

Samantha stopped sobbing and said, "That's ok, it's not your fault."

Then Sara said, "Well, at least that's the worst part of it for you, in a sense anyway. Physical recovery is usually relatively quick, but mental recovery can depend on a lot of things."

Samantha sighed and said, "And I don't have a lot of time to make this decision either."

Saratoga

"Unfortunately, you don't," said Sara. "So let's move on. Next we have adoption. Although it is generally less dangerous than abortion, it can be just as difficult emotionally." Sara looked briefly at her notes and said, "You will feel your child growing in you, and eventually will feel her or him kicking and moving around in you. Most likely, you will develop an emotional attachment to your child long before giving birth to the child."

Then Samantha started sobbing but quickly controlled herself and said, "How soon would I have to give the baby up?"

"It would depend on what type of adoption you chose," said Sara. "There are two types, closed and open."

"So it's an open-and-shut case," said Samantha with a smile.

"Good," said Sara. "Nice to hear your sense of humor again, but gettin' back to business, a closed adoption basically means that you give up the child completely, with no contact ever again. An open adoption means that you can maintain whatever level of contact with the child that you and the adoptive parents agree to."

"Wow. I never knew you could do that," said Samantha. "That's something I'll keep in mind."

"I'm glad that you like that option," said Sara, "but remember we're here today to discuss all of your options. Although you need to decide soon, you need to weigh **all** of your options."

"I will," said Samantha.

"Now for the third option," said Sara. "Keeping the baby. You may have two options within this option; raising the child while still living with your parents or raising the child by yourself."

"May is the key word there," said Samantha. "I don't know how my parents would feel about that, and I'm not sure I would want my baby to be around my father sometimes. I know that he loves us all, but to put it bluntly, he can be rudely critical at times."

Sara took a deep breath and said, "That's one difficult part of a difficult situation, but I really believe that you can sort things out and make the best decision for yourself."

Then Samantha started sobbing again and said, "I wish I hadn't said that about my father. He really means well. He's very hard on himself too, not just my mother and sisters and me. People don't see the things he does for us…..partly because people rarely come over to our house. I know that he loves us, but I just don't know about exposing a child to that kind of atmosphere." Samantha wiped away her tears and said, "Sorry I started crying again."

"Totally understandable," replied Sara as she looked at her watch. "But I'm afraid we're out of time here. Mike's going to do an oil change on my car, and I have to be at his house soon. Then I'm treating him to pizza."

"Well, thank you very much for your help, and consider yourself the recipient of a very big hug," said Samantha.

"You're welcome," said Sara as she put her notes away and started her car.

As Sara drove through the parking lot, Samantha asked, "It's been a while since you've been to my house. Do you remember how to get there?"

Sara laughed and said, "I know how to get there, but for the life of me I couldn't tell you the name of the street. I just know it's sorta on the way to Mike's house."

"Strange how that is," said Samantha. "I know how to get to your house too, but I couldn't tell you the name of your street either." When they got near Samantha's house, she said, "You can just drop me off at the end of the driveway. You're runnin' late, and I don't want to hold up the pizza party."

"Ok. Thanks," said Sara as she pulled over near Samantha's driveway and let Samantha out of the car.

As she got out of the car, Samantha said, "Thanks again, and I'll keep you posted."

"You're welcome," said Sara. After Samantha closed the door, Sara gave Mike a quick call to let him know she was on her way, then drove over to his house.

Two days later, Sara was in her bedroom doing homework when her cell phone rang. She picked it up and saw that it was Samantha calling. Sara didn't even have a chance to say anything before she heard Samantha sobbing.

"What's the matter?" asked Sara. "Are you ok? Do you need help right away?" Samantha managed to control her sobbing enough to tell Sara that her parents were kicking her out of the house. She had wanted to tell her parents about her pregnancy, but she had kept chickening out. When she finally found the courage to say something, her father became furious and told her she could no longer live in his house.

"Where are you now?" asked Sara.

"I'm in my bedroom," replied Samantha. "My father wanted to kick me out right now, but my mother persuaded him to let me stay one more week. I'd rather find someplace else to stay sooner than that if I can. My father is so….." Samantha's voice trailed off and she started sobbing again.

"All right," said Sara. "Today's Wednesday. I'll find someplace for you to stay before the weekend at the latest, even if you have to stay at my house for a few days. I'm sure my parents will understand."

Samantha stopped sobbing and said, "Thank you. Thank you very much. I don't know what I'd do without you."

"You're welcome," said Sara. "And I want you to remember that although this is a very difficult situation for you, you need to remain as positive as you can. I'll help you as much as I can, but you need to help yourself as well."

"I will," said Samantha. Then she sighed and said, "I hope you can find something soon."

"I'll get on it right away and keep you posted," said Sara.

"Ok thanks. Talk to you soon," said Samantha.

"Will do," said Sara.

Hmmm, thought Sara after she had spoken with Samantha. *Well, there's only one way to find out.* Sara went downstairs to look for her mother and found her in the living room, reading a book.

"Do you have a few minutes?" asked Sara.

Her mother put her book down and said, "Of course I do. What's on your mind?"

"Well, I know that Dad has to be in on this," said Sara, "but it might be better if I spoke with you alone about this first."

"Uh oh," replied her mother.

"No, don't worry Mom," said Sara. "This is about a friend of mine. She's pregnant and her father just basically kicked her out of the house. She has a few days to find someplace to go but...."

Sara paused for a moment and her mother said, "So you're asking if she can stay here for a while?"

"Only if she can't find anything else," said Sara. "And I think I can help her find someplace soon. I haven't actually contacted any of the places that I have in mind, but I will do that ASAP."

Sara's mother sighed and said, "Well, it's a possibility, but I'm not going to make any promises. We'll have to discuss it with your father, and then he and I will make a decision."

"Thanks Mom," said Sara. "I'll go start making some phone calls now."

A little while later, Sara heard her father's car pull into the driveway. She went downstairs and joined her mother in the living room. Her mother set her book down and said, "Let your father get settled before we say anything."

"Good idea," said Sara as she picked up a book she had been reading last weekend. When Sara's father walked into the house, Sara and her mother greeted him and asked how his day was.

"Relatively quiet at work today," said Sara's father, "but Rick called and reminded me we have a drill at the fire station this weekend. How's things on the home front?"

"Well, now that you mention it," said Sara's mother.

"Uh oh," said her father. "What happened now?"

"Sara has something that she needs to discuss with us," said her mother. "So I guess it's best if I just let her speak."

"I'm listening," said Sara's father.

"Well, I'll get right to the point then," said Sara. "A friend of mine is pregnant, and her father doesn't want her living in his house any more. I'm trying to find her a place to go, but as a last resort, and **only** a last resort, I'm hoping that she could stay here for a few days if need be."

Sara's father sighed and said, "How soon would this be?"

"A few days from now," said Sara, "and I really think I can find someplace else for her before then. I've done some research online and found a few possibilities. I just have to make some more phone calls."

Sara's father sighed again and said, "All right. Your mother and I need to discuss this privately, then we'll let you know."

"Ok. Thank you," said Sara as she got up and went back upstairs to her bedroom. A few minutes later, Sara came racing down the stairs and said, "Great news. Samantha called and said her aunt is going to let her stay at her house for a while until she can find something else."

"Great. Solves that problem. Well, sort of," said Sara's mother. "I hope that everything works out for her."

"I do as well," said Sara's father. "But does she need any help moving? My truck holds more than your Baja, so I can help if need be."

"Thanks Dad," said Sara. "I'll let you know."

When Sara's father got home Friday afternoon, Sara said, "Thanks again for offering to help Samantha move tomorrow, but she's not taking much stuff and I think we can fit it all in my Baja. Mike's gonna help us load and unload, and Samantha's aunt lives in Lafayette too, so this shouldn't take very long."

"Ok," said Sara's father. "But let me know if you need any help." Then he added, "I heard there might be some showers tomorrow, so bring a tarp and some rope."

"In the Baja already," said Sara, "along with some bungee cords."

The next morning, Sara was driving over to Mike's house when she thought, *Sara Senecal. It does have a nice ring to it, but I'm nowhere near ready for that now*. Sara had thought about the situation that Samantha was in, and was glad that she herself had decided to remain a virgin until after she got married. She didn't care if some of her friends thought she was "old fashioned" in that regard, and Samantha's situation just reinforced her decision. She wanted to help Samantha, but was also determined to not put herself at risk of being in the same situation as Samantha.

When Sara got to Mike's house, she parked in the driveway and was just getting out of her car when Mike came out of his house. He looked up at the sky and said, "Might get some showers today. Do you have a tarp and some rope?"

"All set," said Sara. "But do you have a jacket?"

"In my car," said Mike. He walked over to his car, got his jacket and then got in the Baja with Sara.

She started driving to Samantha's house and Mike said, "I hope everything works out for Samantha, but I don't know what to say to her today. I'm a little bit worried about that. What do I say to her? I hope I don't just blurt out 'how ya doin'. I don't mind helpin' her move, but I need some help with what to say."

"Maybe the weather, fall foliage, Halloween, or," said Sara, "you could remind me that we need to go back and see Joe sometime. I'm not havin any problems with my Baja, but it would be nice to see Joe again. I wouldn't worry about what to say to Samantha though, cause this won't take too long, and we won't be sittin' around the kitchen table socializin'."

"That's true," said Mike. "I just don't want to make a bad situation worse."

"Oh, stop worryin'," said Sara, "and just follow my lead."

"Ok. Thanks," said Mike.

A few minutes later, Sara said, "Ooopps. I think I just drove by Samantha's house. I've got her address taped to my glovebox; can you check it for me?"

Saratoga

"I saw that earlier, and yes, you did go past it," said Mike. Sara turned around and went back to Samantha's house. When she pulled into the driveway, Samantha was on her porch waiting for them.

"Thank you both very much," said Samantha as Mike and Sara got out of her car.

"You're welcome," said Sara and Mike.

Then Sara added, "But we should get goin' here. Might be gettin' some showers soon." She was tempted to say, "And these won't be baby showers either," but decided against it.

Then Samantha surprised Sara and Mike by saying, "And these showers won't be the baby kind either."

Sara laughed and said, "I almost said that, but I didn't dare."

"That's ok," said Samantha. "I have come to terms with what has happened and realized that a little bit of humor can be very helpful."

"Yes, it can," said Mike. "But that sky isn't lookin' very humorous right now."

Sara looked up at the sky and said, "Yes, we'd best get a move on movin'."

Samantha smiled and said, "Ok. Everything, and it isn't much, is upstairs in my room." Then she added, "Oh! My mother made a pot of coffee for us before she left this morning. My father insisted that no one else be here; just the way he is."

After Sara and Mike declined the offer of coffee, they followed Samantha into the house and up to her bedroom. "Let's see," said Sara. "We should probably take the bureau first."

"Good idea," said Mike. "But we should take the drawers out first. We can put them back in after we put the bureau in the car."

Sara looked at the bureau and said, "If we have the drawers facing forward after we put them back in, we can slide the bureau up against the back of the cab of my car. Then just bungee and/or tie the bureau in place."

"That should be fine, so let's do it," said Mike.

After Samantha took the drawers out, Mike and Sara took the bureau downstairs. Samantha followed them with one of the drawers. When they got to Sara's car, Mike and Sara put the bureau in sideways so they could put the drawers back in. Mike put the drawer Samantha had carried out back into the bureau, then they brought down the rest of the drawers. After Mike put the drawers back into the bureau, Sara helped him move the bureau and secure it to the back of the Baja cabin.

"Any other big stuff?" asked Mike.

"Just a rocking chair, and I think that will fit behind the bureau," said Samantha. "I have some clothes packed in a suitcase and some more in large plastic bags. At least some of that should fit in the back of the car."

"I'll bring the rocking chair down," said Mike. "And you two can bring whatever else. We'll see what fits in with the rocking chair, then I'll cover everything with a tarp."

"And while you're tyin' up the tarp," said Sara, "we'll fit what we can in the car. If we can't fit it all in, we can make a second trip."

When they got back to Samantha's bedroom, Sara asked Mike, "Do you need help with the rocking chair?"

Mike picked it up and said, "No, I don't think so. Maybe on the stairs though; let's see about that now." He took the rocking chair over to the stairs and said, "Nope. I'll be fine if I just slowly take one step at a time."

After they got the Baja cargo area loaded, Mike put the tarp over everything and secured it while Sara and Samantha brought the rest of Samantha's stuff down and put it in Sara's car.

"That's it," said Samantha after she put a bag of clothes in the car.

"There's still a little bit of room here," said Sara. "Are you sure that's everything?"

"Yes, it is," said Samantha. "I really don't need a lot. My aunt said I can have my cousin's room. She got married and moved to California last year and left a lot of stuff behind."

"Let's roll then," said Sara.

Saratoga

"Spin them wheels," said Mike as they all got in Sara's car.

After Sara took her keys out and started her car, Samantha said, "Do you know how to get to my aunt's house?"

"I think so," said Sara. "You said her house is on Hemlock Park Drive, right?"

"Yes, said Samantha. "Ten Hemlock Park Drive."

When they arrived there, it was raining, but not very hard. Sara pulled into the driveway, parked her car and said, "Well, at least it's not pouring, so let's go."

Mike took Samantha's suitcase and backpack out from under the tarp while Sara and Samantha each grabbed a bag of clothes from in the car. Samantha's aunt had seen Sara pull into the driveway and opened the front door of her house to let them in. "Follow me," she said as she walked upstairs to Samantha's new room.

After they unloaded Sara's car, Samantha's aunt said to Sara and Mike, "Thank you both very much for helping Samantha. Can I take you to lunch somewhere as a token of appreciation?"

"Oh, thank you for the offer," said Mike, "but I have to get goin'. I've gotta help my brother fix my mother 's car."

"Well, thanks very much for helping me," said Samantha.

"You're welcome," said Sara as she gave Samantha a hug.

"Glad I could help," said Mike.

Then Sara and Mike walked out to her car and got in. Sara started driving Mike home and said, "Just be glad you're not a girl."

Mike was a little bit hesitant to say anything, but said, "Well, I hope everything works out for her."

"So do I," said Sara. "But I'm not talking about that. I'm talking about my monthly friend, and that "friend" is being rather nasty right now."

Damn thought Mike *doesn't seem like a real good time to ask her out. Quick; think of something else to say*. "Sorry to hear that," said Mike. "Wish there was something I could do."

"That's ok," said Sara. "Hopefully, it won't last too long. If it does, I'll just take something for it when I get home."

"Hope you feel better soon," said Mike. "And I'm just curious here, so if you don't feel comfortable tellin' me that's fine, but is Samantha gonna keep the baby?"

"She's not sure right now," said Sara. "But she does need to make up her mind very soon." Then she sighed and said, "I'm tempted to say this to Samantha, but I don't know. I don't want to come across as too pushy. I just don't understand how people who are in favor of allowing abortion would be up in arms if you did the same thing to the fetus of an animal for whatever reason. You can't do it to an animal, but it's ok to do it to a human?"

Mike thought for a moment, then said, "That's true, and a very good point."

A few minutes later, Sara said, "Thanks again for helping today," as she pulled into Mike's driveway.

"You're welcome, and don't forget, we gotta go back to see Joe sometime. I hope his arthritis isn't any worse," said Mike as he got out of Sara's car.

"Maybe next week," said Sara as she waited for Mike to close the car door.

He was walking towards the garage to go help his brother when Sara got out of her car and said, "Wait a second." She went up to Mike and gave him a hug and said, "I really appreciate your help today."

"Glad I could be there" said Mike, but before he could screw up the courage to ask her out on a date, Sara turned around, went back to her car, and drove away.

Damn, thought Mike, *where's my courage when I need it*. He wistfully watched Sara drive away, then turned around and went to help his brother with their mother's car.

7. The Battle for the Bell

"Big game Saturday. You goin'?" asked Reggie as he walked out the door after school with Sara.

"Of course I'm going," replied Sara. "But I don't know who to cheer for, you or my cousin."

"Your cousin?" asked Reggie.

"Yep. He's the quarterback for the Warriors," said Sara.

"Well, you're one of my best friends, and I hate to say this, but I'm gonna make your cousin look like mincemeat," replied Reggie.

Sara laughed and said, "Well, you got the friendship part right, but I don't know about the mincemeat. My cousin's a damn good qb."

The Lafayette Lancers were playing the Wilmington Warriors in the annual Battle for the Bell. The rivalry had been going on for nearly seventy years, and was always a huge event in both towns. There was even a tug-o'-war between the Town Councils of each town just before the game. This replaced the usual coin flip to determine which team kicked off to start the game. The game was always played on the first Saturday in October, starting at one pm, and it was usually over by three thirty, giving the students from the winning school plenty of time to celebrate with their prize before dark.

The prize was a large bell set up on a wagon. Right after the game ended, members of the winning team would pull the wagon around the inside of the stadium, just in front of the stands, while several of their teammates stood on the wagon taking turns ringing the bell. This did not sit well with the home town fans if the visiting team won, but that just made the rivalry even more intense.

After the ceremonial circling in the stadium, the winning team would hook the wagon to a pickup truck and lead their supporters on a parade through their town. The team captains had the honor of ringing the bell during the parade, and always rang it with great gusto. Lafayette was hosting the game this year, and looking to win the rivalry game for the first time in four years. Reggie and the rest of the seniors on the team were especially determined to win the game. They did not want to go through high school without beating their arch rivals the Warriors even once.

Several years earlier, someone in Wilmington had started a petition to change the name of high school sports teams to the Spiders. They felt the name Warriors was offensive and gave the town a bad name. They especially disliked the mascot, a high school student dressed up as an Indian warrior. Some supporters of the Warriors name countered that the name was honoring those who fought unsuccessfully to preserve their way of life back in colonial times. Other supporters said it was just trying to intimidate opponents, getting an advantage any way they could.

Sara thought it was just nitpicking to try to change the name to Spiders, and basically ignored the whole fuss. She felt that Native Americans had definitely gotten a raw deal ever since the first colonists had arrived, but she also felt there were better ways to rectify the situation than to fuss over something like this.

"Well, I'm a damn good defensive lineman, and I chew up qbs and spit 'em out every game," retorted Reggie.

They went back and forth like that for a few minutes, then Sara said, "Enough trash talkin'. We'll see what happens Saturday, but right now I've gotta get goin'. I rode my bike to school today, and it's lookin' like it might rain soon. I'd best get peddlin' to avoid a soakin'."

Reggie looked up at the sky and said, "Yes, you'd best get goin'. Don't want you meltin' before you get home."

Sara smiled and said, "Gracias, mi amigo. Hasta luego."

"Hasta luego," replied Reggie. Then Sara scurried over to her bike, and was soon peddling homeward.

The morning of the big game, Sara got up and looked out the window of her bedroom. There were only a few scattered clouds in the sky and Sara thought, *good. I hope the weather holds for the game.* She got dressed and went downstairs to the kitchen. Her mother was making breakfast, and Sara asked, "What can I do to help?"

"Hmm," replied Sara's mother. "You can make some toast. We've got cinnamon swirl bread in the breadbox."

"Oooh. That sounds good," said Sara.

Then her mother said, "One slice for me, two for your father and whatever for you."

"Ok," said Sara. "Speaking of Dad, where is he?"

"Ready and waiting for breakfast," said Sara's father as he came into the kitchen. He had been outside stacking firewood in the wood shed, and came in anticipating that breakfast would be just about ready.

"You're just in time to set the table," said Sara.

"Wait," said Sara's mother. "Let me see your hands first before you touch any dishes."

"Oh come on," said Sara's father. "I was wearin' gloves. My hands are fine. See?" He flashed his hands at Sara's mother, but before she could actually check them, he started taking plates out of the cabinet.

"Too late now," said Sara. "I guess we'll just have to trust him."

"Well, he hasn't steered us wrong yet, so I suppose we'll let it slide one more time," said Sara's mother.

A few minutes later, Sara said, "Two slices of toast buttered and ready, two more on the way," as she put two slices of cinnamon swirl bread in the toaster.

"Bacon and eggs are ready, and the water for the instant oatmeal is boiling, so I think we're just about set," said Sara's mother. She put the bacon and eggs on the table, and got three packets of oatmeal out of the cabinet.

"Beverage call," said Sara's father.

"Apple juice for me," said Sara's mother.

"Ditto," said Sara.

"Milk for me," said Sara's father as he got the beverages out of the refrigerator. Then they sat down at the table, said grace and ate breakfast.

Saratoga

After breakfast, Sara's father said, "Thank you two for the delicioso breakfast. I'd help with the dishes, but I'd really like to get the rest of that firewood into the shed. Can you help me with that, Sara?"

"Go ahead, Sara. I'll take care of the dishes," said Sara's mother.

"Volunteering my services again, are we? Thanks a lot," joked Sara. Then she said, "Estoy bromeando. Of course I'll help stack the wood. I love sitting in front of a cozy fire in the fireplace, and stackin' firewood will help burn off a few of these calories that I just consumed." She put on a jacket and work gloves and went out to the wood pile with her father.

After Sara and her father loaded the garden wagon with wood, Sara said, "I'll grab a few pieces and carry them to the shed if you'll pull the wagon over to the shed."

"Ok," said Sara's father.

About an hour later, Sara's father said, "That's all she wrote" as they stacked the last load of wood in the shed.

"Good," said Sara with a smile. "I'm gettin' tired of readin' wood." Then she looked at her watch and said, "Hmmm. Yeah, I've got enough time for a quick shower before I ride my bike over to the pep rally at the high school."

Sara always rode her bike to the pep rally, unless it was raining. If the game was in Wilmington, her parents would pick her up at Lafayette High School and drive to the game from there.

"Oh! Did you get the tickets for the game?" asked Sara's father.

"Kinda late to be askin' now, but yes, I did," said Sara "I'll meet you and Mom at the South Entrance to the stadium as usual."

"Ok. And thanks for your help with the wood," said her father as they walked back into the house.

"You're welcome," said Sara. Then she went up to her bedroom and picked out the clothes she wanted to wear to the pep rally. After she took a shower and got dressed, she gave her mother a quick hug and said, "Time to get peddlin'." She went outside, got on her bike and rode to the high school.

"Bout time you got here," said Naomi as Sara parked her bike. Sara and Naomi always sat together at the pep rally, and Naomi had been waiting for Sara at the bike rack at school. Sara got off her bike, locked it in the bike rack and walked into the gym with Naomi. The gym was packed already, but Naomi and Sara managed to squeeze in on the back row of seats.

"Nothin' like the nosebleed seats," said Sara.

"Well girlfriend, if you had gotten here a little earlier, hint hint," said Naomi with a smile.

"I know. Sorry about that," said Sara. "Next year" but before she could finish her sentence, the cheerleaders came running out and the crowd roared. Sara cheered and clapped her hands along with the crowd, but at the same time wistfully thought, *why is it that the girl cheerleaders are always scantily clad while the male cheerleaders are not?* Then she decided that now is not the time to worry about such things, and got into the spirit of the pep rally.

After the pep rally, Naomi said, "I have to go meet Tim. I won a pair of tickets to the game, and I asked Tim if he wanted to go to the game with me." Naomi knew that Sara always bought tickets for the game for her and her parents ahead of time, and besides, she liked Tim a lot and wanted to spend more time with him. She happened to have several classes with Tim this year, and was intrigued by him.

"Ok. I have to go meet my parents at the South Entrance to the stadium anyway," said Sara. "So if I don't see you after the game, I'll see you Monday in school."

"Hasta luego, mi amiga," said Naomi. Then she went to look for Tim, and Sara walked over to the South Entrance to meet her parents. Sara's father was standing on his toes looking for Sara when she saw his bright orange winter hat. He always wore it to the game to help Sara find him in the crowd. He usually took it off after Sara found him, but sometimes it was chilly enough for him to leave it on.

"Decisions, decisions," said Sara's father after Sara joined them outside the stadium.

"Yes, I haven't decided yet either," said Sara. "It's either a chili dog or a hamburger."

"I think I'll try a veggie burger," said Sara's mother, "just to see what it tastes like."

"Actually, I know what I want to eat," said Sara's father. "I'm just tryin' to decide whether to keep the sore thumb on or not."

"Sore thumb?" queried Sara's mother.

Sara just rolled her eyes and said, "Yep, that's Dad speak for his bright orange hat."

Sara's mother just smiled, shook her head and said, "All right, let's quit fiddlin' an' diddlin' and get a move on."

"Yes ma'am," said Sara and her father as they all walked into the stadium. They went to the concession stand, got their food, and headed over to their seats. They were just about to sit down when the PA announcer asked everyone to stand for the national anthem. They carefully set their food down on their seats, and put their hands over their hearts for the national anthem.

Sara's father almost sat down on his food after the anthem, but Sara's mother grabbed his arm and stopped him just in time. "Good save, Mom," said Sara. "That would've been quite the mess, two chili dogs with extra mustard and a cherry cola."

"Thanks. I owe you one," said Sara's father.

"One? More like a dozen," said Sara's mother with a smile.

"At least that many," added Sara.

Sara's father sighed and said, "Surrounded by assassins again."

A little while later, Sara's mother shivered, and Sara's father said, "Gettin' a bit chilled, milady? Would you like to borrow the sore thumb?"

"Thank you, but no," replied Sara's mother. "I have a hat in my jacket pocket if I need it. I was just looking at the cheerleaders and thinkin' I'm glad I'm wearin' more clothes than they are."

Then Sara added, "Not fair, as usual. The girl cheerleaders are scantily clad, but the guys aren't. Why can't they show off their six pack abs?" Sara knew some of the male cheerleaders, and although she thought some of them were handsome, she was more upset that society continued to value girls more for their bodies than guys.

Then she thought, *Well, some girls liked the attention that being scantily clad gave them, and used it to their advantage. Who's to say there's anything wrong with that?*

Suddenly, the crowd roared, bringing Sara back to reality. Reggie had broken through the Warriors' offensive line and practically demolished the quarterback, Sara's cousin. *Reggie's gonna razz me about that on Monday morning for sure*, thought Sara.

"Oh, I hope he's ok," said Sara's mother. She had seen how hard Reggie had hit her nephew and was worried that he might be hurt.

"Relax Mom. He's a tough kid. He can take it," said Sara as her cousin ran off the field.

Then Sara's father added, "It's fourth down now, so he'll have a few minutes to recover. He'll be fine."

"I hope so," said Sara's mother.

The two teams fought back and forth in an epic battle, but eventually, the Lancers prevailed. It took a goal line stand by Reggie and the rest of the defense at the end of the game to keep the Lancers on top, twenty-four to twenty. Reggie put the finishing touch on the game by sacking Sara's cousin before he had a chance to throw the ball on the final play of the game.

After that play, Reggie and the rest of the team rushed over to the wagon with the prize bell on it, and Reggie, due to his game-saving heroics, had the honor of ringing the bell as his teammates pulled the wagon around the inside of the stadium.

As they left the stadium, Sara said, "Well, even though I had mixed emotions about who to cheer for, it was a great game. But boy, am I ever gonna hear it from Reggie on Monday."

"I'm just glad your cousin didn't get hurt," said Sara's mother. "He was gettin' banged up all afternoon."

Saratoga

"Yep. All part of the game," said Sara's father. "I'm sure he'll be fine. Well, except for losin' the game. But he's only a junior, so we'll see what happens next year."

8. Mount Monadnock

    Sara woke up to the sound of birds, but not from outside her window. October nights were too cold to leave her bedroom window open, even just a smidgeon. But her father knew she loved to wake up to the sound of birds chirping and had found an alarm clock that used a recording of actual birds chirping as its' alarm. He had snuck into Sara's bedroom and set it up last Christmas Eve to go off at 5 am Christmas morning to surprise Sara. She definitely was surprised, and thought it was great. Now she could wake up to the sound of birds chirping year round.

    Sara got out of bed, put on her bathrobe, and went downstairs to the kitchen. Her mother was already up, making a pot of coffee. "No coffee for me," said Sara. "I don't want to be dehydrated today. I'm hiking Mt Monadnock with Bob."

    Her mother thought for a moment, then said, "Oh, Bob Kendall, the boy you met at the river cleanup a while ago."

    "Yes, that's right. He should be here in a about an hour," said Sara as she looked at the clock in the kitchen. She had even gone to bed a little bit early last night to make sure she got a good night's sleep. She liked to hike, and was looking forward to spending time with Bob. He liked many of the same hobbies and activities as Sara, and she felt comfortable around him.

    Sara did not have a specific boyfriend yet but was growing fond of her friend Mike. However, she did want to spend more time with Bob. At some point in time, perhaps, she would ask him out, or maybe he would ask her out. She didn't worry too much about things like that. Occasionally, she wondered how and when she would meet her future husband, but today, she had hiking on her mind.

    "Bacon and eggs?" asked her mother as she opened the refrigerator.

    "You know me well," replied Sara. She always had a breakfast of bacon, eggs and cereal when she went hiking. It seemed to boost her

Saratoga

energy without making her feel stuffed. She went back upstairs to get dressed while her mother cooked breakfast. It was a little bit chilly that day, but Sara knew they would warm up once they started hiking. She dressed warm enough for the start of the hike, figuring she could take off her wool sweater when she started to get warm.

Then she put on wool socks and her hiking boots, and went back downstairs. She had already packed her backpack yesterday, making sure she had rain gear and an extra sweater. She also packed a winter hat and pair of gloves, just in case. A sunny fall day could turn rainy and chilly rather quickly. And, the top of Mt. Monadnock was above the tree line, and it could get extra chilly there if it was windy.

"Smells good; thank you for cooking," said Sara as she poured a bowl of cereal.

"You're welcome," replied her mother. Sara sat down at the table, and her mother took a muffin from the bread box, then sat down with her.

"Ooops. We forgot juice," said Sara. "Let's say grace, then I'll get it." After they said grace, Sara got up to get the juice.

"What juice for you?" asked Sara while she walked to the refrigerator.

"Apple cider, please," replied her mother. Then she added, "You have to try this. Grammy and I had some last week. Put the cider in a coffee cup, heat it in the microwave, and then stir in a tablespoon of lemon juice."

"Oooh! That sounds interesting," said Sara. She poured two cups of cider, then put the cups in the microwave.

"A minute and a half should be fine," said her mother. When the microwave beeped, Sara took the cups out and brought them over to the table. Her mother stirred some lemon juice into each cup, and handed one to Sara.

"Wow," said Sara after she took a sip. "This is great. We should bottle this and sell it."

"Hmmm. Something to think about," replied Sara's mother.

Sara had just finished her breakfast when she heard a car in the driveway. "That's probably Bob," she said as she got up and went to the kitchen sink to rinse off her breakfast dishes. Then she put them in the dishwasher and went to the front door. Just as she got there, the doorbell rang.

She opened the door, and Bob asked, "Ready to hike?"

"Who, me," joked Sara with a mock look of surprise on her face. She liked to kid around with Bob, as he did with her.

"Come on in, Bob," said Sara's mother. "Sara needs to fill her water bottle, and I have a muffin for each of you."

"Thank you," said Bob as he came into the kitchen. Then he added, "Pleased to meet you, Mrs. Parmenter."

"Pleased to meet you as well, Bob," said Sara's mother as Sara filled her water bottle and put it in her backpack.

"These will make a nice snack on the trail," said Bob as he took the muffins from Sara's mother. Sara picked up her backpack and they went out to Bob's pickup truck. Bob checked to make sure he had filled his water bottle while Sara put her backpack into the truck.

"Where's your hiking stick?" asked Bob as he closed the tailgate.

"Good catch," laughed Sara. "I put it next to the front door to remember it, and I forgot it anyway." Sara went back and got her hiking stick while Bob made sure that he had the money to get into Monadnock State Park. The fee was not very much, but Bob generally did not carry much cash. If Sara wanted to pay her own way, that was fine with Bob, but he had asked her to go hiking, and felt that he should pay the fee for both of them.

Sara's mother waved goodbye from the doorway, and they were off. "Pick any CD you want, and fire it up," said Bob. Sara took the CD case from between the seats and opened it up.

"Very eclectic collection here," she said as she looked through the case. Sara liked to mix things up, and was impressed by Bob's variety of musical genres in his CD case. She picked out a classical music CD and put it in the player. "Very soothing," said Sara.

"Just like being in the great outdoors," replied Bob.

"Yes, and I'm really looking forward to this hike," said Sara.

It took a while to get to Monadnock State Park, but Sara didn't mind. She enjoyed the scenery and talking with Bob. She was glad he kept the volume on his CD player down. Too many of her friends cranked the music volume in their cars, making conversation difficult. When they got to the park, Bob paid the entrance fee, and drove over to the parking lot.

"Wow, Pennsylvania," said Sara, looking at the license plate on one of the cars in the parking lot.

"That's a bit of a drive, I would say," commented Bob. He found a parking spot, and parked his truck. Then he got out of the truck, and opened the tailgate. Sara took her backpack and put it on, while Bob rummaged through his pack.

"Uh oh. Did you forget something?" asked Sara.

"I don't think so," replied Bob. "I just want to make sure I have my whistle. I know we probably won't need it here, but I just like to have it with me whenever I hike." Then Bob explained that a whistle was good to have in case you got lost or hurt while hiking. Its sound carried farther than a human voice, and a person would not get hoarse using a whistle to call for help.

Being prepared was one of the things that Sara liked about Bob. He always seemed to think ahead and rarely got caught by surprise. One time, though, he had been mountain biking on a hot day with some friends when they came across a swimming hole in a river. Bob had jumped off of his bike, and done a cannonball into the water when realized he still had his wallet in a pocket of his shorts. By the time he got out of the water, the wallet was soaked and ruined. Luckily, nothing in the wallet was wrecked, but he did have to buy a new wallet.

"Do you have a Ziploc bag for your wallet in case it rains?" laughed Sara. Bob had told her about the wallet incident, and Sara could not resist teasing him about it occasionally. Bob just chuckled, put on his pack, and took the hiking sticks out of the truck.

He looked at his trail map, and said, "Let's take a more challenging way to the top today. We'll take the Lost Farm Trail over to the footpaths, and go from there." He showed Sara the trail map, and indicated where the footpaths were. The listings in the legend on the trail map even stated; "FOOTPATHS may be more challenging."

That was all Sara needed to see. "I love a challenge. Let's do it," said Sara.

Bob looked at his watch, and said, "Plenty of time. And, if it takes us too long to get to the top, we can just take the white-cross trail down."

They started walking over to the Lost Farm Trail when Sara paused with a pensive look on her face. Bob kept walking, but when he realized Sara had stopped, he turned around and inquired, "Second thoughts about the hike?"

"No," replied Sara. "I just have a nagging feeling that we forgot something." Bob leaned on his hiking stick and thought. Then Sara remembered and said, "Oh! We left the muffins on the front seat of your truck."

"Don't want to leave those behind, especially homemade blueberry muffins," said Bob as he went back to the truck to get them. He had just enough room in the top of his pack to fit them in without squishing them.

They had been hiking for a while when Bob mentioned, "I could use a snack; how about you?"

"What do you think I am, a gingerbread woman?" laughed Sara. Then she said, "Actually, a snack sounds like a good idea." They were about to sit down on a big log when Sara checked it with her hand and said, "Yep, it's wet. It must have rained here recently, and the moss on the log has not dried out yet."

"How about that rock over there?" said Bob as he pointed to a somewhat flat rock further up the trail.

"Perfect," said Sara. "As long as it is dry." They walked up to the rock, found that it was dry, and sat down to eat their muffins. After they finished eating, Bob took their rubbish and stuffed it in his rubbish pocket. He had one pocket on his hiking jacket that he used only for rubbish. He even brought a small trash bag on every hike in case his

Saratoga

rubbish pocket got filled. He always picked up rubbish that others left behind, and was disappointed that, occasionally, he did need to use the bag.

"Did you hear that?" asked Sara.

"I did, but I'm not sure what kind of bird that is," replied Bob. They looked around for a minute or two but could not find the bird.

"She knows we're looking for her, so she either flew away or is hiding," said Sara.

"Strange how birds, and even other animals, can sense that," said Bob.

Sara took another look around the tree tops, then said, "I know. If I could speak animal, I would let them know we only want to look at them."

They stood there in the relative quiet for a moment, then Bob said, "I love the sound of a breeze whispering through the pine trees."

"I may be going there next year," said Sara.

A puzzled look came over Bob's face and he said, "Going where?"

"Whispering Pines College," replied Sara. "They have an excellent Environmental Engineering program there, and they participate in ROTC as well. I'm going to apply there for both programs soon."

"Yes, I've heard many good things about their Environmental Engineering program, and ROTC is a great way to serve our country," said Bob. "I may apply there myself."

"Great," said Sara. "Let me know if you do."

"Certainly," replied Bob.

Then they put their packs back on, and resumed hiking. They found the footpaths to be a bit of a challenge, but Sara was glad they had gone that way. She liked tackling challenges, and the feeling of accomplishment she felt after successfully conquering another challenge. They reached the top of Monadnock around noontime, and found a sheltered spot out of the wind to have lunch.

Suddenly, a plastic bag blew by, but Bob was quick enough to grab it before it blew away. "Good catch," said a young girl as she came over to take back the bag that had blown away from her. Then she added, "Carry In, Carry Out."

"That's great," replied Bob. "I'm glad that you do that."

After lunch, they looked around and enjoyed the view from the top of the third most climbed mountain in the world. "There's a little bit of color left," said Bob as he gazed over the valley below.

"Yes," said Sara with a sigh. "I love the colorful fall foliage, but it always seems to disappear so quickly." They took one last look around and then headed down the mountain.

When they got back to Bob's truck, Sara said, "Thank you for bringing me here. I had a great time. I'm really looking forward to hiking Mt Washington with you some day."

"You're welcome," said Bob. "I'm looking forward to hiking Washington as well, but we'll need to hike at least a couple of 4,000 footers before we tackle Washington."

"Fine with me," said Sara. "We can talk about it on the way home." They put their gear in Bob's truck and headed for home.

On the way home, Bob said, "My least favorite day of the year is coming up sorta soon."

Sara thought for a moment, then said, "Oh yeah, fall-back day. Not my favorite either. Gets dark early enough as it is at that time of year." Then she added, "If we go hiking, we'll just have to make sure we start early enough in the day so we can get back to the car before dark."

"Speaking of winter hiking, if you are interested in going, you'll need additional gear," said Bob.

"I'm definitely interested, so what do I need for gear?" replied Sara.

Bob thought for a moment, then said, "Well, for starters, you'll need micro spikes and mountain snow shoes."

"Micro spikes?" asked Sara.

"Basically, they are small spikes that use rubber strapping to attach the spikes to your boots. You'll need them in icy conditions," replied Bob.

"You'll also need a good pair of tinted goggles. The sun reflecting off of the snow can get very bright."

"Ok," said Sara. "Where can I get all of this stuff?"

"There's a sporting goods store near my house. I'll bring you there sometime and you can take a look."

"Just thought of this," said Sara. "I do have snow shoes, but it sounds like I might have to get new ones."

"Yes," replied Bob. "Most likely, you'll need new ones, but I'll take a look at what you have. On less rigorous hikes, you might be able to use the shoes you have now."

A few minutes later, Bob said, "Ooopps. I almost forgot one very important item. Hiking poles."

"Hiking poles?" asked Sara.

"Yes," said Bob. "Much different than the sapling hiking sticks that we used today. Those are good enough for the hiking we have done so far, but for winter hiking, you'll need something better."

"I'm guessing these poles are sort of like ski poles," said Sara.

"Similar, but not the same," said Bob. Then he added, "I will say that you can get away without using poles, or you could use just one, but I use two myself. It depends on your comfort level."

"Hmmm. Something to think about," said Sara.

Then Bob said, "Shoot. I missed the road."

"Missed the road?" asked Sara.

"Yes. The road to your house. I guess I'm just on automatic pilot to go to my house." Bob thought for a moment, then said, "Better just turn around and go back. I was tryin' to think of a different way to get to your house, but…. oh well."

"I have no idea where we are," said Sara. "So, yeah, might as well just turn around." Bob found a safe place to turn around, then went back and turned on to the road he had missed. A little while later, he was pulling into Sara's driveway.

When Bob parked his truck in front of Sara's house, she said, "Thanks again for hiking with me. I had a great time."

"So did I," replied Bob. They got out of his truck, and Sara took her gear out. "Got everything?" asked Bob.

Sara checked her pack and said, "Let's see; hat and gloves are in there, and I've got my hiking stick here, so, I'm all set."

"Ok," said Bob as he closed the back of his truck.

Hmmm, thought Sara, followed by, *oh, just do it*. She impulsively gave Bob a quick hug and said "I'm really looking forward to hiking with you again. I'll give you a call soon."

Bob, being somewhat shy, was happily surprised by Sara's hug but all he could think to say was "Sounds good." Then he got in his truck and as he drove away, he thought, *she just might want to go out with me. If only I wasn't so dang shy*.

Meanwhile, Sara stood in the walkway to her house and watched as Bob drove away. She liked Bob a lot, and was glad she had hugged him, but had mixed emotions about it. She liked Mike a lot as well, and hoped that she would not have to someday decide between the two of them. Of course, someone else could come along and capture Sara's heart, but for now, she decided to not worry about it, and just live her life.

9. The Wolf Whistle

Sara was walking down the hall in school when she heard the wolf whistle behind her and turned around to see who it was. She chuckled and said, "I thought that might be you," to her friend Cheri.

"Lookin' sharp today, girl. What's the occasion?" asked Cheri.

Sara smiled and said, "Hmmm….I don't know, but I'll think of something. You know me, always thinking."

"That's true," replied Cheri. "I don't think there's anything you haven't thought about."

Sara liked to mix things up occasionally, and dressing up for no special reason was one way to do that. She just felt it wasn't worth it to fuss over makeup, nail polish and all that stuff every day. She preferred to just throw on a pair of jeans and a shirt and go. Jeans and shirts were a lot easier to clean than fancier clothes, too, and Sara hated doing laundry. But today, Sara woke up in a "dress-up" mood and dressed accordingly.

Suddenly, their conversation was interrupted by "Cheri, Sara, come over here immediately." Cheri and Sara looked in the direction of the voice and saw Ms. Warren standing in the doorway to her classroom, scowling at them.

"Uh oh," said Cheri.

"But what did we do?" asked Sara.

They walked over to Ms. Warren and saw that she was writing out a detention. "A week's detention for each of you ought to teach you to never use a wolf whistle again," said Ms. Warren sternly, with an emphasis on "never".

"What?" said Sara incredulously.

"I was just sayin' I think Sara's very pretty when she dresses up, and ought to do it more often," said Cheri.

Saratoga

"A wolf whistle is a sexist insult that has no place in today's society whatsoever," insisted Ms. Warren as she handed the detentions to Sara and Cheri.

Cheri started to protest again but Ms. Warren interrupted her with, "Perhaps you would like two weeks detention."

Cheri said, "No, I would not, but..." and Sara quickly cut her off with, "Come on Cheri, we have to get going or we'll be late to our next class." Sara took her friend by the arm and walked away with her.

When they had gotten out of Ms. Warren's hearing range, Cheri said, "I can't believe that old battleax gave us a week's detention. I am so pissed...oh, this just fries me to no end."

"Me too," replied Sara. "People need to put things in context. I understand that a wolf whistle can be offensive, but if it's between friends, what's the big deal? We need to go see the Principal right now."

"Good idea," said Cheri. "Hopefully he'll have more of an open mind than that old battleax Warren." Sara and Cheri walked to the Principal's office, and even though the door was open, Sara knocked on it.

"Come in, come in," said Principal Smythe. "The door is always open here; no need to knock." Principal Smythe felt it was very important to keep the lines of communication between students and staff open, so he left his door open as often as possible, and encouraged students to stop in any time to discuss any issue.

Sara and Cheri walked into the office, and Cheri shut the door behind her. She knew that eventually, Ms. Warren would find out that she and Sara had discussed their detentions with Principal Smythe, but she just felt more comfortable discussing the issue behind closed doors.

"Hmmm. Serious business, I see," said Principal Smythe as he watched Cheri shut the door.

"Yes, it is," said Sara as she and Cheri sat down.

They explained the situation to Principal Smythe, and he asked a few questions as they went along. When they finished explaining what happened, Cheri said, "I feel that our detentions should be voided completely."

"Absolutely," added Sara. "We did nothing wrong. It was just a playful moment between friends."

Mr. Smythe gave a pensive sigh and said, "This is a unique situation involving important issues facing us today. I believe in freedom of speech, which in a sense, a wolf whistle is. However, I also understand that a wolf whistle, and the vulgar comments that unfortunately often come with it, can make a woman feel very uncomfortable. Society needs to find a way to accommodate both sides of this issue, but that will be extremely difficult." He paused for a moment, then said, "Regarding this incident today, I believe that Ms. Warren came down too hard on both of you. It was just something between friends taken out of context by Ms. Warren. However, I need to get her side of the story before I make a decision. Come back at the end of school today and I will let you know my decision."

"Very well," said Cheri, "and thank you for listening to our side of the story."

"Yes. Thank you," said Sara.

As they got up to leave the office, Principal Smythe said, "Oh, I almost forgot; you'll be late for your next class, so I'll give you a note." He gave them each a note, then said, "Please leave the door open on your way out."

After Cheri and Sara walked out of the Principal's office, Cheri said to Sara, "Well, we'll see what happens. Damn. That old battleax just fries me."

"Yes, I know," replied Sara. "But don't let her get to you. And if I don't see you before then, I'll meet you at the Principal's office after school."

"Ok," said Cheri as they went their separate ways.

Later on, Sara heard her friend Pierre say "Good morning, your majesty," as he caught up to Sara in the hallway. He had noticed that Sara was dressed up and said, "May I escort you to the royal ball this evening, or perhaps just to social studies class this morning?"

"To the class room, if you please, sire, and perhaps the ball later on," replied Sara with a smile. Then she added, "You're dressed to the nines as usual." Pierre almost always wore dress pants, a dress shirt and tie to school. Occasionally he would replace the tie with a vest and a bow tie, but that was only in cooler weather.

"Yes," replied Pierre. "For whatever reason, dressing well helps me to focus better in school. Getting into a good college is important to me, and establishing good study habits will help me get into a good college and do well there."

"Interesting," said Sara, "and it's great that it works for you, but for me, spending time like I did this morning to get dressed up just isn't worth doing every day."

"After you, milady," said Pierre as he opened the door to the class room.

"Thank you, sire," said Sara as she walked into the room. As she walked to her desk, Sara noticed that Debby was scantily clad as usual. Sara did not know Debby very well, but couldn't help noticing the way that she dressed. Sara also noticed the way that many of the boys at school ogled Debby. Sara understood that this was all part of growing up and everyone was different, but it annoyed Sara to no end that women throughout history had been valued more for their beauty than their brains.

Unfortunately, thought Sara, *although progress has been made, the beauty over brains trend continues. Just look at the CD cover of any female singer, and most likely, she's scantily clad and in a sexually suggestive pose.* Sara felt that one of the biggest reasons that sex sells is because Hollywood and Madison Avenue push it so hard. And the harder they push it, the more money they make.

Occasionally, Sara discussed this with Pastor Stanley. In his sermons, he occasionally spoke of how, according to Timothy 6:10, the love of money is the root of all evil. The more Sara thought about it, the more she realized that yes indeed, the love of money, and the love of power and control that large sums of money can bring, is the root of much of the evil in the world today. Not necessarily all of the evil, but a very large portion of it. Sara felt that other aspects of human nature, such as self-preservation, were responsible for some of the evil, but much of it was due to the love of money, power and control.

Suddenly, Sara was startled back to reality when Mr. Roberts said, "Ok, Miss Einstein, what are you thinking about now?"

"Ummm; just thinkin' about thinkin'?" Sara replied meekly with a smile, hoping to wiggle out of the embarrassing situation she found herself in.

"Well, how about thinkin' about paying attention in class," suggested Mr. Roberts with a wry smile. He knew that Sara's friends occasionally called her Miss Einstein, and he played along with it as well sometimes. He wasn't very hard on Sara for not paying attention that day because he knew she always did well in social studies class. In addition to doing well in school, Sara was known for finding the names of women in history that she felt did not get the attention they were due. Whatever the subject or time period that was being studied in social studies class, Sara was sure to have the name of at least one woman whose story had not made the history books.

"Now, where were we before we were so thoughtfully interrupted?" said Mr. Roberts. He thought for a moment, then said, "Ah yes. Computers. Those wonderful wonders of modern technology. Presuming you all read your homework assignment from yesterday, you would know that computers have been around for longer than most people would think." He paused, looked around at the students and said, "John, can you tell me who invented the first computer?"

John looked a little perplexed, then timidly said, "I think his name was Cabbage." There were a few laughs in the room, but Mr. Roberts said, "Now, now. No laughing. He's actually very close. Does anyone know his name?"

Several hands went up in the air and Mr. Roberts said, "Ok, Abigail, who was it?"

Abigail quickly answered, "Charles Babbage. He began working on it in 1822, but he never actually finished it. Lack of funding prevented him from building a full scale functioning version of what he called the Difference Engine."

Just as Mr. Roberts replied, "Very good, Abigail," Sara put her hand up. Mr. Roberts smiled and said, "Ok Sara, who's the missing link here?"

Sara replied, "Ada Lovelace. She worked with Mr. Babbage and is considered to be the world's first computer programmer. Mr. Babbage had written fragments of programs, but in 1843, Ms. Lovelace was the first person to publish a complete computer program. There's even an Ada Lovelace Day, celebrated around the world every year. It is on the second Tuesday of October, and is an international celebration of the achievements of women in science, technology, engineering and math. Two major goals of this celebration are to increase the profile of women in STEM, and thus inspire more girls to seek careers in STEM."

"Amazing," said Mr. Roberts. "I'll have to google her and find out more. Sounds very impressive. So impressive that I have a new assignment that will be due this coming Friday." There were a few groans in the classroom, and a couple of students gave Sara the "thanks for nothing" look, but Sara took it in stride.

Then Mr. Roberts said, "Your assignment for Friday is to write a one page paper on any woman, or perhaps group of women, involved in any aspect of STEM at any point in time." He paused for a moment before adding, in a stern voice, "And no font size larger than fourteen." The last time Mr. Roberts had given the class this type of assignment, Joe Pugh had used font size twenty-eight for his paper. When Mr. Roberts returned the papers after grading them, he told Joe, "Originally, I was going to give you an F for being a wise guy, but then I realized that I had not specified a font size, so I gave you a C for being creative."

At the end of school that day, Sara met Cheri at the Principal's office. Ms. Warren was there as well, and was not pleased with the situation, but said nothing to Cheri or Sara. Principal Smythe called them into his office and they sat down. Mr. Smythe shut the door behind them, then sat down and said, "I have listened to each side of this situation, and have decided to void the one-week detentions. However, school policy mandates that Ms. Warren agree to this." Then he turned to Ms. Warren and asked, "Do you agree?"

Ms. Warren firmly stated, "No, I do not. I strongly believe that a wolf whistle is a sexist insult and has no place in society today at all."

"That's your prerogative," replied Mr. Smythe. Then he turned to Cheri and Sara and said, "Since Ms. Warren did not agree to void your detentions, school policy does not allow me to void them completely. However, I am allowed to reduce them, and they will be reduced to one day." He stood up to indicate that the meeting was over, and as they stood up, Cheri and Sara said, "Thank you."

Ms. Warren stood up, but said nothing as she walked out the door. Cheri and Sara walked out behind Ms. Warren, and she turned and glared at them before she walked away.

"Well, one day is better than five," said Cheri.

"Yes," replied Sara, "but we better hurry, or we'll get a detention for being late for detention."

"Oh, crap," said Cheri, "I hope the old battleax isn't supervising detention today." They quickly walked down to study hall and were relieved to see that Ms. Warren was not supervising detention.

When they walked into the room, Ms. Peterstone said, "Cheri? Sara? It's highly unusual to see you two here." Ms. Peterstone taught environmental science at Lafayette High School, and knew that Cheri and Sara were serious about their studies. Environmental science was Sara's favorite class, and Ms. Peterstone knew that Sara wanted to become an environmental engineer. Cheri had several career choices in mind, and knew that good grades, and a good record, in high school were essential no matter what career she eventually decided to pursue.

Still worried that Cheri might spout off about "that old battleax", Sara quickly said, "We had a difference of opinion with Ms. Warren regarding the First Amendment."

Then Cheri, outspoken as usual, said, "Ms. Peterstone, what is your opinion of a wolf whistle between friends?"

Ms. Peterstone looked perplexed and gave a sigh of relief when the bell rang. "Saved by the bell," she said with a smile. "But I will think about it, and you can discuss it with me after detention, if you want. In the meantime, please join the rest of the miscreants and have a seat."

As they walked to their seats, Sara whispered, "We can stay if you want; Mike will give us a ride home."

"Good," whispered Cheri, and they sat down. Sara did have her own car, but rarely drove it to school. Finding a parking spot was just too much of a fuss. Earlier that day, she had asked Mike if he could give her a ride home, and he was happy to do so.

When detention was over, Sara and Cheri walked up to the desk and let Ms. Peterstone know that they would like to discuss the wolf whistle issue. "Good. Good," replied Ms. Peterstone. "I'd love to have a lively discussion of First Amendment rights." Then she said to Cheri, "I must admit, you caught me off guard with your question. And I'm just wondering, is this issue the cause of your recent disagreement with Ms. Warren?"

"Yes," said Cheri, then she and Sara explained what had happened earlier in the day with Ms. Warren.

"Interesting," said Ms. Peterstone. "That's a very conflicting issue. On one hand, you have freedom of speech, yet on the other is sexual harassment." She sighed, then added, "I have been on the receiving end of a few wolf whistles myself." Sara and Cheri gasped, but before they could say anything, Ms. Peterstone continued, "I was in college, in New York City, a few years ago. To get to my school, I had to walk past a construction site, and you know how those are."

Sara grimaced, and Cheri said, "Disgusting pigs."

"Well, yeah, some of the stuff they said, in addition to the wolf whistles, would put them in that classification," said Ms. Peterstone, "but I dealt with it by completely ignoring them. I was determined to not let it bother me, and I succeeded. As far as I'm concerned, if you let it bother you, you are empowering and enabling them, thus making the situation worse."

"I'da been tempted to march right over and slug one of them," said Cheri.

"Yep. Knowin' you, I wouldn't have been surprised if you had," said Sara with a smile. "Me, I would have done my best to ignore them. It's a sad fact of life that some men act that way, but I don't think we can regulate our way out of that. Freedom of speech is just too important."

"Hmmm," said Cheri. "I can't agree with you on that one, my friend. Sexual harassment is just too prevalent and must be stopped."

Then Ms. Peterstone said, "Let's liven things up a bit by asking "how can you tell if the woman being whistled at considers it sexual harassment, or, maybe she considers it a compliment". How can you tell what she thinks?"

"Oh come on," said Cheri. "With the way those guys carry on, how can anyone consider that a compliment?"

"Believe it or not, some of my classmates got the same treatment and really did consider it a compliment. They weren't happy about some of the comments," replied Ms. Peterstone, "but they knew the guys were just showin' off in front of their friends, and felt it was best just to ignore the whistles and comments while secretly taking them as a compliment."

"Well, as far as I'm concerned, the comments are uncalled for," said Sara, "but you just can't stifle free speech. No matter how vulgar it is, it has to be allowed."

Then Mike said, "Sorry for buttin' in here, but it is getting kinda late, so if you two want a ride home, the bus is leavin' now." He had been waiting in the hallway just outside of the classroom door for a minute or two before he decided that he had run out of time and had to interrupt what he found to be a very interesting discussion.

Ms. Peterstone said, "Quite all right, Mike, I've got to get going too. I'll see you all tomorrow."

Mike, Sara and Cheri said goodbye to Ms. Peterstone and walked away.

"So, what got you two angels into trouble?" asked Mike with a sly smile. He knew Cheri was a little bit on the feisty side, and liked to tease her occasionally. If she got too wound up, he had a knack for being able to unwind her. Maybe it was his easy going personality, or his timely self-deprecating jokes, but whatever it was, it just about always worked.

Sara quickly said, "Please, don't get her started, at least not til we get out to your car."

Cheri said, "I'm so tempted to let off steam now, but I'll be good and wait. But be prepared; I'm already at the boilin' point."

When they got in his car, Mike said, "Ok, steam away."

Saratoga

Cheri laughed and said, "I'll try not to steam too much, but here goes." She and Sara explained what had happened, with a few "old battleaxes" thrown in for good measure.

When they finished, Mike smiled slyly, gave a wolf whistle, and said, "Wow, that's quite the adventure."

"Wise guy," said Sara as she slugged Mike in the shoulder.

"Careful now," said Mike. "You don't want that old battleax seein' you slug someone. She'll give you another detention. Good thing I wasn't drivin'." As soon as he said that, they all realized they were still sitting in the school parking lot.

"I thought you said the bus was leaving," joked Cheri. "I should be home by now. What kind of service is this?" Mike laughed, started his car and drove away.

"Who's first?" asked Mike as he pulled out of the high school parking lot.

"I live closer, so I'm first, I guess," said Cheri as she looked toward Sara in the front seat.

"Fine by me," said Sara.

"Oops. Forgot to ask which way to go," said Mike.

"This way is fine. I live on Meadowbrook Road," said Cheri.

"Ok. I know where that is," said Mike. "Just give me a holler when I get near your house." *Cool*, thought Mike, *I get some time alone with Sara after I drop Cheri off*. Mike was feeling more comfortable alone with Sara, but still could not muster up the courage to ask her out.

"Ima hollerin'," said Cheri as they got near her house. "Next one on the right."

Mike pulled into the driveway and said, "That'll be four dollars and ninety-three cents, please." He put his car in park and stuck his right hand, palm up, towards the back seat.

Cheri grabbed his hand and kissed it, then said, "Thanks" and got out of the car.

"Best tip I ever had," said Mike.

"Wait til you get to my house," laughed Sara. Then she said, "Uh oh. I'm in trouble now."

"Nah. Don't worry about it," replied Mike. "I know you were just kiddin' around." Then he thought, *damn. I wish she wasn't just kiddin' around.*

"Looks good on my side," said Sara as Mike backed out of Cheri's driveway. Mike had started driving towards Sara's house when he saw a teenage girl walking down the street. He whistled at her as he drove past, then waited for Sara's reaction.

"Oh! You disgusting pig. Stop the car. I'm getting…..only kidding," said Sara.

Mike laughed and said, "Well, she didn't seem too mad. In fact, she smiled a bit after I whistled."

"Yep. I saw that too," said Sara.

Whew, thought Mike, *she's not mad about me whistlin'*. Then he thought, *Relax. Don't be getting' nervous around her, you'll scare her away. Just be yourself.* "Right turn here?" asked Mike as he came to a four-way intersection.

"That's correct," replied Sara. Then she added, with a sly smile, "And don't be whistlin' at that guy walkin' down the street there."

Mike smiled and said, "You don't have to worry about that. If some other guy whistles at him, whatever, but not me."

Sara sighed and said, "That's so sad. There's such a big fuss about LGB whatever. I can never remember the letters. Anyway, why can't everyone just leave each other alone? Don't ask, don't tell, don't flaunt, but do respect the opinion of those who disagree with you."

"My feelings exactly," replied Mike, "but good luck with that nowadays."

Sara sighed again and said, "Yes. Unfortunately, it's getting to the point where you can't even say that you think homosexuality is wrong. Personally, I don't have an opinion one way or the other. Both sides, to me, seem to have valid facts on their side. My concern is with freedom of speech. I am very concerned about that. Did you know that in Canada, you can't say that you think homosexuality is wrong? You can get in huge trouble for that. That's crazy. Fines, jail time, lawyers' fees, lose your job, the whole nine yards."

Uh oh, thought Sara, *he's gonna be thinkin' "here she goes again."* Sara enjoyed spending time with Mike and didn't want to "scare" him away, but she felt very strongly about the First and Second Amendments and was not afraid to speak up about them. But before Mike could say anything, Sara said, "Sorry about being a wind bag, but I just feel strongly about certain things."

"Well, don't worry about it. Everybody's gotta let off steam every once in a while," replied Mike. A few minutes later, Mike pulled into Sara's driveway. Her mother was unloading groceries from her car, and Mike volunteered to help her. When they finished, Sara's mother offered Mike a piece of pie, but Mike said, "Well, thank you very much, but I have to get goin'. I told my brother I'd help him fix the brakes on his car. It's a two-man job, and he really needs to get it done today."

As Mike walked toward the door, Sara said, "Awe, I wish you could stay, but I understand." Then she came over, kissed him on the cheek, and said, "Thanks for the ride home, and for helping my mother."

"You're welcome," said Mike. Then he turned around and walked out to his car. *Yeah*, thought Mike with a big smile as he started backing out of Sara's driveway. *That definitely was a better tip than Cheri gave me.* Suddenly, the honk of a car horn brought Mike back to reality. He had backed out of Sara's driveway and on to the road without checking the road first. At the sound of the horn, he slammed on his brakes, and the passing car just missed his car.

Whew! Close one, he thought. *Oh crap. I hope Sara didn't see that. Maybe I'll just tell her she got me so flustered when she kissed me, I forgot to check the road. Yeah, right. Like Charlie Chicken is gonna tell her that.* Mike sighed and started driving home. *I have to do something*, he thought. *She kissed me on the cheek. I think she really likes me. Damn. I gotta quit bein' a chicken and ask her out.*

Meanwhile, Sara had heard the horn, looked out the window and saw what happened. "Wow! Close call," she said.

"What happened?" asked her mother from the kitchen. Sara came back into the kitchen and said, "I didn't see it all, but Mike almost got clipped backing out of our driveway."

Sara's mother smiled and said, "Maybe you got him all wound up with that kiss you gave him."

"Oh, mother, puuulllese," said Sara with a grimace.

"You know, he'd make a nice catch for you," said Sara's mother.

"Jeesh, Mom," said Sara.

"Well," said her mother, "I mean a nice guy to go out with, that's all." Mike had been over to Sara's house a few times, and Sara's parents thought well of him. Sara didn't want to admit it to her mother, but sometimes, she really wished Mike would ask her out.

Maybe he'll get the hint from that kiss, thought Sara. *If not, I just might have to ask him out myself. But then again, what about Bob?*

"Earth to Sara, come in please," said Sara's mother with a smile. She had seen Sara deep in thought and couldn't resist teasing her. Then she added, "And what is the mad scientist thinking about now?"

Might as well spill the beans now, thought Sara. "Well," she said, "it's not something I like to talk about, but I'm kinda torn between two guys right now. I like them both a lot, and really don't want to have to….."

Sara's voice trailed off, and her mother finished the sentence for her with, "Decide between the two of them?" she asked.

"Sort of. I guess so. I don't know. This is all so confusing," said Sara.

"Welcome to womanhood," replied her mother.

Then Sara laughed and said, "Wish I could just flip a coin, but no, it can't be that easy. I just don't know. I have an inkling that Mike wants to ask me out, but Bob is such a nice guy, and I wouldn't want to hurt his feelings."

"Well, you don't have to decide right now, and there's some sweet potato…"

Saratoga

"Awesome. I'm on it right now," interrupted Sara as she took the pie out of the refrigerator. Her mother got out plates and forks, and they sat down to commiserate over sweet potato pie.

10. The Birdhouse

"Chick-a-dee-dee-dee. Chick-a-dee-dee-dee," called Sara. "Where are you, little buddy?" Sara was sitting in her camp chair in her back yard, near their bird feeder. She liked to sit out there and feed any birds brave enough to land on her hand and take a sunflower seed. When she started doing this, she had to sit out there a few times with no visitors before a chickadee was brave enough to land on her hand and quickly grab a seed. Eventually, the birds that frequented the bird feeder felt comfortable feeding from Sara's hand, and at times there would be two or three birds disputing whose turn it was to grab a seed.

Most of her visitors were chickadees, but occasionally a nuthatch, cardinal or some other type of bird would grab a seed and fly off. Chickadees were her favorite, though, because they seemed to Sara to be the most curious, outgoing and friendly birds. At first, when a bird landed on her hand, Sara would not look over at it. She would sit perfectly still and let the bird grab a seed and fly away. Eventually, she was able to watch them on her hand, and some of them would even poke through the seeds in her hand to find one they liked best. The one she called her buddy was missing a front toe, but that did not seem to bother the bird.

Sara did not have to wait long for her buddy to show up. Sara knew it was her, because she was the only bird that always landed on Sara's head before hopping down to her hand. One time, she had pooped on Sara's head just before hopping down to Sara's hand, but Sara didn't get too mad. She knew the bird was just answering Mother Nature's call. Her father had happened to watch the bird poop on Sara's head and was still laughing when Sara came in the house to wash her hair. As she walked in the door, he told her, "You know that would have gone viral on YouTube. Where's my cell phone when I need it?"

Sara had laughed and said, "Remember that when something crazy happens to you," before she went into the bathroom and washed her hair. From then on, whenever Sara went out to feed her feathered friends by hand, she always wore a baseball cap.

Saratoga

Sara watched as her buddy poked through the seeds in her hand. Sara wondered what made the bird reject or accept a seed. The seeds seemed pretty much the same to her, but obviously, the bird thought differently. *Oh, I see you're eating in today*, thought Sara as her buddy took a seed, held it on Sara's thumb, and started pecking at it. When she finished eating the seed, she turned and took another seed. She ate this one at Sara's hand as well, then flew away.

Sara sat out in her yard for a while that day and had quite a few more avian visitors. Then she decided to go back in the house. She had been thinking about building a birdhouse and wanted to do some research on the subject. She knew that different types of birds required different sized houses, and wanted to build one that, hopefully, her buddy would select for her "home". She found the information she needed online and printed the plans for building a birdhouse that chickadees might use. It was late October, but Sara wanted to get the birdhouse in place before winter so that it would be available the following spring whenever it was needed.

The next day, Sara took the birdhouse plans out to the garage and looked for what she would need to build it. She found a four foot long piece of one-by-six lumber, which was all the wood she needed. She also found a small piece of clear Plexiglas that she could cut to the right size and use for one side. She wanted to be able to watch the birds in their house, and having one side made of Plexiglas would enable her to do that. After she brought the plans and materials into the basement of her house, she set up the table saw to cut the wood.

Then Sara put on her safety goggles and started cutting the wood. She didn't notice that her father had come down to the basement while she was cutting the first piece. When Sara finished cutting that piece, he said, "I heard the doctor operating and came down to console the patient."

"Thanks Dad," said Sara with a smile. She knew her father was only kidding.

Then her father noticed the birdhouse plans on the workbench and said, "Who are we inviting to live here?"

"Well, the bird house I'm building is the right size for several types of birds, but I'm hoping to have a chickadee family live there."

"What's the Plexiglas for?" asked her father.

"I'm going to use that on one side of the house so I can watch the birds raise their family," replied Sara.

"Interesting," said her father. "Let me know when you're done so I can call the housing inspector to make sure the dwelling is up to code."

Sara just rolled her eyes and said, "Whatever you say, Dad." Then Sara's father went back upstairs and Sara continued cutting the wood. When she finished cutting the wood to size, she drilled the entry hole for the bird, and sanded the cut edges of the wood as needed. She screwed the pieces together, except on one side, where she used nails at the top so that the side could pivot open for cleaning when the bottom screws were removed. Then she glued a small wooden knob on the bottom of that side to help open it for cleaning. After she finished building the house, she decided not to stain it. She wanted it to be as natural as possible, and knew that eventually, the sun would "bleach" the wood and turn it into a more natural color. Then she brought the house upstairs to show her parents.

Her mother saw it first and said, "Great job. I'm very proud of you."

"Thanks Mom," replied Sara. Just as Sara said, "Where's Dad?", he walked into the house. Sara showed him the bird house and said, "Does the housing inspector approve?"

Her father took the birdhouse, looked at it closely and said, "Well, I'll have to get my building code book out, but...seriously, it came out great. Nice job. You handle the table saw very well."

"Thanks Dad," Sara said, beaming with pride. "And you did a great job teaching me how to use all of your power equipment." Her father had several power tools in the basement, and had shown Sara how to use all of them. He stressed safety first, along with "measure twice, cut once."

When Sara showed her parents how one side of the birdhouse swung open to allow for cleaning, her father saw the wood chips on the floor of the birdhouse and said, "Jeesh. Needs cleaning already. What's up with that?"

Sara smiled and said, "An article I read said to put some wood chips on the floor of the birdhouse before putting it up. The article didn't say why, but my guess would be that the chips make it look more natural to whoever is checking it out."

"Makes sense to me," said Sara's mother.

"Yep. Me too," added her father. Then he said, "So where are you going to put this?"

"Well, I did some research on that, and I think the best place to put it would be in the big maple tree across the yard from my bedroom. There's a place on the trunk where I can put the bird house at the correct height, and I'll be able to see into it from my bedroom window. I'll need to use my binoculars, but I'm sure that will be fine," replied Sara. Then she added, "I'm also going to use the movie camera to make a video of them. I think I can zoom in from my bedroom window and get some good videos."

"That's a great idea," said Sara's mother. "That'd be cool to watch, and post on Facebook too."

"Do you need any help putting the birdhouse up?" asked Sara's father.

Sara thought for a moment and said, "I could probably do it myself, but it would make it easier if you could hold the house in place while I screw it to the tree."

"Ok," said Sara's father. "Let's see; twenty dollars an hour, four hour minimum."

Then Sara's mother cut him off with "My rates are much cheaper, but I don't know if you'll go for this. I'll help you if you'll do your laundry after you put the house up."

Sara laughed and said, "I get the hint, Mom. I'll do my laundry after I write an autographed basketball for Dad's help in putting up my birdhouse."

Sara's father smiled and said, "No checks, cash only....but since it's for a good cause, I'll waive my fee."

"Alrighty then, let's go," said Sara. She went down to the basement and got two screws and a screwdriver while her father went out to the garage and got a ladder. When Sara went out to the maple tree, her father had already positioned the ladder against a branch. "I'm guessin' the ladder is in the right spot; do I need to move it?" asked Sara's father.

"That should be fine," replied Sara as she handed the birdhouse and screwdriver to her father and said, "Can you hand these to me after I get up there?"

"Will do," replied her father.

Then Sara climbed up into the maple tree while her father held the ladder in place. She maneuvered around a bit, and got in position to put up the birdhouse. Sara's father handed it to her along with the screwdriver and said, "Good. I see that you started the screws. We won't have to worry about droppin' one."

"Yes. It'd be hard to find it if I dropped a screw here," replied Sara. She took the birdhouse and positioned it where she wanted it. While she did that, her father checked the ladder and made sure it wouldn't slide along the branch. Then he climbed up the ladder and stood on a branch near Sara. He held the birdhouse in place with one hand while holding a branch with the other. Sara sat on a nearby branch and secured herself by putting her feet under another branch. Then she screwed the screws into the tree and gave the birdhouse a good tug when she was done.

"Yep. It's secure," she said.

Then her father climbed down the ladder, looked up at Sara and said, "Ladder?"

"Nah," said Sara as she handed her father the screwdriver. "I think I'll climb up to the top of the tree and look around. After I climb down, I'll just jump off a branch." Her father put the ladder away while Sara climbed to the top of the tree. She spent a few minutes at the top, then climbed down and jumped out of the tree.

A few days later, Sara noticed a small cardboard sign hanging in the maple tree. It read "house available immediately; small, comfy, no utilities; very reasonable price" and had an arrow pointing to the birdhouse. Sara just smiled and thought, *Yep, that's gotta be Dad.* She got her cell phone out and took a picture, then went back in the house and got a magic marker. She went out to the maple tree and wrote "SOLD" across the sign and took another picture.

When she went back in the house, her mother said, "Oh, somebody moved in already?"

Sara laughed and said, "Nope. I'm just messin' with Dad. Someone might move in, but most likely the house won't be occupied until next spring."

11. Deer Hunting

"Well, I think we have everything," said Sara as she closed the tailgate of her father's pickup truck.

"If we don't, we'll manage somehow," replied her father.

Every Thanksgiving morning, Sara and her father would load up his pickup truck with their gear early in the morning while Sara's mother went to Grammy's to help get breakfast ready. After breakfast, Sara and her father would drive up to the cabin they rented in northern New Hampshire and spend the rest of Thanksgiving weekend deer hunting. They usually had at least one deer to bring to LeMay and Sons in Goffstown for butchering the following Monday. If they were fortunate enough to get two deer, they would donate one to the New Hampshire Food Bank.

Sara and her father had gone deer hunting every Thanksgiving for close to ten years now. Sara's father had taught her how to shoot at an early age, emphasizing the importance of gun safety. Her parents, lifetime members of the National Rifle Association, had given Sara a lifetime membership for her seventh birthday. They had also instilled in her the importance of the Second Amendment, the right to keep and bear arms. Sara understood that part of that right was the responsibility to properly use, maintain, and store any firearms and ammunition that she may acquire.

Soon they were walking into Grammy's house, where breakfast was just about ready. "Perfect timing," said Sara's mother. "You two can set the table, and Grammy and I will bring the food out."

Sara helped her father set the table, then went out to the living room to let Grampa know that breakfast was ready. He was in his chair, absorbed in a book, and Sara was able to sneak up behind him. She covered his eyes with her hands and said in a low voice, "Guess who?"

"Sounds like the big bad wolf," Grampa replied.

Saratoga

Sara took her hands away, tousled Grampa's hair, then gave him a kiss on the top of his head and said, "Breakfast is served, your highness. May we have the honor of your presence at our table?"

"Of course, milady," he replied. "I shall join you momentarily." Grampa put his book down, got up and went out to the dining room with Sara.

Sara's mother came out from the kitchen and said, "Everyone, have a seat please. After Grampa says grace, I'll bring out the pancakes." Sara's mother always made blueberry pecan pancakes for Thanksgiving breakfast, and Grammy had real maple syrup to put on them. Grammy took care of the rest of breakfast, usually scrambled eggs with bacon or sausage on the side. And she always made fried apple slices, another one of Sara's favorites.

After breakfast, Sara helped clear the table while her father took one last look in the back of his pickup truck to make sure they had everything. When he came in, they did a group hug, then Sara and her father went out to his truck. Just before they got in the truck, Grammy came out with a small cooler. "I almost forgot these," she said. "I made some sandwiches for you, and there are a couple slices of apple pie and two sodas in there too."

"Great. Thank you," said Sara. Her father gave Grammy a hug while Sara found a spot in the back of the truck for the cooler. Then they got in the truck, buckled their seatbelts and were on their way.

They had been on the highway for a little while when Sara said, "Well, it wouldn't be until next summer, but I might start coming up this way a bit more often."

Sara's father thought for a moment, then said, "That's right. Whispering Pines College is up this way."

"It is one of my top three choices," said Sara. "It has a very good Environmental Engineering Department, they have ROTC there, and the school is relatively close to home."

"Well, being close to home is nice, but your education is more important," said Sara's father, "and if that means you go to a college far from here, so be it. Your mother and I will miss you, but we'll just have to deal with it."

"Hopefully, we'll find out soon," said Sara. "I applied to several colleges a while ago, and should be hearing back from them in the near future."

A little while later, Sara's father asked, "Are we lookin' for Winchester Road?"

"Hmm. We only come up here once a year," said Sara, "but I think you're right." She checked the directions her father had written down and said, "Yep. That's the one we want."

Her father said, "Ok. That's the next exit." A few minutes later, he took the exit and said, "Should be about another half hour to go."

"Good. We'll get there just about lunchtime, maybe a little later," replied Sara. "I'm glad Grammy made sandwiches for us so we don't have to fuss with that."

"Me too," said her father. "We'll be able check our blind this afternoon, before it gets dark." Sara and her father had been renting the same cabin every Thanksgiving for several years, and had built a blind out of tree branches and other natural cover in an area that was perfect for deer hunting. They even made a bench for it by nailing a six foot piece of two-by-eight lumber onto two stumps. They had to touch up the blind every year, but there was always plenty of dead wood nearby for them to choose from.

After a while, Sara's father said, "I think we take a right turn soon." Then he added, "Yes. I remember turning just after that giant oak tree in the field over there."

Sara checked the directions and said, "Yes, that should be Miller's Way."

When they got near the road, Sara's father laughed and said, "Oh yeah. I remember that road sign." Someone had put up a handmade sign with "thataway" and an arrow pointing to the right underneath "Miller's Way."

Saratoga

The road had been paved at one time, but it was not maintained very well. Sara's father slowed down accordingly, and said, "What are we looking for next?"

Sara checked the directions and said, "In about five minutes we should see a dirt road on the left with a gate across it." A few minutes later, they almost went past the road. It was on the other side of a small hill, and on a curve.

"One of these years that big rock will remind me that we're almost there," said Sara's father.

"Yes, the one on the right, just before we went over the hill. I always forget about it too," replied Sara.

After he turned around, Sara's father pulled into the dirt road and stopped in front of the gate. He had given Sara the key Roy had given him, and she got out and unlocked the gate. She swung it open and closed it after her father drove through. Then she hung the lock on a nail in the gatepost. "Tallyho," said Sara as she got back in the truck.

"You got it," replied her father, and he started driving down the dirt road. Soon, they arrived at the cabin, and after he parked the truck, Sara's father said, "I'll start unloading the truck if you'll get lunch set up."

"Deal," said Sara as she got out of the truck. She unlocked the cabin, then took the lunch cooler out of the back of the truck and started unloading it onto the picnic table near the cabin.

"Awesome," said Sara. "Grammy made roast beef sandwiches with spinach and onions, and she gave us a container of tomato slices."

"Great. I'll be there in a minute, but first I'm gonna turn the refrigerator on and put the food from the other cooler in there." The cabin had four rooms; a kitchen with a small table, a bedroom, a bathroom and a small storage room with a propane refrigerator. In addition to the refrigerator, the cabin also had a two-burner electric hot plate, a microwave, and a wood stove.

Sara laughed the first time she saw the "shower stall" in the bathroom. It was just an old bathtub with a hook above the bath tub for holding a shower bag filled with water. There was no toilet in the bathroom, but the outhouse next to the cabin had a composting toilet, which Sara thought was really cool.

After Sara's father put the food away, they sat down at the picnic table, said grace, and started eating lunch. "Oh yeah," said Sara. "We need to check the generator after lunch."

"Good idea," replied her father. There was a shed near the cabin with a generator inside. An underground cable brought the electricity from the generator into the cabin. After they finished eating lunch, they walked over to the shed to check on the generator. Sara unlocked the door and they walked in. "I think there's a rechargeable lamp in here somewhere," said her father.

"Yep. On the shelf above the generator," replied Sara as she walked over and turned the lamp on. Then she said, "Good. The instructions for starting the generator are still on the wall next to the lamp."

"Ok," said her father. "Go ahead and fire it up, and I'll go finish unloading the truck." Her father was just about to walk out the shed door when he saw a gas can in the corner of the shed near the door. He picked it up and said, "Uh oh, there's not much gas in here. Roy told me he'd leave a full five gallon can here."

"Ooopps. My bad," replied Sara. "Roy called last night while you were out and said he would come out this afternoon with a full can of gas and swap it for the empty one."

"Right on cue," said Sara's father as Roy drove up to the cabin.

"Good afternoon," said Roy as he got out of his truck and walked over to the shed with the full can of gas. "Sorry about the empty. I plumb fergot to swap 'em last Monday when I came out to check the cabin."

"Not a problem," replied Sara's father. "The old Boy Scout in me had me bring a one-gallon can just in case, so we probably would have managed. We just don't use the generator that much."

"I noticed that," said Roy, "but it's strange how some people come out here to get away from it all yet bring every electronic device they can get their hands on."

Then Sara walked out of the shed and said, "The tank on the generator is full, so we're all set there." After Roy put the full five gallon

Saratoga

can in the shed, Sara's father gave him the empty gas can and he secured it in the back of his pickup truck.

"Might as well run the generator while I'm here," said Roy. "Should be fine, but ya never know." Then he added, "Don't forget to turn on the exhaust fan."

"Will do," said Sara as she walked back into the shed. She had to pull the cord a few times, but she got the generator started, and turned on the exhaust fan. "Smooth as silk," she said as she walked out of the shed.

"All set then," said Roy as he walked back to his truck.

"Yep, we're good to go," replied Sara's father.

Roy got in his truck, put down the window and said, "Nice to see y'all again, and happy huntin'."

"Nice to see you again as well," replied Sara.

"Ditto," added her father as Roy turned his truck around and drove away.

After Roy drove away, Sara's father walked over to the back of their truck and said, "There's a little bit of stuff left in here, but we can unload that after we check the blind."

"That's right. We haven't done that yet. Let's go," said Sara. "If I remember correctly, it's about a forty five minute walk."

"Yeah, about that long," Sara's father replied.

When they got out to their blind, they saw that it needed a little bit of touching up, and the top half of a spruce tree had snapped off and covered about half of the bench. Sara touched up the blind with some dead branches she found on the ground while her father moved the spruce tree. "That's perfect right there," said Sara's father after he moved the tree out of the way. "Gives us a little more cover for deer approaching us at the blind."

"Good. I think we're all set now," said Sara.

They took one last look around, then started walking back to the cabin. When they got there, Sara's father said, "I think we did fairly well.

A little bit noisier than I would have liked when I moved the spruce tree, but we'll see what happens tomorrow morning."

"Yeah, quiet and scent free is always best, but that's much more important tomorrow morning than today," said Sara. "In fact, we made more noise and left more scent when we built the bench, yet we got that big buck the next day."

"That's right," said Sara's father. "Biggest buck either one of us ever got."

A few minutes later, Sara said, "Gettin' more than a bit chilly here. I think I'll collect some kindling and start a campfire. But first I have to rake away the leaves and sticks from around the fire pit."

"While you're doin' that, I'll fill the watering can and put it on the picnic table," said Sara's father. "Then I'll collect some more kindling before it gets too dark."

"And, as usual, Roy left us a nice stack of fire wood in the shed," said Sara.

"Yes, Roy takes good care of us," said Sara's father as he went into the cabin to fill the watering can. There was no water supply at the cabin, so Sara and her father brought two six-gallon jugs filled with water. While Sara's father filled the watering can, Sara got the fire started and set up their camp chairs so they could sit by the fire and enjoy the warmth and camaraderie. Then she fed the fire some more, gradually adding thicker wood as the fire grew.

"I think that's enough kindling for now," said Sara's father as he added another armful to the pile he had made near the shed.

"Yeah, that should be fine," said Sara.

"Did you bring your book?" asked Sara's father.

"Yep. It's on the table in the cabin," replied Sara.

"Ok. I'll bring it out and we can read and write by the fire," said Sara's father. He went into the cabin, got Sara's book and his crossword puzzle magazine and brought them out to the campfire. They sat down by the fire and Sara started reading while her father started working on a crossword puzzle.

A few minutes later, he said, "What's a four letter word for a flightless bird?"

"Oh come on, Dad, that's easy," replied Sara. "It's kiwi."

"Huh. I thought that was a fruit," said Sara's father.

Sara couldn't resist and said, "Takes a fruit to know a fruit, but I love you anyway." Then she added, "And yes, you are correct about it being a fruit. The Chinese gooseberry is also known as kiwi."

Sara's father filled in 'kiwi' in the crossword puzzle, then said, "What's the mad scientist reading about today?"

Sara smiled and said, "I'm reading a biography of Mary Edwards Walker. During the American Civil War, she was the first woman surgeon in the Union Army, and at one point in time was arrested by the Confederates as a spy. For her services to our country during the Civil War, she was awarded the Congressional Medal of Honor, the only woman so far to have received that honor. Later on in her life, she worked on issues such as health care, temperance, women's rights and even dress reform for women."

"Dress reform?" queried Sara's father.

"Oh yeah," said Sara. "And wait til you hear this; she was frequently arrested, yes arrested, for wearing men's clothing."

"Imagine that. Getting arrested for wearing men's clothing. That's crazy," said Sara's father.

"Yes it is," said Sara. "And thankfully, we have come a long way from that in regard to women's rights, but we still have much work to do."

"Speaking of work," said Sara's father, "should we feed the fire, or perhaps let it die down so we can go have supper?"

Sara looked at her watch and said, "Yeah, it is gettin' late for our situation, so we probably shouldn't feed the fire."

"I wish we could stay by the fire longer too," said her father, "but we do have to get up early tomorrow morning."

"You're right Dad," said Sara. "We can read and write for a little bit, then go have supper."

After a little while, Sara looked at her watch and said, "Yep. Time to give the fire a shower."

"Ok. If you water the fire, I'll fire up the generator and go heat up supper," said Sara's father as he got up and put his crossword puzzle magazine on the picnic table.

"Deal," said Sara as she got up from her camp chair and walked over to get the watering can. Sara's father got up, went into the shed and started the generator. Then he went into the cabin, plugged in the microwave and started heating up supper.

After Sara finished putting out the fire, she brought her book and her father's crossword puzzle magazine into the cabin. She put them down on the table and said, "Cook! Cook! Where's my hasenpfeffer?"

"You'd best watch out or I'll turn you into hasenpfeffer," replied Sara's father with a smile. Then the microwave dinged and Sara's father said, "Supper's just about ready." He took the big bowl of beef stew out of the microwave, stirred it up and said, "All set here. We just need beverages and we're good to go."

Then Sara said, "It's not freezin' in here yet, but maybe I should get the wood stove goin' before we eat supper."

"Oh yeah. I forgot about that. It's actually ready to roar," said Sara's father. "I loaded the stove up earlier today. Just needs a match."

"Ok. Thanks Dad," said Sara as she took a long stick match and lit a fire in the woodstove. Then, just after she blew the match out, she said, "Testing, testing," and put the match head up near the smoke/carbon monoxide detector. Shortly after she did that, the fire alarm emitted a loud "beep, beep, beep."

"Glad it works," said her father as he shut the detector off, "but I'm even gladder that you warned me. I woulda jumped through the roof if you hadn't."

"I do like to tease you, Dad," replied Sara, "but I don't want you to have a heart attack."

Then Sara's father put his hands around the bowl of stew and said, "Still warm enough for me. Let's eat."

"Sounds good," said Sara. "But we almost forgot. We need to heat up some water to wash the dishes in after supper. I'll fill the teapot and put it on the stove if you'll divvy up the stew and get the cider out of the fridge."

"Ok," said Sara's father. After Sara filled the teapot about three quarters full and put it on the wood stove, they sat down, said grace and started eating supper.

"This is a tasty stew," said Sara. "But hopefully, we'll soon have some venison for stew making."

"Yes indeed," said Sara's father. "And I know I'm preaching to the choir, but I am glad to live in a country where we have the right to keep and bear arms. That's an extremely important right, and for many more reasons than just being able to hunt."

"Amen and hallelujah to that," said Sara. "Far too many Americans today don't understand the importance of our Second Amendment. The right to keep and bear arms is vitally important to maintaining freedom. A disarmed civilian population is much easier to control than an armed one. That's why the British were going after the arms and ammunition in Concord back in 1775."

"Agreed," said Sara's father. "And I see that your mother and I have taught you well in that regard."

"Yes, and thank you also for having taught me to shoot well," said Sara. "Hopefully, I'll need that skill tomorrow morning."

"Speaking of tomorrow morning," said Sara's father as he put some more wood in the stove, "we need to fill the watering can and leave it on the stove so we'll have warm water for taking a shower before we get dressed."

"A warm shower on a cold morning is not my favorite," replied Sara. "But you're right. We need to get rid of at least some of our scent. And our clothes are all set because Mom switched to scent-free detergent a few years ago."

"I remember that," said Sara's father. "We used to have to wash our hunting clothes separately in our own detergent before that. She didn't want to switch, but you convinced her it was better for the environment."

"Every little bit helps," said Sara.

Suddenly, the whistle from the teapot startled both of them. "Wake up call," said Sara.

"Oh, that woke me up all right," replied her father. "Woke me up to the fact that one of us is going to have to do the dishes. I'll flip you for it."

"Acrobatically, or a coin?" asked Sara with a smile.

"Wise gal," said Sara's father as he got a quarter ready to flip. Then he said, "Tails you win, heads I lose. I mean….."

"Too late. You're washin' tonight," laughed Sara as she took the small plastic wash tub from under the sink. She put the dirty dishes and some dish detergent in the tub, then put it on the counter next to the sink and said, "Fill'er up my good man, and wash away."

Sara's father just smiled and put some hot water from the teapot in the tub and adjusted the water temperature to bearable by adding cold water from a water jug. Then he filled the kitchen sink with water to about three-quarters full for rinsing the dishes. While he washed the dishes, Sara filled the watering can and put it on the stove. Then she checked the fire in the stove, added a few of pieces of wood and said, "The watering can is just about full, so by the time it starts to think about boiling, the fire will be low enough to keep the can from boiling over."

"Ok, Miss Mad Scientist," joked Sara's father. Then he said, "Hmm. It's a bit late to be askin' now, but did you bring the alarm clock?"

"Uh oh…..just kidding," said Sara. "That was one of the first things I packed, and I checked the batteries before I put it in my suitcase."

"Good," said Sara's father. "After I finish the dishes, it'll be lights out and time to hit the sack."

"Ok," said Sara as she went into the bedroom, set the alarm clock and put it on the small table next to her bed.

A few minutes later, Sara's father finished washing the dishes and said, "Job's done, so I pulled the plug," as the water drained from the sink.

"I guess that means it's time for lights out," said Sara as she put her book down.

"Yes ma'am," said Sara's father, "and if you'll go shut off the generator, I'll turn on the rechargeable lamp so we can see while we're getting ready for bed."

"Will do," said Sara as she got up and went out to shut off the generator. After she shut off the generator, she made a quick stop at the outhouse. When she came back into the cabin, she got ready for bed. Soon she and her father were snuggled in their sleeping bags. When the alarm went off the next morning, Sara's father was already up and putting wood into the wood stove. When Sara came out to the kitchen, she carefully touched the watering can and said, "Not hot, but at least it's warm."

"You'll be pleased to know that, as usual," said Sara's father, "I got up in the middle of the night and fed the wood stove a little bit before I went out to see a man about a horse."

"Thanks Dad," said Sara. "I really appreciate that."

"You're welcome" replied Sara's father. "And if you want to take a shower now, I'll put some water in the teapot for two bowls of oatmeal and heat it up."

"Sounds good," said Sara as she got the shower bag ready to fill. After Sara's father put the teapot on the stove, he helped Sara fill the shower bag and hung it up in the "shower stall" for her. Then he went back out to the kitchen and shut the bedroom door behind him.

Sara unwrapped the scent free soap, got undressed and took a very quick shower. She didn't even bother with washing her hair. That would have to wait until she got home. Then she got dressed, went out to the kitchen and said, "Your turn to freeze."

"Oh, it's not that bad," said Sara's father. Then he added, as he patted his belly, "But I do have a little bit more insulation than you."

"You said it, not me," laughed Sara as her father disappeared into the bedroom. While he was in the shower, Sara got the oatmeal ready and warmed up a couple of pieces of raisin bread on a piece of tinfoil on the wood stove. When Sara's father came back out to the kitchen, Sara said, "Breakfast is just about ready."

"Thanks," said Sara's father. "I'll butter the "toast" if you'll get the juice out."

When everything was ready, they sat down, said grace and started eating breakfast. "Nothing like homemade apple butter on homemade raisin bread," said Sara's father.

"Yes, and nothing like a hunting weekend with my father," replied Sara.

"Yes indeed. Two of my favorite pastimes: hunting and spending time with my daughter. Wish I could do more of both, but ya can't always get what ya want."

"I know," sighed Sara, "but we need to quit ramblin' on, finish eatin', and get huntin'."

"Yes ma'am," said Sara's father. "I'm just about done here anyway." Then he picked up the last bit of his raisin bread "toast" and put it in his mouth.

Sara finished her breakfast and said, "Let's leave the dishes til later. I'm hungry for huntin'."

"Sounds good," said Sara's father as they got up and went to the bedroom closet to get their rifles and ammunition.

While she was taking her rifle out of the closet, Sara said, "Oh yeah. Do you have the written permission from Roy to have loaded rifles in the cabin?"

"Yep. Right here in my wallet with my hunting license," replied Sara's father. "I checked to make sure of that while you were in the shower."

"Good. Most likely, we won't need to show it," said Sara. "But if we didn't have it, the Fish and Game Warden would sniff us out for sure and we'd be in a heap o' trouble."

"Speakin' of paperwork and trouble," said Sara's father, "where's your hunting license?"

Saratoga

"Right here in my pocket," replied Sara as she pulled it part way out of her pocket, then stuck it back in.

"Last but not least," said Sara's father, "I've got my knife, which I sharpened last night. Do you have the rest of the guttin' gear?"

"Yep. I already checked and made sure it's in my backpack along with the draggin' tarp," replied Sara. The draggin' tarp was a heavy duty six foot by eight foot tarp with reinforced grommets. Whenever Sara or her father shot a deer, they gutted it somewhere nearby, then wrapped the tarp around the deer to make it easier to drag the deer back to the cabin.

"Then it's time to lock and load," said Sara's father as he and Sara brought their rifles and ammunition out to the kitchen. After they locked and loaded their rifles, they each took some spare ammunition to put in their hunting jackets, and Sara put the rest of the ammunition back in the bedroom closet. While she was doing that, her father took some soft granola bars from their food bin and put them in his jacket pocket. They had taken the granola bars out of their wrappers and wrapped them in paper towels to reduce the chance of making any noise when it came time to eat the bars.

When Sara came out of the bedroom, her father said, "Do you have your "gourmet" lunch?"

"No, I don't," replied Sara. "Thanks for reminding me." She opened the food bin, took some granola bars and put them in her jacket pocket. Then she said, "Last call for the outhouse."

"Yes. Very important," said her father. "Don't wanna be needin' to tie a knot in it when a big buck comes along. You can use the outhouse and I'll go out in the woods and hide." When they finished their "last call", they went back in the cabin, got their gear and started walking down the old logging road that the cabin was on.

About twenty minutes later, Sara said, "There's the stone wall up ahead." When Sara and her father got to the stone wall, they got off the road and followed the stone wall. The stone wall eventually led to a perfect hunting spot near a pond.

They walked along the stone wall for a while, then Sara saw a big birch tree and softly said, "Time for silence." Sara's father just nodded his head in agreement. When they first started hunting here, they decided that it would be best to maintain silence after they reached the big birch tree. A while later they were at their blind, and Sara looked at her watch and saw that they had a little over twenty minutes before they could start hunting. It was light enough to see well, but they had to wait until actual sunrise to shoot. Earlier in the week, Sara had checked the sunrise/sunset chart on her computer at home to find out when they could legally shoot if they saw a deer.

A watched pot never boils, thought Sara as she sat on the bench at their blind resisting the temptation to check the time again. It seemed like an eternity before her father slowly held out his fist with a thumb up to indicate that it was ok to shoot. Then Sara almost burst out laughing as she thought her father might be thinking *here bucky, bucky, bucky* while waiting for a big buck to come along.

She managed to stifle herself, then thought, *focus, Sara, focus*, as she scanned the stream that emptied out of the pond. Although the surface of the pond was frozen, parts of the stream were not frozen over, and deer liked to stop there to drink on their way to their feeding grounds in the morning. They had been sitting on the bench for about an hour when Sara saw a deer approaching the stream. She slowly tapped her father once on his leg, and he knew that meant that Sara had seen a deer. Since Sara saw the deer first, she got to attempt to shoot it.

That's a nice buck, thought Sara as the deer slowly came closer to the stream. Sara was raising her rifle very slowly when she saw the deer's ears swivel towards her. Sara froze in place and watched as the deer cupped its ears. When the deer licked its nose, Sara knew the deer was trying to enhance its sense of smell to detect any danger in the area. Suddenly, the deer took off, running back in the direction it had come from. *Damn*, thought Sara, *that was a good-sized buck*.

A little while later, Sara saw another deer. This time, as she reached over to tap her father on his leg, her hand felt his hand coming over to touch her on the leg. They had both seen the deer at the same time. That meant her father got to shoot because he had won at rock paper scissors last night in the cabin. *Might be the same one I saw*, thought Sara. She sensed her father raising his rifle and watched as the deer lifted its head back up after taking a drink from the stream. The deer stood there for a moment, swiveling its ears, before Sara's father squeezed the trigger. After getting hit, the deer took one or two steps, then fell to the ground.

"Great shot, Dad," said Sara as she and her father walked over to the deer.

"Thanks," replied her father. "And it's nice to not have to track it like we had to do last year with the one you got."

"Yes, I remember that," said Sara. "I made a good shot, but not as good as yours. We were lucky to find that deer and get it back to the cabin before it got too dark."

"Yes we were, but that's enough memories; time to get to work," said Sara's father. They dragged the deer to a small clearing nearby and positioned the deer with its back on the ground. Then Sara took the deer's front legs and held them slightly apart.

"Is the patient ready?" asked Sara's father.

"As ready as he'll ever be," said Sara with a smile. Then Sara's father put his gloves on, took his knife out and began to gut the deer. He worked slowly and made sure he did not cut any internal organs, which would taint the meat. After dealing with the rectum and reproductive organs, he cut the sternum and pelvic bone in half with a small saw and removed the internal organs. When her father finished gutting the deer, Sara laid out the draggin' tarp and they positioned the deer on the tarp. Then Sara's father tied the deer's hind legs to the middle of its chest and the front legs to its neck.

"Oh yeah," said Sara. "Don't forget the tag."

"Good catch," said Sara's father. He took his gloves off, removed the deer tag from his hunting license and attached it to the deer's ear. Then they wrapped the tarp around the deer and secured two of the grommets to the base of the deer's antlers.

"Can you tie this up please," said Sara's father as he bunched the tarp together just beyond the tail of the deer. Sara took a piece of rope out of her pack and tied the tarp while her father held it together.

"Sew up the grommets and we're done," said Sara's father. Sara took another piece of rope out of her pack and "sewed" together the side grommets, thus preventing the deer from sliding out of the "bag" they had just created.

Then her father said, "Time for the coin flip."

Sara was puzzled for a second or two, then smiled and said, "I'll take the head for a while. You can start with the tail end and we'll swap after a while." Sara took the deer by the antlers and her father grabbed the tarp where they had tied it together near the tail of the deer. They started dragging the deer bag to the cabin, resting for a couple minutes every twenty minutes or so. About two hours later, they arrived back at the cabin with the deer.

"Whew! Glad the draggin's done," said Sara. "I could drink like a camel and I'm famished to boot."

"Well, you can eat your boots if you want," said Sara's father. "But I'm slappin' together a ham sandwich or two."

"One for me please," said Sara, "and I'll peel a couple of oranges." Sara's father got the ham, mayonnaise and mustard out of the refrigerator and made three sandwiches while Sara peeled two oranges and poured two glasses of apple juice. Just the sound of the juice pouring into the glass induced Sara's father to take a break from sandwich making and join her in guzzling some juice.

Then he said, "I might need a little bit of prune juice to recharge things."

"Oh please, Dad. No prune juice. That's even worse than you eatin' baked beans," laughed Sara as her father went back to making sandwiches.

When they finished eating their lunch, Sara said, "Now comes the fun part: lifting that heavy load into the truck. But my taste buds will be thanking me later."

"Yes indeed," said Sara's father as he walked over to his truck. "I'll back the truck up to the deer and you can tell me when to stop," said Sara's father as he got in his truck. Sara watched him back up the truck and signaled him when he got close enough for them to lift the deer into

Saratoga

the truck without having to drag it any further. When he shut the truck off, Sara opened the tailgate and climbed into the back of the truck. Her father got out and came around to the back of the truck. Sara was kneeling on the tailgate of the truck, waiting as her father started raising the deer by its antlers. When Sara could reach the antlers, she grabbed them and took over lifting the front of the deer. Her father quickly switched to lifting the deer by its rump, and they loaded the deer into the truck.

Soon they were on their way to the deer check station, a local convenience store where an authorized agent of the New Hampshire Fish and Game Department would be available to check their deer as required by law. When they got there, Sara said, "Do we need anything besides ice while we're here?"

Her father thought for a moment, then said, "Yes. We're getting low on juice. No preference here; get whatever you want."

"Ok. Maybe I'll get some snacks too," replied Sara as she walked into the store. While Sara was looking around in the store, Sara's father "unwrapped" the deer and had it checked.

When Sara came out of the store, her father was waiting for her and said, "Paperwork's all set but where's the ice?"

"Oh shoot. I forgot the ice," said Sara. "Two five-pound bags?"

"That should be fine," replied her father. "It's been cold here so far, so we might not even need it, but better safe than sorry." Sara put the bag with the juice and snacks in the truck and went back into the store to get the ice. When she came out, her father took the bags of ice and put them in the chest cavity of the deer. After he retied the deer's hind legs to the middle of its chest, Sara helped him close up the draggin' tarp around the deer.

On the way back to the cabin, they heard the weather report on the radio and Sara's father said, "Good. Upper thirties to low forties for temps, but I hope the rain holds off until the evening like they said."

"Yes," said Sara. "Not fun sittin' in the rain like we did a couple years ago."

"Yep. I remember that," said Sara's father. "All rain and no deer. But it happens, and I still consider that quality time with my daughter."

"Thanks Dad," said Sara. "That's quality time for me too."

When they got back to the cabin, they unwrapped the deer from the draggin' tarp and Sara's father got it ready to hang. He untied the rear legs and cut a slit in each leg between the calf and the ankle. Then he slid a stainless steel bar through the slits. The bar was about an inch thick, two inches tall and eighteen inches long. There was a hole near each end for securing the deer's legs in place and a hole in the middle near the top for attaching a rope. After he slid the bar through the deer's legs, Sara's father said, "Can you get the rope ready while I tie the legs to the bar?"

"On it right away," said Sara as she took the rope and tied a small weight on one end. Then she held the other end and tossed the weighted end over the branch they had selected to hang the deer from. She took the weight off the rope and tied that end of the rope around the tree trunk.

"Ready when you are," said Sara as she walked back over to the truck with the loose end of the rope. Her father took the rope and secured it to the metal bar.

"Ready to raise," said Sara's father.

"Heave ho," said Sara as she helped her father hang the deer up.

After they hung the deer, Sara looked at the tarp and said "Good. It's not very messy at all. I'll clean it up, fold it up, and hopefully, we'll need it again tomorrow."

"Great," said Sara's father. "Then it's time for supper." After she cleaned the tarp, Sara started the generator while her father brought some more fire wood into the cabin.

"I'll get a fire goin' in the wood stove if you'll nuke the soup," said Sara's father as she joined him in the cabin.

"Deal," said Sara. "And we've got homemade peach pie for dessert." She took the big bowl of pea soup out of the refrigerator and started heating it up. Then she set the table and took the pie out of the refrigerator. She took a slice of pie for each of them and put each slice on a plate, then put the pie back in the fridge and took out the juice.

After her father got the fire started in the wood stove, Sara said, "Three more minutes for the soup. I put it on power three so it wouldn't boil."

"That's fine," said Sara's father as he poured two glasses of juice.

When the microwave dinged, Sara took the soup out and said, "Warm enough for me. I'm hungry."

"Me too," said her father. "Let's eat." Sara put the soup on the table and her father took a ladle and filled their bowls with soup. Then they sat down, said grace and started eating.

"Your mother made lip smackin' good soup as usual," said Sara's father.

"Oh yeah," said Sara. "Nothing like pea soup slow simmered with diced ham, onion and sweet potato."

"Wouldn't have it any other way," said Sara's father. "Although I wasn't so sure the first time I saw her adding the diced sweet potato."

"I wondered about that too," said Sara. "But now, like you said, I wouldn't have it any other way." When they finished eating, Sara said, "Well, we forgot to heat up water for dish washing, but I'll fill the watering can and put it on the stove for our showers tomorrow morning."

"Well, it is too late to heat dish washin' water on the stove, but we can nuke it instead," said Sara's father.

"Great idea," said Sara. "I'll rinse out the pea soup bowl and we can heat the water in that." Then Sara's father cleared the table while Sara got the dish water ready. She put a little bit of soap in the dish tub, then added the hot water from the pea soup bowl. After she added enough cold water to cover the dishes, she said, "Lukewarm, but it'll have to do."

"That'll be fine," said Sara's father. "It's gettin' late and you need your beauty rest, so I'll take care of these."

Sara smiled and said, "Thanks Dad." Then she filled the watering can, put it on the stove and got ready for bed.

The next morning, after breakfast, Sara's father went out and sat in his truck to listen to the weather report. When he came back into the cabin, he said, "Sounds good. They said it's a bit cloudy here now, but the rain's still supposed to hold off until this evening."

"Great," said Sara. "Let's go." She got her gear ready and they started walking to their blind.

They had just turned off the logging road and started following the stone wall when they heard barking off in the distance.

"Might be a coyote," said Sara softly.

"Most likely," replied her father softly. "I thought I might have heard more than one, but they're far enough away that they shouldn't interfere with our hunting." A few minutes later, Sara's father saw the big birch tree. He turned around to face Sara and put an index finger to his lips. Sara nodded, and they maintained silence after that.

When they got to their blind, they quietly sat down to wait for sunrise. Then Sara slowly raised her arm and checked her watch. *Got here a little later than yesterday*, thought Sara. *Less than fifteen minutes to huntin' time*. Sara really wanted to get a deer. Even though the deer her father had gotten would provide plenty of meat for them, Sara wanted to get a deer so they could donate it to the New Hampshire Food Bank. Sara loved the taste of venison, and helping others less fortunate than herself to be able to enjoy some venison was very important to Sara.

Sara and her father waited patiently, glad that the rain was still holding off. Every once in a while, it sprinkled a little bit, but it never lasted long. Sara was just about to take a granola bar out of her jacket pocket when she saw a buck walking along the stream about fifty yards away. She slowly reached over and tapped her father on the leg to let him know she had seen a deer, then raised her rifle. She followed the deer in her rifle sight and waited as long as she dared. The deer was still not in ideal range, but Sara didn't want to wait any longer. She squeezed the trigger and watched as the buck staggered from the impact of the bullet.

"Good shot," said Sara's father. Then the buck turned and wobbled away along the stream, disappearing where the stream went behind a small hill. Sara sighed and said, "Yeah, but not good enough to drop him dead. I hope he doesn't get too far."

Her father was just about to say something when they heard a loud noise from where the deer had disappeared.

"That's gotta be him droppin' dead," said Sara's father as they walked toward where the noise had come from. When they went around the hill, they saw the deer a little ways ahead.

"Well, at least he didn't get too far," said Sara.

"Yeah, but it looks like he's tangled up in some blackberry bushes," said Sara's father. They walked over to the deer and sure enough, it had dropped dead right in a big thicket of blackberry bushes.

"Oh boy. This is gonna be fun," said Sara's father.

"Real fun," said Sara. "But at least we have the right tool and gloves for the job." She took her backpack off and got out the brush snippers and two pairs of leather gloves. Sara took the snippers and cut some of the blackberry bushes while her father pulled away the ones she cut.

"That should be enough to let us get the deer out without getting too slashed," said Sara as she put the snippers away.

"Yeah, I think so," said her father.

After they pulled the deer out of the bramble, Sara said, "Uh oh, is that thunder I heard off in the distance?"

Sara's father smiled and said, "No, that's my stomach complainin' about the lack of fuel."

"I'll take that hint and munch on it," said Sara as she took a granola bar out of her jacket pocket.

"I suppose these will do for now," said Sara's father as he took some granola bars out of his jacket pocket. "But I'd really love a steak and cheese sub instead."

"Italian with horseradish cheddar cheese for me," said Sara. "We can get those for supper tonight when we bring the deer to the check station."

"We'd best hurry up then," said Sara's father. "We've got a lot of work ahead of us."

They quickly ate their "lunch" and started dragging the deer toward the small clearing where they had gutted the other deer yesterday. When they got to the edge of the clearing, Sara's father said, "Look: somebody ate the awful offal. It's all gone."

Sara just laughed and said, "Who had waffles?" Then she looked where the pile of deer guts from yesterday had been and said, "Yep, it's gone. Probably coyotes but could've been a fox."

"And now it's your turn to play doctor," said Sara's father. When the deer was in position, Sara took the knife and began to carefully gut the deer. Her father had taught her the importance of not cutting any internal organs, especially the bladder. He had also shown her how to split the sternum and pelvic bone in half with a saw. This greatly helped cool the carcass and made it much easier to remove the internal organs.

When Sara finished gutting the deer, they tied and "bagged" it up the same way they had done it with the other deer yesterday. Before they started dragging the deer back to the cabin, they looked around and Sara said, "I think we've got all the guttin' gear packed up."

"Yep," said Sara's father. "And we left supper for the coyotes. I'm sure they'll be happy with that."

"Oh yeah," replied Sara. "I'm sure they won't complain about a free meal. Too bad we can't get them to drag the deer back to the cabin for us in exchange for their meal."

"Sled coyotes: interesting concept," said Sara's father. "But in the meantime, we gotta get draggin'. I'll start with the head today." He picked up the deer by the antlers and Sara grabbed the "bag" just beyond the tail of the deer. Then they started dragging the deer back to the cabin.

They stopped every twenty minutes or so to rest, then swapped places and started dragging the deer again. When they got back to the cabin, Sara's father said, "Let's get'im done. I'll bring the truck over and we'll load up and head out." Sara stood next to the deer while her father backed his truck up. When he got close enough, Sara raised her hand to

Saratoga

indicate "stop". Just as Sara's father got out of the truck, it started to rain hard.

"Be careful," said Sara's father, "But let's get this guy loaded before we get soaked." Sara opened the tailgate, climbed onto it and got ready to take the deer by the antlers.

"Got him," said Sara after her father lifted the front of the deer up to her. He was lifting the rump of the deer up when Sara slipped in the truck as she was pulling the deer in.

"You ok?" asked her father.

"Yeah, I'm fine," said Sara. "Gonna look like I wet my pants, but I'm fine."

She got back up and they finished loading the deer into the truck. Then Sara's father looked at his watch and said with a sly smile, "Gettin' late. No time for you to get changed. You'll just have to go the check station as is."

"Yeah right, Dad," said Sara. "It aint that late."

Sara was about to jump out of the truck when her father said, "Wait. Let me help you. Kinda muddy and slippery here."

"Thanks Dad," said Sara as her father helped her get down.

"Yep. Does look like you wet your pants," said Sara's father as he followed her into the cabin.

"I'll get changed quickly," said Sara, "and be right out." She went into the bedroom, closed the door and changed her clothes.

When Sara came out of the bedroom, her father said, "I took a look around while you were gettin' changed, and I don't think we need anything at the store except the ice for the deer and the subs for supper."

"Good," said Sara. "Do you remember what kind of sub I want?"

"Italian with horseradish cheddar cheese."

"Good," said Sara. "I don't know what it is, but the horseradish cheddar cheese just makes the sub super."

"Ok," said her father. "I'll order the subs while you're gettin' your deer checked." Then they made a quick dash through the rain to the truck and got in. Sara's father started driving to the check station while Sara turned the radio on to get the weather report.

"We might have to pack the truck in the rain tomorrow morning," said Sara.

"Not good," said her father. "But at least we're not camping. As you know, I like camping, but there's a lot more to pack in the truck than when we stay at the cabin."

"True," said Sara, "And we can just put anything that needs to stay dry behind our seats in the crew area."

When they got to the check station and got out of the truck, Sara said, "Good. It's only sprinkling here."

"Sshhh," said her father. "Mother Nature might hear you and change her mind."

"Oh come on, Dad," said Sara with a laugh. Then she said, "Don't be like me and forget the ice when you get the subs."

"Two bags of ice and two subs comin' up," said Sara's father as he walked into the store. Sara filled out the paperwork and had her deer checked while her father got the subs and ice. When he came out of the store, Sara took the ice and packed it in the deer's chest cavity. Then she retied the deer's rear legs to the middle of its chest and resealed the "bag" around the deer.

"Our work here is done," said Sara with a big smile.

"Yep," said her father. "Time to go hang him up and relax."

"It'd be nice if we can have a campfire," said Sara. "But if not, we can just sit around the wood stove and maybe play cribbage."

When they got back to the cabin, it was still raining. They hung up the deer as quickly as they could and Sara started the generator while her father brought the subs into the cabin and got a fire started in the wood stove. After Sara came in the cabin, she took some juice out of the refrigerator while her father got cups ready. Sara poured two cups of juice and put the juice back in the fridge. Then they sat down, said grace and ate supper.

Saratoga

"I'm stuffed," said Sara's father as he finished the last bite of his sub.

"I can just barely finish mine," said Sara as she looked at the few bites that she had left. "But I will. I'm sure I'll work it off tomorrow morning loadin' those deer into the truck." After they finished eating supper, they played a few games of cribbage and called it a night.

The next morning, they didn't get up until after sunrise. "Nice to be able to sleep late," said Sara's father as they started getting breakfast ready.

Sara stepped outside for a moment, came back in and said, "Even better that it stopped raining and there's not a cloud in the sky that I can see."

Suddenly the teapot whistle sent out its shrill call. "I'm awake now for sure," said Sara as she took the teapot off the wood stove and poured some water into the bowls of instant oatmeal that her father had put on the table.

"Sausage is ready," said Sara's father as he took it out of the microwave. "Glad we cooked this at home. Much easier than fussin' with it now."

"Yes indeed," said Sara as she poured two glasses of juice. Then they sat down, said grace and ate breakfast.

After breakfast, Sara did the dishes while her father started packing things. When she finished washing them, she said, "Dishes are done. I'll dry them and pack them up."

"Thanks," said her father. "I'm just about done here, but let's put the deer in the truck after you pack the dishes."

"Good idea," said Sara. "Then we can fit our gear around the deer." When Sara finished packing the dishes, they went out to load the deer in the truck. Sara's father backed the truck under the first deer and when he shut the truck off, Sara got in the back and laid out a tarp on the truck bed. Then she and her father lowered the deer onto the tarp and Sara's father slid his hand into the deer's chest cavity and checked the ice.

"Plenty of ice here," he said. "I'm sure the other one will be fine."

"Good," said Sara. "Let's wrap him up." They wrapped the deer in the tarp and then loaded and wrapped the other deer. Then they went back in the cabin and finished packing their gear.

After they finished loading their gear in the truck, they took one last look around the cabin to make sure they hadn't forgotten anything.

"Nice and clean, and nothin' left behind," said Sara.

"Alrighty then, let's hit the road," said her father.

Sara sighed, hugged her father and said, "Thanks for bringing me here Dad. I had a great time even though it flew by way too fast."

"Too fast indeed," said her father, "and I had a great time as well." Then they got in the truck and headed for home.

When they got home, after they unloaded their gear from the truck, Sara said, "I'll go get the garden wagon if you'll go open the hangin' shed."

"Will do," said Sara's father as he walked over to the shed he had built specifically for hanging deer. When he got back to the truck, Sara was waiting with the wagon. Sara's father climbed into the back of the truck and slid one of the deer to the back of the truck. Then he jumped out of the truck and helped Sara load the deer onto the wagon. They pulled the wagon over to the shed and brought it inside. Sara unwrapped the deer while her father got the hanging rope ready.

As they got the deer ready to hang, Sara stroked the deer's head and said, "Well, it's a little bit late, but sorry dude, we need food."

"Yes indeed," said Sara's father. "And since you'll be in school tomorrow, I'll have my brother come over and help me bring these guys to LeMay and Sons for butcherin', and as usual, we'll donate one to the New Hampshire Food Bank."

"Thanks Dad," said Sara.

As they walked out of the shed after hanging the second deer, Sara turned around and said, "One last look. Some good memories here, Dad. I know I said it before, but I had a great time huntin' with you."

"I had a great time too," said her father. As he closed the shed door, he added, "And now it's time to close the door on another chapter of deer huntin' with my dear daughter."

Sara smiled, said "Thanks Dad," and gave him a hug.

12. The Debate

"Last one in's a rotten egg," said Tim as he raced past Sara and into school.

Sara hurried in the door and said, "Wait for me," as she scurried to catch up to Tim. Then she said, "I want to talk to you about our debate."

Sara's parents had instilled in her the importance of the founding principles of America, including the freedom of speech enshrined in the First Amendment. Sara had joined the debating club her freshman year in high school, and enjoyed it very much. Her parents had also taught her the importance of listening to all sides of contention before making up her mind about the subject being discussed.

Sara's parents did not allow any electronic devices to be used during supper time. Instead, they discussed and/or debated things that had happened that day in their lives and around the world. Sara's friends enjoyed coming over occasionally for what they called "supper brainstorms" and would eagerly participate in the conversations. They knew to put their cell phones on vibrate at supper time, because these were only allowed for quick research or confirmation of facts during their discussions.

As they walked down the hall, Sara asked "Have you done any research for our upcoming debate?" She had done some research herself, but she expected Tim to do his share as well.

"Ummm," stalled Tim. "You know I always wait until the last minute." Tim usually did wait until the last minute, but he always came up with good material for the debate, whatever the subject was. Sara knew she could count on Tim to do a good job researching the debate subject, but was frustrated by his procrastination whenever she was teamed up with him. The debate resolution this month was "Resolved: the U.S. Constitution prohibits religious displays on government property."

"How about meeting me at the clubhouse after school, and we can do some research together," suggested Sara.

The debating club had its own room, known as the clubhouse, next to the school library. Several years before Sara began high school, one of the social studies teachers, Mr. Roberts, had started a debating club. Mr. Roberts was a firm believer in freedom of speech and debating. His favorite quote was from French philosopher Joseph Joubert, who said, "It is better to debate a question without settling it, than to settle a question without debating it." The first two years, the club met in the library, but Mr. Roberts knew that could only be a temporary situation. The club members had held several successful fundraisers to raise money to purchase computers, dictionaries, reference books, periodicals and other supplies, while Mr. Roberts lobbied the School Committee to provide funding to renovate an old storage room in the high school next to the library.

Mr. Roberts was having a difficult time persuading the School Committee to pay for the renovations when one of the club members suggested debating the subject in front of the committee. Mr. Roberts thought that was a great idea, and made arrangements for the debate. The students were nervous the night of the debate, but the School Committee was so impressed by their performance, both for and against the proposal, that they voted that night to provide the funds.

The debate in front of the committee had given Mr. Roberts the idea to have the debates in the evening so that parents and other adults would be able to attend after work. Previously, the debates had been immediately after school. The debates were a big success, always lively and well attended by both students and adults. They were held in the high school auditorium, starting on the last Tuesday in September and ending on the last Tuesday of the following May. Starting time was six pm, and the debate usually lasted about an hour. They were even televised on the local cable channel.

Tim's eyes had caught Sara's "don't mess with me" look, and he said, "Ok, Ok, I'll meet you at the clubhouse after school." Tim knew that Sara only used that look when she really meant it, and he realized that she was right. The debate was less than a week away, and besides, he liked spending time with Sara. Tim thought Sara was pretty, even though she rarely wore makeup. Sara did not like to spend a lot of time putting on makeup, so she mostly only wore it on special occasions. She liked to mix things up though, so sometimes she would get all dressed up for a regular school day.

Sara was not very concerned with impressing people with her looks. As she said to Tim once, "I prefer to let my thinking do the talking, rather than my body." Maintaining good health was important to Sara, and if that meant she looked attractive, so be it. An occasional splurge on sweet treats, or her mother's sweet potato pie, would be burned off with a whirlwind of activity, such as hiking, biking, snowshoeing, cross country skiing, swimming, or kayaking. There were very few outdoor activities that Sara did not enjoy.

"See you after school then," said Sara as she walked down the hall to her homeroom.

"Will do," said Tim before he turned to go toward the cafeteria. He had slept late again, and had no time to eat before running out the door to catch the school bus. *Vending machine breakfast again*, he thought. *I definitely have to get up on time tomorrow.*

"Another nutritious breakfast, I see," said Mr. Roberts. He came to the cafeteria every school morning and bought a bottle of fruit juice and a granola bar. He wished the vending machines had a larger variety of nutritious food, but at least it wasn't all junk food. And, the profits from the vending machines went to the Student Activities Fund.

"Well, one out of three isn't bad," said Tim, who had bought a chocolate chip cookie, granola bar and bottle of root beer.

"You better finish that before social studies class," said Mr. Roberts as Tim gobbled down his cookie. "You know the rule; if I catch you eating in class, you bring one of what you were eating for everyone in class the next day."

"I'm too hungry to wait," said Tim, as he wolfed down the granola bar. Mr. Roberts took his food and walked toward his classroom.

Rrrrrriiiinnnnggg!!! *The bell for first class came much too soon*, thought Tim. He guzzled down the root beer, then put the empty bottle in the recycling bin and sped down the hall.

After school, Sara went to the clubhouse to meet Tim. Mr. Roberts, as usual, was there. He always went to the clubhouse after school to correct papers, and work on his student plan or various other school chores. On most days, a member or two of the debating club would stop in just to chat with him, or do some research on an upcoming debate. When Sara arrived at the clubhouse, she was pleasantly surprised to see that Tim was already there. As Sara walked in the room, Tim said, "I've done some research here, and I've got some good leads for either side."

"Great," said Sara. "I know which side of this debate I'm on personally, but that's irrelevant. As you know, we won't find out which side we are taking until just before the debate, so we have to prepare for both for and against." Then she added, "And we'll have to be very well prepared. We're going up against Al Friedrich and Elyse. And as you know, Al is an awesome debater. Very smart, thoughtful, speaks very well, and he's always well prepared."

There were two Als in the debating club, and although Sara thought Al Ellis did well debating, she felt that Al Friedrich was the best debater in the club by far. Although Sara did not have much opportunity to interact with him outside of debating club, she always enjoyed speaking with him. He was very inquisitive and encouraged Sara to be so herself.

"Yes, we must be on our toes to tangle with Al, and Elyse is no pushover either," replied Tim.

"We're going up against a tough team, but we can do it," said Sara.

Then she sat down, turned on her computer and said, "Ok, let's get to the actual wording of the First Amendment regarding religion." Sara knew this by heart and stated, "Congress shall make no law respecting an establishment of religion, or prohibiting the free exercise thereof."

Then she asked Tim, "What do you think they meant by that?"

Tim thought for a moment, then said, "Well, it doesn't really matter what I think, we have to find arguments to bolster either side."

"True, true," said Sara. "I mustn't let my feelings about this issue interfere with our research."

Then she sighed and said, "Even though I enjoy playing the devil's advocate, it would be hard to do this time. I really think they only meant that, basically, there should be no 'Church of the United States'. Setting up a Christmas display is no more "establishing a religion" than setting up a Halloween display would be."

"Well, I know, but..." replied Tim.

"Yeah, we gotta get goin' here," said Sara "Time to drop my true feelings and get to work."

"That's my girl," said Tim, "Let's go get'em Miss Einstein."

Sara decided to google "arguments against allowing religious displays on government property", and Tim googled court rulings on the subject. A little while later, Tim said, "Well, from what I've been reading, a Christmas crèche is allowed on government property if secular holiday images are included in the display."

"Great," said Sara. "That means Hudson is allowed."

"Hudson is allowed?" queried Tim.

"Yes. Hudson, New Hampshire, down by the Massachusetts border, has an awesome Christmas display every year. My cousin lives there, and I've seen the display a few times. It's really cool, especially at night. In addition to the manger scene, they have Snoopy on a doghouse, four soldiers from the Nutcracker, and a pavilion that's decorated with lights. I wish we had something like that here in Lafayette. Decorating the big spruce tree on the common with lights is nice, but it's just not the same."

"Uhhh, we're getting' off track again," replied Tim.

"Ooops. Sorry about that," said Sara as she turned back to look at her computer. "I did find a few things here, mostly claiming that a crèche scene by itself would be, in effect, a government endorsement of Christianity."

They continued researching the subject on their computers, commenting occasionally on items they found. After a while, Sara said,

"Well, it's getting late. How about if we make a pro and con list before we go home."

"Sounds good," said Tim. "I actually set one up before you got to the clubhouse today. We can add to that, and I'll email it to you when we're done today."

"Elizabeth, it's the big one," said Sara with one hand on her heart and the other extended straight out to the side.

"Huh," asked Tim?

"That's a line from an old TV show my parents like to watch, Sanford and Son. From back in the days when TV show producers didn't all think you had to be dirty to be funny. I'll explain it some other time, but basically, I was just sayin' I can't believe you actually did something ahead of time. Glad that you did, but very surprised."

Tim just smiled and said, "My reputation promotes me."

Just like my Dad, thought Sara. *Well, the mixing up words part, but not the procrastination.* Sara played along and said, "Yes, you're promoted to lead typist. So get typin', my man."

"Yes ma'am, on the double," said Tim as he called up the pro/con list on his computer.

When they finished the list, Sara stood up to stretch, looked at her watch and said, "Uh oh, it's getting' late and I forgot to call my father for a ride home."

"I could give you a ride home," said Tim hopefully. He liked Sara a lot, and was even thinking of asking her out.

Sara thought for a moment, then said, "Ok. I'll take the ride, and would you be interested in having supper at my house? My mother is making venison stew."

"I'm game for that," said Tim with a sly smile. He liked playing with words and couldn't resist that one.

Sara laughed and said, "No wonder you and my father get along so well. Two pods in a pea, just like me." Then she added, "Ooops. I should call my mother first. I'm sure she won't mind but I'll call just to let her know you're coming over." She called her mother, then said, "All set."

"Great. I'll text my Mom and let her know," said Tim. "She might be with a customer right now and I don't want to interrupt her. A text will be fine; I do it that way all the time." After Tim texted his mother, he and Sara said good night to Mr. Roberts and left the clubhouse. Then they walked down the hall and out the door to the school parking lot. They started walking out to Tim's car and Tim thought, *Damn. Am I gonna have the guts to ask her out today?* Then he sighed and thought, *but what do I say? If only I could put my feelings into words. Ahhh!! Words, why are you deserting me now in my time of need?*

That was the frustrating part for Tim. He had a way with words, except when it came to asking girls out. There were several girls he was interested in asking out, and Sara was one of them. He thought she was very smart, funny, sexy and just plain fun to be around. When they got to his car he thought, *Better focus on driving now. Don't wanna crack up the car with Sara in it.* After they got in the car, they buckled their seat belts and Tim started driving to Sara's house. On the way there, they talked about the upcoming debate and a few things that had happened in school recently. Tim hinted around a bit about going out, but did not directly ask Sara out.

Sara had mixed emotions about Tim, but did not respond to his hints. She liked him a lot and enjoyed spending time with him, but did not feel comfortable about his tendency to procrastinate. Sara herself procrastinated sometimes, especially regarding laundry, but she felt that Tim's habit of procrastination was too high a hurdle to overcome in establishing a serious relationship.

When they got to Sara's house, they went in and walked into the kitchen. "Smells delicious, Mom," said Sara.

Tim sniffed the air a couple times and said, "Yes indeed it does, but my nose doesn't knows what else is in the stew pot besides venison. Just curious, as I am sure the stew will be deciduous." He had been over to Sara's house for supper many times, and knew that Sara's mother was a very good cook.

"Well, thank you for the compliment," said Sara's mother. She knew Tim well and was used to his playful way with words. Then she said,

"In addition to venison, it has tomatoes, sweet potatoes, green beans, onions, parsnips and carrots."

"And all from our own garden," added Sara with pride.

"Wow," said Tim. "I'm foamin' at the mouth already."

Sara and her mother just laughed and said, "Yep. Just like."

"Me," said Sara's father as he cut off their sentence while he walked into the kitchen. Then he said, "Good to see you again, dueling partner. Are you ready to rumble tonight?"

"I can duel with the devil any time," replied Tim. He and Sara's father sometimes kiddingly called each other the devil because they often played devil's advocate against each other in supper-time discussions. They were on opposite sides of the political spectrum, but they both felt it was important to keep an open mind. Playing devil's advocate was a great way to do that.

Sara's mother looked at the kitchen clock and said, "The stew will be ready in about five minutes."

"Ok. I'll set the table," said Sara.

"Shoo, shoo," said Sara's mother to Tim and Sara's father. Then she playfully added, "Get out the way. Can't you see that Sara and I are busy here?"

Tim smiled and said, "Yes ma'am, on the double," as he and Sara's father walked out to the living room and sat down. Sara set the dining room table while her mother added just a little bit of seasoning to the stew and stirred it in. After they sat down in the living room, Tim decided to ask Sara's father how he felt about religious displays on town property.

Sara's father sighed and said, "Well, you know, it just doesn't make any sense to me. For years and years, before it ended up in court, people were puttin' up Christmas mangers on town commons, and what was the harm in it? Christmas is the only holiday that it is done on. It isn't done on other Christian holidays, and as far as I know, there are no other religions that have displays for any specific holiday. How is that a government endorsement of Christianity? The commercialism is getting out of hand, though."

"Yes, it is," agreed Tim. "They start playing Christmas music way too early." Before Tim could say anything else, "ding-a-ling, ding-a-ling" came the sound of the supper bell from the dining room. "One of my favorite sounds," said Tim as he got up to go to the dining room.

"Mine too," added Sara's father. He waited for Tim to walk by, then got up and followed him out to the dining room.

"I took the liberty of filling everyone's bowl with stew so that it can cool down a little bit," said Sara's mother.

Then Sara brought out a gallon jug of cider and said, "We have other things to drink in the fridge if anyone wants something else."

"Homemade cider gets my vote," said Sara's father.

"Homemade? That's for me for sure," said Tim.

Sara and her mother wanted cider as well, so Sara poured four glasses of cider and said, "I'll put the cider back in the fridge, then we can say grace."

Tim was basically agnostic, but whenever he ate a meal at Sara's house, he always politely bowed his head and remained quiet when Sara's family said grace. After Sara returned from the kitchen and sat down, her mother began saying grace. When she finished, Sara added a few words about a friend in need. Then Tim surprised everyone by saying, "And may everyone in the world learn to live together in peace."

Sara's father added, "And in a country whose government truly is of the people, by the people, for the people." After a brief pause, they all said, "Amen."

Following grace, Sara's mother said to Tim, "That was very nice of you to mention world peace."

"Yes," said Sara's father. "That's something that we all need to learn how to do. I added the part about government because, although we in America are fortunate enough to have such a government, far too many people in the world do not."

"Agreed," said Tim. "And although I am not a practicing Christian, our upcoming school debate about religious displays reminded me that the Christmas season is supposed to be one of peace and joy.

Saratoga

Unfortunately, humanity doesn't follow that script very often, so that's why I mentioned world peace during grace."

Sara, after finishing a bite of stew, said, "Yes, unfortunately, the Christmas season script is not followed anywhere near as much as it should be, and I would love to see everyone in the world learn to live together in peace, but how do we achieve that goal?"

"It's a long and winding road," sang Sara's father to the tune of the Beatles song.

"Oh jeesh," said Sara and her mother.

"Ok, seriously," said Sara's father. "Regarding world peace, one thing I've thought a lot about recently is the United Nations. A very good idea in theory, but in practice, it has not worked out very well, especially in regard to free elections. I think we should start a new world organization whose first requirement for membership is truly free and fair elections within each member nation."

"Au contraire, mon ami," said Tim. "Although it does have some faults, I think the U.N. has worked out very well. It is indeed a long and winding road, but I think the best way to achieve world peace is working within the framework of the U.N."

"Well Tim, I'm with my father on this one," said Sara. "One of the most important principles of the founding of America was laid out in the Declaration of Independence. And that is that governments derive their just powers from the consent of the governed. An international organization such as my father proposes would be a great way to promote that principle. What do you think, Mom?"

Sara's mother looked at Sara's father and said, "I think your new organization is a good idea, but what would we do about the U.N.?"

"That's a tough one," said Sara's father. "The U.N. is so ineffective, I think we should just leave, but it might be a good idea to stick around and try to make it better. I just don't see how we can do that though. The founding principles of the U.N. have been ignored for too long to be able to repair the damage. Free and fair elections are enshrined in the U.N. Charter, but look at how many members of the U.N. have never had a free and fair election. And don't get me started about the U.N. Human Rights Council."

The lively discussion had continued through supper when Sara said, "Yes indeed, it is a rocky road to world peace."

"Rocky road? My favorite ice cream," said Sara's father.

"We do have some of that, and homemade peanut butter cookies as well," said Sara's mother.

"Oh, I'm too full for dessert," said Tim. "The stew was awesome, thank you very much, and every nook and cranny in my gastronomical suitcase has been stuffed with it."

Sara smiled and said, "No room for dessert here either. It'll have to find someplace else to park."

"I'm very tempted, but there's no room in my parking lot either," said Sara's father. "In fact, it's so full, I'd best clear the table and load the dishwasher to keep from havin' to loosen my belt."

"I won't have to loosen my belt, but I do need to get goin' now," said Tim. "I have a homework assignment that was due yesterday, and I really, really have to finish it tonight."

Sara thought about commenting on Tim's procrastination, but just smiled and said, "Well, thank you for the ride home, and I'm glad you enjoyed the stew."

"And I gotta get goin' with these dishes," said Sara's father. "But I just want to say thanks, Tim, for stopping by and I hope you enjoyed sparring with the devil again."

"It's always fun duelin' with the devil, but I'd best be headin' home," said Tim as he stood up to leave.

"Well, it was good to see you again Tim, and thank you for bringing Sara home," said Sara's mother.

Sara got up and walked with Tim to the front door. She opened the door and said, "Good luck with your homework, and I'll see you tomorrow."

"Thanks. See you tomorrow," said Tim. Then he gave Sara a quick kiss on her cheek and disappeared out the door. When he got to his car, he turned to wave to Sara, but she had already shut the door.

Rats, thought Tim. *I hope she's not mad at me for kissing her. Well, I'll find out tomorrow*. He got in his car and drove home, hoping he hadn't messed up his friendship with Sara.

Sara had shut the door, but was still standing there looking pensive when her mother came out and said, "Is something wrong, dear?"

"Oh, I don't know," replied Sara. "Tim gave me a quick kiss on my cheek just before he went out the door, and it caught me by surprise."

"Well, as you know," said Sara's mother, "I don't intrude in your love life, but I'm just curious as to what you think of him. If you don't feel comfortable talking about it, just say so."

"Maybe some other time," said Sara. "Right now, I've got homework that I need to get working on."

"Ok. But you know you can speak to me at any time about anything," said Sara's mother.

"I know. Thanks Mom," said Sara. Then she went up to her bedroom to do her homework.

What do I do about Tim? thought Sara as she started doing her homework. She was working on her geometry homework, but could not stay focused on it. Her mind kept wandering back to Tim. *He's a nice guy, and very smart, but his procrastination is just too much*, thought Sara.

After a few minutes of thinking about what to do about Tim, Sara thought, *enough, enough. I've got to get this homework done*. Then she decided she would not say anything to Tim about the kiss, and hoped he would not try to push their relationship beyond friendship. If he did, she would have to tell him she was interested in friendship only.

Once she focused on her homework and stopped thinking about Tim, Sara was able to finish her homework quickly, much sooner than she had anticipated. *Good*, thought Sara. *I can catch up on my sleep tonight*. She had been working for the past week on a report on hurricanes for her environmental science class. She stayed up late several nights while working on it, and had finally finished it after midnight the previous night.

She went downstairs to say good-night to her parents, then went upstairs, brushed her teeth, and went to bed.

Several hours later, the raucous sound of a blue jay woke Sara up. *Why did I put my alarm on random*, thought Sara? The bird call alarm clock that Sara's father had given her had several alarm options, and one of those was letting the clock's computer randomly select one of the calls stored in the clock. *Well, it certainly woke me up*, thought Sara, *so, up and at'em. Let's go*. She got up, got dressed and went downstairs to the kitchen.

When she got there, her mother had just finished a bowl of cereal and said, "Oh, sorry. You're on your own for breakfast this morning. I forgot I have to bring Grammy to a specialist in Concord this morning, and I have to leave now."

"I think you mentioned that a few days ago, and I forgot as well. That's ok, I'll just make some instant oatmeal and have a pear and maybe a granola bar to go with it," said Sara.

After breakfast, she went back upstairs and brushed her teeth. Then she went to her bedroom, picked up her school backpack and thought, *is everything in here?* She took a quick look at her desk and thought, *yep. All set*. Then she went back downstairs, put on her jacket and went out to catch the school bus. *A little bit chilly today*, thought Sara as she waited for the school bus. *I'm glad I have a sweater in my locker at school. I might need it today.*

When the bus stopped for Sara, she got on and sat down next to her friend Brenda. "A wee bit chilly today," said Sara.

"Yes, gettin' to be that time of year," said Brenda. "Before you know it, the snow will be flyin', and it'll be time to go shoein again."

Sara knew Brenda meant snowshoeing and said, "Yes. Let's do that as soon as we get enough snow."

Then they started singing the Christmas carol "Let It Snow, Let It Snow, Let It Snow", getting through a few choruses while their amused bus mates looked on before the bus arrived at school. They got off the bus, and when Sara walked into school, her friend Naomi was waiting for her.

Saratoga

"Mornin', girlfriend. Got a minute?" asked Naomi as they walked down the hall.

"Sure," said Sara as she looked at her watch, then said, "Times a tickin' so hurry up." Then she quickly added, "Estoy bromeando, mi amiga."

Naomi laughed and said, "Yo se. But gettin' serious here, I have a question or two about a certain someone." Sara had spoken to Naomi recently about Tim, and Naomi knew that, although Sara liked Tim, at this point in time she was not interested in going out with him.

"A certain someone?" queried Sara. "Could that be a certain Tim?"

"Certainly is," said Naomi. "You know me well." Naomi thought that Tim was hinting around to her about going out, and she was definitely interested in dating him, but wasn't sure how a biracial relationship would go over at Lafayette High School. Although Naomi and her family felt comfortable living in Lafayette, not many blacks lived there.

Billy Hamilton was currently the only male black student at Lafayette High School, and Naomi just didn't happen to be interested in dating him. Naomi knew Billy very well, and like most everyone else at Lafayette High School, she had the utmost respect for him. Billy always had a smile on his face and lived by the golden rule. But as much as Naomi respected Billy, she had her sights set on Tim.

"I'm askin' you because I know you'll tell me straight," said Naomi. "Is Lafayette High School ready for a biracial relationship?"

Sara thought for a moment and said, "I think so. I really do. I know it's not the same, but Billy Hamilton is very popular here. He's a good athlete, and that's probably part of it, but he has tons of friends here."

"Ok," said Naomi. "But I have a bigger concern: Tim's parents. I've never met them and I have no idea how they would feel about me dating Tim."

"I think they'd be fine with it," replied Sara. "I've been over to Tim's house a few times, and although this subject has not specifically come up, I really think they'd be fine with it."

"Well, thanks for your input," said Naomi as she continued down the hall to her homeroom class.

"You're welcome," said Sara. She stopped at her locker and took out the sweater. *Glad I have this here*, she thought as she put it on and headed to her homeroom. When Sara went to her social studies class that morning, Tim just happened to arrive at the classroom at the same time as Sara and thought, *well, I'll find out now if she's mad at me for that kiss last night*.

Sara had pretty much decided to just ignore the kiss and see what happened, so she just said, "Good morning, Tim. Were you able to finish that overdue assignment last night?"

Whew, thought Tim, *she's not mad at me*. Then he said, "Yes, I did finish it. I stayed up later than I wanted to, but at least I got it done."

"Good," said Sara as she sat down at her desk. Tim, glad that Sara did not seem to be mad at him, walked over to his desk and sat down.

Wow. That was quick, thought Tim as the bell rang and class ended. He had spent practically the whole class time thinking about the upcoming debate, and about Sara as well. He was glad Mr. Roberts hadn't called on him, because he hadn't paid much attention in class. Still relieved that Sara wasn't mad at him, Tim decided to temporarily set aside his feelings for Sara and focus on their debate instead. He stopped at her desk on the way out and said, "I think we're almost ready for our debate, and if we stay after school today, we could finish our preparation."

"Sounds good," said Sara as she and Tim walked out of the classroom. "I'll meet you at the clubhouse after school."

"Great. See you then," said Tim as he walked down the hall.

"Ok," said Sara. Then she thought, *shoot. Forgot my sweater*. She went back in the room, got her sweater and went to her next class.

After school, Sara went to the clubhouse, but Tim was not there yet. Sara sighed and thought, *well, I hope he didn't forget. I'd like to finish this today*. She talked with Mr. Roberts for a while, then sat down and started reviewing their research.

Then Tim walked in the room and said, "Yep, I remembered…..when I got out to my car. Actually, no, I didn't get quite that far but anyway, I'm here, rarin' and ready to go."

Saratoga

When he sat down, Sara said, "I think we've got enough information here. We just need to organize and prioritize it."

"Yes, we need to priorgatize it," said Tim as he started his computer.

Mr. Roberts couldn't help but laugh at Tim's comment and Sara said, "Yep, that's our Tim."

After a while, Tim said, "Ok, time to write some music."

"Yeah, I think we're all set here," said Sara as she took out some note cards from her backpack. She knew that Tim meant it was time to start writing notes on the index cards they were allowed to use during the debate.

She gave some cards to Tim and said, "You can write the cons and I'll do the pros."

"Awe, you always stick me with the just kiddings," said Tim.

Sara just laughed and started writing her notes while Tim did the same. After a while, Sara heard a knock on the clubhouse door. After he opened the door, Mike said, "Ready when you are, Sara." Then he added, "Tim, do you need a ride home too?"

Sara had just finished writing her notes and said, "I'll pack things up and be ready to go in a jiffy."

"I'm all set, Mike," said Tim "but thanks for the offer." Then he thought, *and don't be askin' Sara out while you're bringin' her home*. He had noticed the way Mike and Sara interacted and was afraid that Mike would ask Sara out before he worked up the courage to do so himself.

"You're welcome," said Mike as he and Sara walked out of the clubhouse and down the hall. Sara had been having some trouble with her Baja, and had asked Mike to take a look at it after school that day. She told him that she needed to stay after school for a short while to work on the upcoming debate and Mike had said he could run some errands and then come back and get her.

When they got to Sara's house, Mike checked a few things on Sara's Baja and said, "I think it just needs a tune-up, and you probably should replace the air filter as well. Shouldn't be too much money for parts, and a couple of pieces of sweet potato pie for my labor."

"Great," said Sara. She knew her mother had just made a sweet potato pie, and Sara was willing to sacrifice her share of it to get her car running well again. Then Sara impulsively gave Mike a quick kiss on his cheek and said, "You're a sweetheart."

Now's the time to ask her out, thought Mike, but before he could say anything, Sara's father walked into the garage and said, "Car trouble?"

Damn, thought Mike. *Just when I was gonna ask her out*. Then he quickly recovered and said, "Nothin' major. Just needs a tune-up."

"That's good," said Sara's father. Then he added, "I hate to be the bearer of bad tidings to the princess, but the queen mother has informed me that Mount Laundry is in danger of reaching the stratosphere."

Sara laughed and said, "The stratosphere? That's a wee bit of a stretch, but yes, it does need to be tackled." Then she turned to Mike and said, "I'm sorry, but I really have to do my laundry now. Seems like I just did it, but the mountain never stops growin'. Plus I've got a lot of homework to do tonight."

"That's ok," said Mike. "I've gotta get goin' too. I'll get the parts soon, and we'll go from there." As Mike started backing his car down the driveway, he could still hear Sara saying "you're a sweetheart" in his mind. Then he remembered the time he had almost gotten hit backing out of Cheri's driveway and thought, *damn, pay attention to the road man*, but he couldn't get his mind off of Sara. *Damn*, he thought. *I wish her father hadn't come out to the garage. I finally get the courage to ask her out and what happens?* He was disappointed at the outcome that evening, but glad that he was finally getting the courage to ask Sara out. He decided that if the opportunity to ask her out did not arise before then, he would try again when he went to her house to work on her car.

After Mike left, Sara went back in her house and started a load of laundry. As she loaded the washing machine, she thought about having called Mike a sweetheart. She sighed and thought for a moment, *I wish he was my real sweetheart* before thinking, *but what about Bob?* Sara really liked Mike a lot, but had some fairly strong feelings for Bob as well. *What should I do?* thought Sara. *Well, now's not the time to decide something like that. It'll just have to wait.*

When Sara finished loading the washing machine, she made a mental note of the time so she would know when to come back and take her clothes out and hang them on the clothes line in their back yard.

After supper, Sara went upstairs to her bedroom and started working on her homework. A little while later, she heard her mother call up from the bottom of the stairs, "Sara, it's eight o'clock. You said your laundry should be done by now, so I'm just lettin' you know."

Sara got up from her desk, went downstairs and said, "Thanks, Mom." Then she added, "Oh, did you happen to hear the weather forecast? I don't want to hang my clothes outside if it's supposed to snow."

"Should be fine," said her father from the living room.

"Ok. Thanks Dad," said Sara as she went down to the basement. She took her clothes out of the washing machine, went outside and hung them up on the clothesline. Then she went back in the house and up to her bedroom to start working on her homework again. She had been working on her homework for a while when she yawned and thought, *Getting tired here. What time is it?* She looked at her watch and thought, *Yep. Past bedtime. I'll finish this Monday in study hall*. Then she shut her computer down, put her books away and went to brush her teeth. When she finished brushing, she went downstairs, said good night to her parents, and went back upstairs to bed.

"Who cooks for you? Who cooks for you?" The call of a barred owl on Sara's alarm clock woke her up on Monday morning. *Up an at'em, sleepy head*, thought Sara as she dragged herself out of bed. She was tempted to get dressed up for school, but thought, *Nah, I'm too tired for that today. Jeans and a shirt will be fine*. She got dressed and went downstairs for breakfast.

After breakfast, Sara helped her mother clear the table, then checked her back pack to make sure she was ready to go to school. Then she put on her jacket, hugged her mother and went out to wait for the school bus. *I hope Mike can fix my car soon*, thought Sara as she waited for the bus. She didn't drive her car to school very often, but liked having the option of doing so if she wanted to.

When she got off the bus at school, Tim was waiting for her. "Are you ready to rock tomorrow night?" asked Tim as they walked into school.

Sara thought for a moment, smiled and said, "Well, if you think about it."

"Uh oh," said Tim. "Think about what?"

"Just kiddin'," said Sara. "I'm rarin' and ready to go."

"That's my girl," said Tim. Then he thought, *maybe I should ask her out now*, before quickly deciding that this was not the time or place to do something like that. Instead, he asked Sara, "Do you need a ride to the debate tomorrow night?" Tim knew that Sara had her own car, but impulsively asked her anyway.

"Thank you, but my parents are bringing me. They don't mind getting here a little bit early," said Sara as she stopped at her locker.

"Ok. See you later," said Tim as he continued down the hall towards his locker.

"Hasta luego," replied Sara.

When Sara got home after school on Tuesday, she did some homework and then reviewed her notes for the debate. A little while later, she looked at her watch and thought, *just a few more minutes, then it's time to take a shower and get dressed for the debate*. There was no dress code for the debate, but Sara felt it helped to dress well for the occasion: no flashy colors or revealing clothing. *All set here*, thought Sara as she finished looking at her notes.

Her mother was in the kitchen, about to start heating leftover stew for supper, when she came halfway up the stairs to ask Sara, "Supper before or after the debate?"

"I had a piece of pie when I got home, so I'm all set for now," said Sara. She didn't like to eat a lot before a debate. It seemed to make her sluggish, and she wanted to be bright tailed and bushy eyed, as Tim

Saratoga

would say. After Sara took a shower, she looked through her closet and decided to wear a modest black skirt with a light green blouse. She got dressed and took a darker green sweater out of her closet and put it on, thinking, *Well, I can always take it off if it gets too warm in the auditorium.*

Then she took her note cards and a pen, put them in the cell phone case that was the perfect size to hold them, and went downstairs to the kitchen. Her parents were there, just finishing their supper.

"If you're ready to go, we can clean up here when we get home from the debate," said Sara's mother.

"Ok, thanks Mom. I'm ready to go," replied Sara.

Sara and her parents put on their jackets and went out to her mother's car. Then Sara said, "Hmmm. Something just doesn't seem right here." She thought for a moment and said, "Oh, jeesh. I left my notes in the house."

"I'll warm up the car while you go back in and get your notes," said Sara's mother. It was a cold December night, but the storm that had been forecast for that day had stayed north of Lafayette, and the sky was filled with stars. After Sara got her notes, she came back out and got in the car with her parents.

"I'm so glad I have heated seats in my car," said Sara's mother.

"Yes, nice and toasty warm," said her father.

Sara, sitting in the back, said, "I don't need a heated seat. My adrenaline is so pumped, I'm plenty warm enough."

"Any butterflies yet?" asked Sara's father.

Sara laughed and said, "Not yet. They always wait until just before I go on stage, and then when I start speaking, they fly away."

"They'd probably carry me away if I was up on stage," said Sara's father. "Public speaking just gives me the jitters."

"Not me," said Sara's mother. "I don't mind it at all." Sara's mother was well known in town as one who would speak her mind at town meeting, no matter how unpopular her words may be. If she felt strongly about something, she spoke out about it.

Soon they arrived at the high school, and Sara's mother was glad she found a parking spot relatively close to the school. It was cold that night, and Sara's mother did not want to have a long walk out to the car after the debate. After they went into the school, Sara's parents went to the auditorium and sat down while Sara went backstage to get ready for the debate. She looked for Tim, but he was not there yet. *Ahh! Tim and his procrastination. Drives me crazy sometimes*, thought Sara. The butterflies had arrived a little bit earlier than usual, and Tim's being late did not help things.

Then she heard, "Relax. Relax. I'm here and all is well," said Tim as he walked up from behind Sara.

She turned around and said, "Yes. All's well that begins well and hopefully ends well as well." Sara and Tim laughed at her manipulation of words and Sara thought, *Good. The butterflies have flown away too*.

Then she started to panic a bit when she saw Tim fumbling around, looking for his note cards, but she breathed a sigh of relief when he pulled them out of one of the back pockets of his pants.

"Time for the coin toss," said Mr. Roberts as he came backstage from the auditorium. "Is everybody ready?"

No one asked for more time, so Mr. Roberts said, "Let's go," and walked out to the auditorium. The debaters followed him, and lined up on stage. As predetermined by Mr. Roberts, Sara and Tim got to call the coin flip. They called heads, but the coin came up tails, and the other team chose to speak first. That meant that Sara and Tim got to choose either the "pro" side or the "con" side. Sara knew how she felt about this issue, but was determined to not let her true feelings interfere with her debate performance. When Mr. Roberts asked them which side they wanted, Sara quickly said, "Pro."

Tim was a little bit surprised by Sara taking the "pro" side, but it didn't really matter to him. After Sara took the "pro" side, Mr. Roberts introduced the debaters and the judges. After introducing the participants, Mr. Roberts said, "The subject for tonight's debate is as follows." He paused for just a moment and said "Resolved: the U.S. Constitution prohibits religious displays on government property." Then he set his timer for four minutes and said, "Team A, Speaker 1, you have

Saratoga

four minutes to present your team's case when you are ready." After Elyse walked to the podium and indicated to Mr. Roberts that she was ready, Mr. Roberts sat down and started his timer.

When Elyse had started walking to the podium, Sara thought, *Great. That means I'm up against the best*. Elyse and Tim would be speaking first for their respective teams, which meant that Sara and Al would each be refuting the opposing team's case. After their refutations came Sara's favorite part: the crossfire. She and Al would alternate asking and answering questions, just as Elyse and Tim would do after each presented her or his case. The crossfire part of the debate could be very daunting, but Sara loved verbal sparring, especially against someone as erudite as Al.

After Mr. Roberts started his timer, Elyse looked at the audience and said, "The opening line in the First Amendment to the U.S. Constitution states that: Congress shall make no law respecting an establishment of religion, or prohibiting the free exercise thereof. This clearly indicates two things. First, there shall be no "Church of the United States", and second, there shall be no laws prohibiting the expression of religious beliefs. Prohibiting religious displays on government property clearly is prohibiting the expression of religious beliefs, thus violating the First Amendment to our Constitution."

While Elyse was speaking, Tim listened and took notes as best he could. Sara listened as well, and checked their "blocks", the pre-written responses to arguments they expected Al and Elyse to make. She put a red check mark next to the ones that they could potentially use, and added a remark or two as needed. Sara's mind was racing, trying to keep up with everything and she thought, *I love this. It's a difficult challenge, but very exciting*. Then she caught herself and thought, *Pay attention, dammit*. She had missed a few words of Elyse's presentation and could only hope that Tim had not missed it as well.

When Elyse finished speaking, she went back to the small table on her team's side of the podium and sat down. Now it was Tim's turn to speak. He gave a quick thumbs up to Sara, then got up and walked to the podium. He briefly looked over the audience, then said, "When government allows the display of religious symbols on government property, it is endorsing and supporting the religious traditions to which those symbols are sacred. Prohibiting these displays protects the religious liberty of all Americans. Government property should not be used to advance one particular religion over all others."

He paused for a moment, taking a quick look at his notes before saying, "Prohibiting religious displays on government property is not prohibiting expression of religious beliefs. These expressions are freely allowed on private property at the discretion of the property owner." After elaborating on these points, he concluded by saying, "President Jefferson himself declared that the First Amendment built a wall of separation between Church and State. Allowing religious displays on government property clearly breaches that wall."

When Tim finished his presentation, he remained at the podium and Elyse joined him there for the first "crossfire" of the debate. For three minutes, they would alternate asking and answering questions. Since Elyse had spoken first, she was entitled to begin the session. She began by asking Tim, "If all religions are allowed to set up displays on government property, how can the fact that only one religion chooses to do so be considered government advancement of one particular religion over all others?"

Tim responded by saying, "It does not matter how many religions do or do not set up religious displays on government property. What matters is the fact that any religious display on government property establishes government endorsement of that religion."

To Tim, the three minutes seemed to go as quick as a wink. When the time was up, he walked back to their table and Sara gave him a quick, "Good job". Then they got ready to listen to Al and take notes as needed.

When Al got to the podium, he briefly scanned the audience before saying, "Allowing a religious display on government property cannot be considered an endorsement of said religion when any and all religions are allowed to set up displays. It is not the fault of the government that not all religions choose to set up religious displays on government property."

Al briefly elaborated on that statement, then said, "Regarding the separation of church and state, the wall that President Jefferson alluded to was intended to keep government from interfering with religions. The wall is there to prohibit the government from preventing the free exercise of religious beliefs by the citizens of America."

Good point, thought Sara as she tried to think of a way to counter that point while at the same time trying to listen to Al and take notes. A very challenging task, but one that Sara loved.

When Al finished his presentation, he turned and briefly nodded at Sara before walking back to his team's table. *Interesting*, thought Sara. She knew that Al was very polite, but wouldn't put it past him to be trying to distract her in order to get a competitive edge. Sara quickly put it out of her mind, stood up and walked to the podium. She began her presentation by saying, "Allowing the display of a religious symbol on government property establishes government support and/or endorsement of the religious traditions of that symbol. The Establishment Clause of the First Amendment clearly prohibits this in order to protect the religious liberty of all Americans. A Nativity Scene on government property sends a message to non-Christians that their beliefs, whatever they may be, are not supported by the government."

Sara briefly looked down at her notes, then continued her presentation. She made what she felt were some good points, but her four minutes were up before she could get in as many points as she wanted to. She didn't have time to worry about that though, because her crossfire session with Al was next.

When Al walked up to the podium for their crossfire session, Sara looked at him, nodded and smiled. *Two can play this game*, she thought before she quickly thought, *focus, Sara, focus*. As in the first crossfire between Elyse and Tim, since Al had spoken first, he got to ask the first question.

Al briefly looked out at the audience, then looked at Sara and asked, "How is the setting up of a religious display on government property establishing a religion?"

Sara responded by saying, "It is not establishing a religion per se. However, one definition of the word establishment is: the action of establishing something. And in this case, it is establishing government support and/or endorsement of that particular religion."

Then Sara asked Al, "Since very few religions want to set up displays on government property, how is allowing this activity maintaining the religious neutrality expressed in the First Amendment?"

Al responded by saying, "As I stated before, it is not the fault of the government that not all religions want to set up religious displays. The government maintains its neutrality by allowing any and all religions to set up displays."

Al paused briefly to think before asking Sara, "How is allowing religious displays on government property breaching a wall that was clearly intended to keep the government from interfering in religious matters?"

Sara responded by saying, "My esteemed opponent has misinterpreted the wall of separation between church and state. This wall is intended to keep church and state totally separated. Allowing religious displays on government property clearly breaches that wall and therefore, religious displays on government property are prohibited by the First Amendment."

Sara was about to ask Al another question when the timer went off. Mr. Roberts said, "Crossfire time is up. Let's move on to summarization." Since Elyse and Tim had spoken first for their teams, they each had a turn summarizing the points their team had made. After Elyse and Tim had made their presentations, it was time for Al and Sara to each put forth the reasons why they believed their team had won the debate.

Al went first and began by reviewing what he felt were the strongest points that he and Elyse had made during the debate. Then he closed by stating, "For our debate this evening, the relevant part of the First Amendment states as follows." He paused briefly then said "Congress shall make no law respecting an establishment of religion, or prohibiting the free exercise thereof. Elyse and I have clearly shown that setting up a religious display on government property does **not** establish a religion and that prohibiting religious displays on government property **does** prohibit the free exercise thereof. Therefore, the First Amendment does **not** prohibit setting up religious displays on government property." Then he added, "Based upon this reasoning, it is clear that Elyse and I have won this debate."

Saratoga

Then it was Sara's turn. She walked up to the podium, scanned the audience and reiterated the main points that she and Tim had made during the debate. Then she stated, "Most importantly, the First Amendment builds a wall of separation between church and state. Setting up religious displays on government property clearly breeches that wall. Therefore, the First Amendment **does** prohibit setting up religious displays on government property." She closed by saying, "And contrary to what my esteemed opponent said moments ago, it is clear that Tim and I have won this debate."

When she finished speaking, Sara returned to her team's table and sat down. Then Mr. Roberts stood up, looked at the judges and said, "Judges, have you reached a decision?" The judges all nodded and/or said yes, so Mr. Roberts walked over to their table and collected their ballots. Then he walked to the podium, counted the ballots and said, "Ladies and gentlemen, we have a close decision tonight. By a three-to-two count, the judges have determined that the "pro" side has won the debate. Congratulations to Tim and Sara for winning, but also to Elyse and Al for making this another great debate." Then he added, "And of course, thank you to our audience for coming here to listen to our debate. We appreciate that very much."

After the announcement of the winner, the audience started to file out of the auditorium. Sara turned to Tim and said, "Well, it was nice to win, but I'm disappointed too." Then she sighed and said, "It's not the end of the world, but I just don't agree with what we were saying tonight."

"But that's why you're such a great debater," said Tim. "You play a great devil's advocate."

"Thanks," said Sara. "And you did very well tonight too."

"Congratulations. You both did very well," said Al as he and Elyse came over to Tim and Sara's table.

The four of them talked about the debate for a few minutes before Sara noticed her parents waiting for her. She laughed and said, "It's past my father's bedtime, so I gotta go. Thanks for a great debate everyone." Then she walked out of the auditorium with her parents and they went home.

13. Shoein'

"Oh shoot," said Sara as she looked at her cell phone. "That's Brenda calling. I'll bet she wants to go snowshoeing."

"What's wrong with that? I thought you liked going snowshoeing," said Sara's mother. They were in the kitchen on a Saturday morning, cleaning up after breakfast.

"I'd love to go, but I have to help Dad shovel the driveway and walkways," replied Sara. About twelve inches of snow had fallen the night before, and Sara's father had gone out right after breakfast to start shoveling their driveway.

"Oh, go ahead and go snowshoeing," said her mother. "I'm sure your father will leave some snow for you to shovel. Call Brenda back, and I'll let your father know you'll shovel later on."

"Ok. Thanks Mom," replied Sara.

Sara called Brenda and said, "I'll shoe over and see you in a bit. I still have to get dressed, but that won't take long. I'll be there in about half an hour." Then Sara went up to her bedroom and got dressed for shoein'. After that, she went downstairs to get her jacket, mittens and snowshoes.

Soon she was on her way to Brenda's house. *Nothin' like fresh snow for shoein'*, thought Sara. She was glad her friend lived nearby, and that they could snowshoe over to the Lafayette Town Forest from Brenda's house. There were lots of trails at the Town Forest, and a variety of terrain there as well.

Brenda had just started putting on her snowshoes in her back yard when Sara arrived and said, "Great day for shoein'."

"Perfectomondo," replied Brenda. Then she finished putting on her snowshoes, and off they went, singing "we're off to see the blizzard, the wonderful blizzard of snow". After about thirty minutes, they arrived at the Town Forest. Then Sara noticed that some windblown snow had stuck

Saratoga

to the bronze plaque honoring the Marquis de Lafayette at the entrance to the forest. She brushed off the snow with her mitten and said, "I'm glad that this is here to remind us of the sacrifices that were made to secure our independence. Far too often today, Americans take our freedom for granted."

"Sad but true," said Brenda.

Then Sara said, "I remember when they dedicated this plaque. I was six years old and my parents brought me here for the ceremony. I remember my parents telling me the importance of the founding principles of our country, and how Lafayette had been so impressed by them that he came over here during the Revolution and helped us to win the war."

"Well, I don't remember the dedication ceremony," said Brenda, "But I know that several of the soldiers who served with Lafayette settled here after the Revolution and named the town in his honor."

"Yes, and Lafayette came here in 1824 when he toured America," said Sara, "And that's when the town decided to build the statue of him on the Town Common."

Then Sara sighed and said, "But it's very frustrating, though, to realize that our country has not always followed through on those founding principles. I will admit that it is not easy, especially as the world, in a sense, shrinks and yet gets more complex at the same time. But I still firmly believe that America is an exceptional country."

"Well, I love our country and would rather live here than anywhere else, but I'm not so sure about the exceptional part," said Brenda. "I mean, right from the get-go, only propertied men could vote, we had slavery of blacks, and women weren't much better off than slaves as far as I'm concerned. Plus look what we did to Native Americans."

"Speaking of Native Americans," said Sara, "They definitely got a raw deal from most Europeans who came here, but keep in mind that, unfortunately, just like far too many other humans, they weren't always nice to each other. Tribal warfare, slavery, human sacrifices; rather nasty stuff." Then she added, "But getting back to exceptionalism…."

Sara had paused for a moment, trying to put her thoughts into words when Brenda said, "Yes. We have some exceptional shoein' conditions here, and we're just standin' here blabbing away. Come on, girlfriend, let's get shoein'."

Sara laughed and said, "Yes, yes, we must get shoein' while the shoein's good." Then they started shoein', taking a trail that eventually went around a large beaver pond. When they got to the pond, they saw that several members of the Lafayette High School boys and girls hockey teams were already shoveling off a space to play hockey. Sara saw her friend Reggie there, wearing his number forty-two hockey jersey. He had specifically asked for that number so that he could honor Jackie Robinson, the first Negro player in Major League Baseball. Sara had heard a little bit about Jackie Robinson, but was appalled when Reggie told her all of the things that Jackie had gone through during his Major League career, especially in his first year.

Sara strongly believed that a person's skin color does not matter; it is the content of their character that counts. She had seen a video of Dr. Martin Luther King Jr's "I have a dream" speech, and sincerely hoped that one day in the not too distant future, his dream would come true.

By the time Sara and Brenda were half way around the pond, enough people had shown up to have a spirited game of co-ed hockey. "Wow! Did you see that? I don't know who the girl with the long blond hair is, but she just put a spin move on Reggie and blew right past him," said Sara. "I'll have to razz him about that on Monday for sure." Reggie was a defenseman on the Lancers boys' hockey team, and was one of the better players, but this girl had made him, as he was fond of saying about opponents, look like mincemeat.

"**Two** spin moves," said Brenda. "She got the goalie with another one."

"Yes, I saw that," said Sara. "Absolutely amazing."

They watched the hockey game for a few more minutes, then continued shoeing. "I love this," said Sara as they climbed up a slight hill. "So peaceful and quiet."

Saratoga

"Yes. It's awesome out here," said Brenda. Then she said "Huh. That's strange. There's a hole in the snow over there." They went over to investigate when suddenly a ruffed grouse exploded out of the snow.

"Whoa! What was that?" exclaimed Brenda.

"I'm not totally certain," said Sara, "But I'm pretty sure it was a ruffed grouse. I didn't get a good look at it, but I know that ruffed grouses will actually dive into the snow, then tunnel in a little bit and make an "igloo" to shelter in. When we got too close, it felt threatened and we saw how they get out of their shelter."

"Wow. That's really cool," said Brenda, "But how did you find out about that?"

"I read about it on a nature blog called "Naturally Curious with Mary Holland," replied Sara. "She has something new every day, and I've read some very interesting stuff there."

"I'll definitely have to check that out," said Brenda as they walked back to the trail. A few minutes later, they came to an intersection of trails.

"Which way shall we go, which way shall we go?" asked Sara. Brenda was about to make a suggestion when Sara's cell phone rang.

"Hi Mom. What's up?" asked Sara.

"Pizza is what's up. Are you in for some?" asked Sara's mother.

Brenda's eyes and face lit up and she said, "Homemade?"

Sara's mother heard her and said, "Of course."

"Then we're in for sure," said Sara.

"Awesome," said Brenda.

"Ok. It'll be about an hour," said Sara's mother.

"Perfect," said Sara. "We're on our way." Sara put her cell phone away and said, "We should be getting' to my house just about when the pizza's comin' out of the oven."

"Fantastic," said Brenda. "A great day of shoein' topped off with the best homemade pizza in the world."

"On behalf of my mother, thank you for the compliment," said Sara "But we'd best get goin' or my father will vacuum the pizza before we even get a bite."

A little less than an hour later, they arrived at Sara's house and she said, "We should be in time for pizza, but that Mr. Hoover acts quickly."

"Mr. Hoover?" queried Brenda.

Sara laughed and said, "I'm just raggin' on my father. He loves pizza and I like to tease him about how fast he vacuums it. I just can't convince him that if he ate it more slowly, he'd enjoy it more."

"Sounds like we'd best get inside then," said Brenda.

"Yes indeed," said Sara as they walked into the house. When they got to the kitchen, Sara's mother said, "Sorry girls, but Mr. Hoover here vacuumed the entire pizza."

"Surrounded by assassins," said Sara's father as he came out to the kitchen. Then he said, "Let's see; four plates, four cups, and a boatload of napkins." He put the plates and cups around the table and put a few napkins next to each plate. He knew pizza was finger food for his family, but asked Brenda, "Would you like a fork for yours?"

"Nah. Pizza's finger food for sure," replied Brenda.

"Time to slice and dice," said Sara's mother as she took the pizza slicer out of the drawer. She sliced the pizza, separated the pieces, and then put the pizza pan on the middle of the kitchen table.

They sat down and said grace, and before everyone said, "Amen", Brenda added "And thank you for the good shoein' conditions today."

Then Sara's father said, "Speakin' of snow, I did **all** of the shovelin' today, so I should get **all** of the pizza."

"Well, thanks for shovelin'," said Sara. "But you could have left some for me to do."

"Tell you what," said Sara's mother to her father. "You can have **all** of the pizza if you'll eat the whole thing right now."

"Careful, Mom, he just might take you up on that," said Sara.

Brenda looked at the pizza and said, "No way. One person couldn't possibly eat that whole thing. There's way too much stuff on there."

"You don't know my father's appetite for pizza," said Sara.

"I'm very tempted," said Sara's father. "And after shovelin' all that snow, I'll bet I could eat the whole thing, but I'll be nice and share."

"Time to quit yappin' an' start shovelin'…..pizza that is," said Sara. "But company first."

"Decisions, decisions," joked Brenda. "Oh, I'll just take this one. They're all awesome anyway, so this'll be fine." She took her plate and put it next to the pizza pan and slid a slice of pizza from the pan onto her plate.

"Thank you for the compliment Brenda," said Sara's mother as she took a piece for herself.

"Oh yeah. We forgot beverages," said Sara as she got up from the table. She opened the refrigerator and said, "We've got OJ, milk, apple juice, a few cans of soda, and a few bottles of Red Stripe beer."

"Red Stripe for me," said Sara's mother. "It's perfect with pizza."

"Make that two Red Stripes please," said Sara's father.

"How about you Brenda," asked Sara?

"Milk or juice and pizza just don't mix well for me, so I'll just have any kind of soda. That'll be fine," said Brenda.

"Me too," said Sara as she got two Red Stripes and two cans of soda out of the refrigerator and brought them to the table. She passed them out accordingly, then sat down.

"So how was the shoein' today?" asked Sara's father.

"Awesome," said Brenda.

"Yes, it was great," said Sara. "We went out to the Town Forest, and I got to play dentist."

"Dentist?" said Brenda with a quizzical look on her face.

Sara smiled and said, "I cleaned off the Lafayette plaque."

Sara's mother just shook her head and teasingly said, "Of all the things you could have inherited from your father…"

"Jeesh, I thought that was pretty good," said Sara's father.

"Speaking of the Lafayette plaque," said Sara as she looked at Brenda. "That reminds me of what I wanted to say to you about America being an exceptional country."

"Well, as I mentioned before, I love our country," said Brenda, "but I just don't think it's exceptional. However, keeping an open mind is important to me. Therefore, I'm willing to debate the subject right now despite being outnumbered three to one."

"Rock, paper, scissors for the advocate?" asked Sara's father.

"Nah. I'll play devil's advocate this time," said Sara's mother.

"Cool," said Brenda. "I love how you guys do that. I know that you all disagree with me on this, but all of you are willing to take my side for purposes of discussion. Great pizza and a great debate; it doesn't get any better than that."

"Since this obviously isn't a formal debate," said Sara's mother, "I'll begin by saying that believers in American exceptionalism seem to think that, due to our position of strength in the world, we should be allowed to act independently of international organizations such as the U.N."

"Precisely," said Brenda, "and those people need to understand that such an attitude is counterproductive, and alienates our country from other nations. And that helps our adversaries to gain ground against us."

"I'll defer to my esteemed colleague to open for our side," said Sara's father, "seein' as how she already has an opening statement prepared."

"Let's see now," said Sara. "Where was I before I was so thoughtfully introduced. As I recall, I was about to pontificate on American exceptionalism. Therefore, I shall do so momentarily." She paused for a moment and her mother cut in with, "Spoken like a true politician, evading the subject whilst babbling on."

"Now, now," chided Sara's father. "I'm sure she's just thinking of the best way to rebut the fallacious statements of you and your mendacious colleague."

Sara smiled and said, "Ok, I'll get right to the point; America is an exceptional country not because of what we have done, but because of how our country was founded and the principles it was founded upon."

"That's all well and good," said Sara's mother. "But actions speak louder than words, and unfortunately, too many of the actions of our country have fallen short of those principles. And the notion that America is the envy of the world leads us to think that the American way is always the best, no matter what. Excessive national pride is a dangerous thing. It leads to arrogance and believing that we know what's best for the whole world. In other words, "it's our way or the highway"."

"And," said Brenda, "We really need to realize that we are not the world's policeman and must work together with other countries in such organizations as the U.N. to achieve world peace." Then she added, "But I do know what's best for me, and that's another slice of pizza."

While Brenda took another piece of pizza, Sara's father held up his finger indicating he wanted to make a point. He took a sip of his Red Stripe then said, "Regarding America being the envy of the world, perhaps envy is too strong a word, but if everyone in the world could choose to live anywhere they wanted, I'd be willing to wager that a very large percentage of them would choose America. And regarding being the world's policeman, I think a better way to put it would be that, as President Kennedy was going to say in a speech that he never got to make in Dallas, "we are the watchmen on the walls of world freedom"."

"Agreed" said Sara. "I like to think of it as being the world's big brother rather than the world's policeman. The big brother I'm thinking of is someone whose younger siblings look up to, and who protects them, but only steps in when absolutely necessary. And it's absolutely necessary for me to take the last piece of pizza. Any objections?"

"I'm all set," said Sara's mother.

"I'd object, but I'm sure I'd be overruled," said Sara's father.

"Due to your past transgressions, the court has been keeping an eye on you," said Sara's mother with a smile. "So don't even think about it."

"Fifty fifty?" asked Brenda.

"Sure," said Sara as she took the pizza cutter and split the last piece in half.

Brenda took a slice, put it on her plate and said, "Unfortunately, too often the watchmen end up being policemen. Attempting to police the world portrays us as thinking we know what's best for everyone and we don't have to listen to others. As I mentioned before, this only breeds more anti-American feelings and doesn't help foster world peace. Working within the framework of the United Nations is the best way to bring about world peace."

"Ay carumba," said Sara's father. "A very frustrating situation, but I just don't think the U.N. is the answer. It's bad enough that our own government is becoming a government of the people by the bureaucrats for the bureaucracy, but the U.N. is even worse. Plus, too many countries just flat out don't comply with the principles as set forth in the U.N. Charter. Just look at some of the countries on the Human Rights Council; China, Cuba, Saudi Arabia and who knows how many other countries that violate the U.N. Declaration of Human Rights with impunity."

"Sad but true," said Sara. "The U.N. looks great on paper, but it has not come close to fulfilling its promise. At least America has come much closer to fulfilling its promise, but far too often we have strayed from our founding principles, and need to do a better job of advancing those principles throughout the world. I try to be optimistic, but it can be very disappointing to realize how many people in the world look up to America yet feel that we have let them down in a sense. Ironically, Ho Chi Minh had a point when America was supporting the French colonialists in Indochina after World War Two. He said, "Is the Statue of Liberty standing on her head?"

Then Sara looked at her father and said, "But on the other hand, as you said, I believe that, given a choice, more people would want to live in America than anywhere else in the world."

"Well, I'll concede on that point," said Brenda, "But not on exceptionalism."

"Well, whether America is exceptional or not," said Sara, "I just wish that everyone in the world could live together in peace, live by the golden rule, and live in a country whose government truly is of the people, by the people for the people."

"And not a government of the people by the bureaucrats for the bureaucracy," added Sara's father.

"Amen to that," said Sara's mother. "And to the fact that we've got homemade chocolate chip cookies if anyone has room for some."

"Well, I'm all debated out," said Sara's father. "But there's no debatin' that I'll always have room for my sweethearts awesome chocolate chip cookies."

"No doubt they're awesome," said Brenda, "but I can only make room for one. And I've gotta get goin anyway. I've got a lot of homework and I need to get started on it soon."

"Just one for me as well," said Sara.

After Brenda finished her cookie, she stood up and said, "As I mentioned earlier, great pizza and great debatin'; it doesn't get any better than that." She put her jacket on, then turned to Sara's mother and said, "And thanks for teamin' up with me for the debate today."

"You're very welcome," said Sara's mother.

"Don't forget your shoes," said Sara as she and Brenda walked toward the door.

"Yes, thank you," said Brenda. "And thanks for shoein' with me today. I had a blast."

"My pleasure," said Sara as Brenda picked up her snow shoes and walked out the door.

14. The Chickadee Family

Sara had kept an eye on the birdhouse she had built and put up, but no one made it their winter quarters. If any birds had done that, Sara's research had told her to clean the birdhouse out in early spring to prepare it for the nesting season. In mid-April, Sara's mother came in to the kitchen and saw Sara cutting short pieces of yarn and piling them on the table. "Ok, I give up. Are you making miniature mittens or socks or what?" asked her mother.

Sara picked up a small mesh bag and said, "I'm cutting these pieces for birds to use to line their nests. When I have enough pieces, I'll stuff them in to this bag, and hang the bag in a tree."

Sara's mother laughed and said, "But won't the birds get mad at you when they figure out the yarn isn't food?"

"No, I'm sure Dad will put a sign up to let the birds know what it is," joked Sara.

"You know your father well," replied her mother with a smile.

One day in early May, Sara was looking out her bedroom window and noticed a chickadee hopping around in the maple tree near her bird house. Sara thought it might be interested in her bird house, but she was doing homework and did not have time to watch the bird for long. A few minutes later, Sara happened to look out the window again and was thrilled to see a chickadee leaving the bird house. Sara quickly got her binoculars and focused them near her bird house. Soon, the chickadee returned, and Sara noticed she had a mouthful of moss. *Yay*, she thought, *someone's moving in to my bird house*. She hoped it was her little buddy, but the bird was moving around too much for Sara to be able to notice whether the bird was missing a toe or not.

Then Sara focused on the inside of her bird house and saw that there was about two inches of material in the bottom of the house, including some of the yarn she had put out in the mesh bag. She couldn't tell exactly what else was there, but she knew that chickadees used wool, hair, moss, feathers and other soft material to make a nest inside a bird house. Instead of weaving a nest with twigs and straw, the nest box is simply filled with soft material to a depth that allows the bird to hollow out a nesting area. When the nesting area is completed, the bird lays her eggs.

Sara was thrilled that someone was using her bird house, but wanted to see if it was her buddy moving in to the house. She decided to go out and sit in her chair near the bird feeder with some seeds in her hand. She sat down in the chair with some seeds in one hand and waited. She was just about to give up when a chickadee landed on her hand. Sara had just enough time to notice the bird was not missing any toes before it grabbed a seed and took off. The bird flew to the maple tree, landed near the bird house and ate the seed. When the bird finished eating the seed, it hopped over to the bird house and went in. Sara was disappointed that it was not her buddy, but maybe it was her buddie's mate. Anyway, she was happy that a bird was using her house. Sara stayed out in the chair for a few more minutes, but then went in her house because she wasn't dressed for the cooler weather. She had run outside without putting on a jacket or sweater, and the cool spring weather drove her inside. When she got inside, she said, "Dad, where's the movie camera?"

Her father got up from his chair in the living room and said, "Lights, camera, action coming right up."

When he came back with the camera, Sara said, "Oh, good. You got the tripod too."

"Yep, and the batteries are fine. I just checked them," replied her father.

"Great. Thanks Dad," said Sara as she took the camera and tripod and quickly went upstairs to her bedroom. She set the camera up at her bedroom window and zoomed in on the bird house until it filled most of the frame. Just then, the female chickadee returned to the bird house, hopped in and settled down on the nest. She wiggled around a little bit, then made some adjustments to the nest area. Sara had turned the movie camera on as soon as the bird had returned to the house. Then she got her binoculars and watched in amazement as the bird laid her first egg. After a while, Sara shut the movie camera off. She left it in place, ready for action, but Sara knew that it could take several days for the bird to finish laying her eggs. Then it would be about twelve days before the eggs started hatching.

When she went back downstairs, her father said, "Catch anything?"

"Nothin' but goose eggs…..I mean one chickadee egg," replied Sara with a smile. "It was quite the show, but it makes me wonder about having kids myself though. A lot of fuss to go through just to have a little brat like me."

Sara's mother smiled, looked at Sara's father and said, "Yes indeed, it is quite an ordeal, but we're very glad to have you in our lives, right dear?"

Sara's father made a pensive face and said, "I'll have to think….only kidding. You are absolutely correct, milady." Then he took his wife's hand and kissed the back of it.

"Silly lovebirds," said Sara.

A few days later, when the female came out of the bird house to be fed by the male, Sara saw there were six eggs in the nest. Sara kept a close eye on the bird house, hoping to watch a bird hatch. Occasionally, she saw the mother turn the eggs as part of the incubation, but she was not able to witness the birth of any of the birds. After the eggs hatched, Sara was amazed at how small the baby birds were, and that they were born without feathers. About ten days after the eggs had all hatched, Sara was showing her mother a video of the young birds in the nest when her mother asked "So when are they going to be able to fly?"

"Actually, they'll leave the nest before they can fly," replied Sara.

"Before they can fly?" said Sara's mother with a querulous look on her face.

"Yes," said Sara. "They'll hop out of the bird house and sort of flutter to the ground. Then they'll hop and/or flutter around on the ground and in low branches for a few days until their wings are strong enough for them to fly. The parent birds will continue to feed and care for them until they can fly on their own."

"What about predators?" asked Sara's mother.

Saratoga

Sara sighed and said, "Unfortunately, predators do take advantage of the situation, but that's just part of nature. After a few days, the fledglings will be able to fly, and hopefully evade any predators."

A few days later, Sara noticed that the fledglings had left the bird house. She used her binoculars to look for them in the area underneath the maple tree, but she did not go out and sit in the yard. She did not want to disturb the fledglings at this critical time in their lives. She got an occasional glimpse of one, sometimes while one of the parents was feeding it. The parents only fed the fledglings for a few days, though; after that, the fledglings were on their own.

When Sara was sure that the chickadee family was no longer using the bird house, she took it down and cleaned it out. She went out to the woods behind her house, opened the side that swung out and emptied out the nesting material onto the ground. Then she scrubbed the inside of the house with a weak bleach solution, making sure she got all the corners and the entrance hole. When she finished scrubbing, she thoroughly rinsed the house with clean water. Then she left the bird house outside in the sun to dry, making sure she left the swinging side open. Her mother had watched her out the kitchen window, and when Sara came back in the house, her mother said, "And now it's time for your favorite pastime, laundry."

Sara laughed and said, "Not today, Mom. I'm done with cleanin'. I'll get to that tomorrow."

Then Sara's father chimed in from the living room with "We've heard that song and dance many times before."

"Jeesh. Surrounded by assassins," said Sara.

"I thought you liked hiking, and mount laundry is right there for the climbing," said Sara's mother with a smile.

"Alright. It's not like its Mt Washington," said Sara "but mount laundry is getting a bit tall. I'll do it now."

Later on that day, Sara checked the bird house and found that it was completely dry. She brought the bird house in to the garage and put it on a shelf. Then she decided to go out to her birdwatching tree stand for a while. She liked the serenity of just sitting quietly and observing nature, whether it was red squirrels chasing each other, birds looking for food, or just leaves falling from trees. Even if "nothing" was going on, Sara enjoyed spending time at her tree stand. She had been sitting there for a while when she saw a sharp shinned hawk come darting through the trees and grab a chickadee. The chickadee had heard the hawk coming at the last second and tried to fly away, but the hawk was too quick. *Awww*, thought Sara, *but, the hawk has to eat too*. Nature's balancing act fascinated Sara and helped inspire her desire to become an environmental engineer.

    She was glad that, in general, humanity had finally figured out that it could not continue to wantonly abuse the earth without suffering the consequences. As an environmental engineer, Sara hoped to help maintain the crucial balance between humanity and nature. She saw it as being similar to whenever there was an overabundance of one species, a natural increase in predators of that species would balance things out. It was like the pendulum of life. The Industrial Revolution had swung the pendulum too far away from nature, but there was no need to slam on the brakes and go back to living in caves. Sara was very confident that humanity could find a way to coexist with nature without abandoning the quest to improve life on earth for all.

    That night, Sara decided to go star gazing from the roof of her garage. She secured a ladder to the side of the garage and carefully climbed up the ladder and on to the roof. She took the pillow she had tossed on to the roof and put it under her head after she laid down. *Someday*, thought Sara, *travel in outer space will be as common as air travel is today. Perhaps even I will be able to fly to the moon, or maybe even Mars*. Sara had considered a career as an aeronautical engineer but had decided to become an environmental engineer instead. She loved being outdoors, and felt that being an environmental engineer would enable her to help protect and preserve the great outdoors that she so loved.

    Sara scanned the sky, looking for constellations as well as meteors. Sara hoped to see at least a few meteors while she was star gazing but she also enjoyed looking for various constellations. When she first started star gazing, she had used a planisphere to help her find the constellations in the night sky, but now she knew them well enough to find them on her own. She was fascinated by their history, and sometimes, her mind wandered into the future, where interstellar travel was common.

Although Sara knew that interstellar travel would not occur during her lifetime, she believed that mankind would eventually explore and colonize various planets and/or moons in outer space. She felt that it was an important mission for mankind, and having colonies in outer space was, in a sense, like having a backup place for humanity to live in case a horrific disaster made Earth uninhabitable. Sometimes, especially while she was star gazing, Sara felt a twinge of disappointment that she would not live to see human colonization of outer space, but she did not dwell on that. Instead, she focused on her desire to become an environmental engineer and hoped that some of the things learned here on earth could be used to help humanity coexist with nature in outer space. She even thought that maybe one day, one of her children could be an environmental engineer on Mars.

Sara had been on the garage roof for quite a while when her mother came out and said, "Earth to Sara, come in please; it's two am."

"What!" exclaimed Sara.

She sat up, looked down at her mother, and her mother said, "Gotcha. In our time zone, it is eleven pm." A few years ago, one time when Sara's mother had asked her what time it was, Sara added three hours to the actual time. Her mother had looked perplexed, and Sara had said, "Well, that might not be in our time zone, but it is four pm somewhere." Sara and her parents liked to tease each other occasionally, and the time zone trick had become part of their repertoire of trickery.

"Well, I suppose it is time to climb back down to reality," said Sara. She picked up her pillow and tossed it to her mother, then carefully went over to the ladder and climbed down off the garage roof.

"Did you see any shooting stars?" asked her mother.

"Only three or four," replied Sara. "But it was awesome just to spend time up there wandering amongst the stars and planets."

"Well, I'm glad that you decided to come home, Dorothy," said Sara's mother.

"Yes, there's no place like home, Auntie Em," replied Sara.

Then Sara's mother said, "Well, it's past my bedtime, so that's where I'm goin'."

"Me too," said Sara as they walked in to the house.

15. Fried Eggplant

"The lilacs are blooming, so it's time to plant the garden," said Sara as she walked in the house with the mail. She had been keeping an eye on the lilacs near their mailbox, and noticed that they had started blooming. A few years ago, her Grampa had said, "It might be an old wives' tale, but waitin' for the lilacs to bloom always worked for me." So every year, Sara and her father waited for the lilacs to bloom before they planted their garden.

"Great," replied her father. "My green thumb's been gettin' an itchy finger."

"Are you going to plant fish again?" teased Sara's mother.

"Of course," replied Sara. "I'm sure they'll sprout soon, and before you know it, we'll have enough for a good chowda." Whenever Sara or her father caught any fish, after cleaning them, they would mix the fish heads, guts and bones in to their compost pile. Her mother kept a container in the kitchen for vegetable scraps and coffee grounds, which she mixed in to the compost pile when the container got full.

"Hmmm," said Sara's mother. "Well, I think it's still too early for my sweet potatoes. I'll wait another week or so, then transplant them." She always started them indoors, and usually waited a week or two after the lilacs had bloomed to transplant them into the garden.

"Well, I'm ready to dig in," said Sara's father. "I'll get the digging fork and the rake, and you can grab the seed packets and seedlings, please."

"Right behind you," said Sara as she followed her father out the door. Her father took the tools from the garage and went out to the garden. Sara brought the seed packets and seedlings out, then set them down near the garden.

Then her father said, "I'll turn over the soil, and you can level it off with the rake afterward, please." Sara picked up the rake and waited while her father started turning over the soil.

"Moistly fair, just like the weather," her father said. "We won't need to water it too much after we finish planting."

When they finished preparing the garden for planting, Sara's father said, "Let's see. I think we had the corn at this end and the beans at that end, so we'll swap those around."

"Yep," said Sara. "And the tomatoes were next to the beans, so we'll put them over there this year." They planted basically the same things every year, but rotated their location to help the garden to grow better. Sara and her father planted the garden themselves, but her mother would help maintain and water it as needed. One thing she refused to do was to sprinkle the rodent repellent around outside the edge of the garden. The active ingredients in the repellent were dried blood, putrescent whole egg solids, and garlic oil. She was glad that the pellets kept the rodents and other animals out of the garden, but could not stand the smell of it. She had sprinkled it around the garden once, and refused to do it again. So Sara or her father would apply it as needed.

Sara was just about to plant the zucchini squash when she said, "Oh, I almost forgot. I bought a Japanese eggplant at the nursery last week when I bought the tomato and hot pepper seedlings. I think I'll plant the eggplant in place of some of the squash. Naomi's mother fries eggplant, and it is absolutely scrumptious. I think you and Mom will love it."

"Looks interesting," said Sara's father as he looked at the eggplant, "but what part do you fry?"

"Oh, Dad, come on now," replied Sara with a sly smile. "You fry the eggs the plant produces from the flowers". Then she said, "Gettin' serious here, Japanese eggplant produces something similar in size to a zucchini squash. You slice it up, dunk it in beaten eggs, and coat it with bread crumbs. Then you fry it up, and watch it get vacuumed by me."

"Sounds good," said her father. "I'll just have to be quick enough to get some before it gets vacuumated by you and your mother."

Her father picked up the tools they had used to plant the garden and said, "I'll put these away, then give you a shower."

Sara looked at him and said, "Huh?" Then she realized he was going to set up the sprinkler for the garden. She sniffed one of her armpits and said, "Nah, I'm all set. Maybe next week."

Her father just smiled, walked over to the garage and put the tools away. By the time he had set up the sprinkler, Sara had finished planting the squash and eggplant. She put the seed packets back in the garage so that they could refer to them to determine when to expect each different vegetable to start growing. Then she went back out to the garden. Her father had just turned the water on and was standing near the sprinkler. "I'm presuming you set the sprinkler for a half spread," said Sara.

"Ooopss. Forgot to check that. We'll find out soon," replied her father.

"Uh oh," said Sara. Sure enough, the sprinkler was set for a full spread, and Sara and her father had to dash out from under the sprinkling.

"I'm melting, I'm melting," joked Sara as she imitated the Wicked Witch of the West in the Wizard of Oz. Sara's father shut off the water and re-set the sprinkler.

"Ok, now we should be all set," he said as he turned the water back on.

"Yep," said Sara. "It covers everything."

"Ok. Remember, we don't need to run the sprinkler very long today," said Sara's father. "When the watering is done, one of us can sprinkle Ma's favorite around the outside edge of the garden."

"Nothing like putrefied eggs to keep the rodents away," said Sara as she held her nose. A little while later, Sara went out and shut the water off. Then she sprinkled the rodent repellent around the edge of the garden, and put the repellent container back in the garage.

When she went back into the house, her father said, "I'd say I can hardly wait for some fresh veggies from our garden, but time flies fast enough. I'll just be patient and they'll be ready soon enough."

"Speaking of veggies," said Sara's mother. "I do have some frozen sweet po." Sara's mother did not finish her sentence before Sara said, "Yesss!! Sweet potato pie. I'll go get the sweet potato from the freezer right now."

"Awesome," said Sara's father as he looked at her mother. "Sounds like you might be willing to make one of the most scrumptious pies in the world."

"Flattery will get you everything, including a sweet potato pie," replied Sara's mother with a smile. At the end of sweet potato season, Sara's mother would make one last pie, and divide the remaining mashed sweet potatoes into pie sized portions for freezing. When she wanted to make a sweet potato pie, she would just thaw out a portion, and the resulting pie tasted just as if she had used fresh sweet potato.

Sara practically flew down the stairs to the basement. She took a package of sweet potato out of the freezer, and noticed that there were two packages left after that. She brought the package back up to the kitchen and said, "Is it ready yet; is it ready yet?"

Sara's mother laughed and said, "If only I had my rolling pin in my hand." Then she said, "You'll just have to wait, and if you don't like it, you'll just have to wait."

"How long should I nuke the package of sweet potato?" asked Sara as she put it in the microwave.

"One minute on power two," said Sara's mother. "It can finish thawing out in the fridge and will be ready when it's time to make the pie tomorrow afternoon."

"Awe, we have to wait until supper tomorrow for your fabulous out of this world pie," whined Sara.

Her mother looked at the clock and said, "Well, I'm tempted, but it's too late to start fussin' with makin' a pie from scratch today." Then she added, "And we have some other out of this world business tomorrow morning. It's called church."

"Oh yeah. That's right, today is Saturday," replied Sara. While the package of sweet potato was in the microwave, Sara's mother looked for and found all of the remaining ingredients necessary to make the pie.

When the microwave bell rang, Sara took the package of sweet potato out, put it in the fridge and said, "I'll be tastin' you tomorrow."

When they got home from church the next day, Sara said to her mother, "Since you're making my most favorite scrumptious food, I'll cook brunch."

"Uh oh," said Sara's father as he looked at her mother. "We better watch out for the extra protein potion in the eggs."

"That "potion" does have egg solids, Dad, and that's good protein. Plus you love garlic," joked Sara.

"I don't love garlic that much," replied her father.

"Well, ok," said Sara. "We do need to save the potion for the garden. Gotta keep those freeloadin' rodents away."

Then Sara's mother looked out the window at the garden and said, "Looks like we might have some asparagus ready. How about a ham, cheese, and asparagus omelet for brunch."

"Sounds great," said Sara. "I'll go check the garden." She went out to the garden with a pair of scissors and found some asparagus that was ready to pick.

"Not much asparagus, but enough for three omelets" said Sara as she came back into the kitchen. "Hot peppers, anyone?" asked Sara.

"Hmmm. Not today," said Sara's mother.

"I'm **always** game for hot peppers," said Sara's father.

"That reminds me," said Sara. "I have to make some bug juice for the garden." Sara's father used to apply chemical pesticides as needed to control insects in their garden, but Sara had discovered a few years ago that she could make an effective insecticide from vegetables. To make the pesticide, she chopped up hot peppers, onion, and garlic. Then she put a half cup of each one in to a blender and ran the blender until the contents became a thick, chunky paste. She mixed the paste and two cups of warm water in a jar, covered the jar, and let it set in a warm location for twenty four hours. Then she strained the mixture to remove the vegetable matter. The remaining liquid was a very effective pesticide.

Saratoga

"Good. We've got plenty here," said Sara as she took a bag of chopped frozen hot peppers out of the refrigerator freezer. She set aside enough for two omelets and her pesticide potion, then sealed the bag and put it back in the freezer. "Ooops. I forgot the ham," said Sara as she opened the freezer again and looked for the diced ham. "Uh oh, no ham," she said.

"Bottom shelf of the fridge," said Sara's father. "I bought some yesterday." Sara's mother hated grocery shopping, and Sara's father did not mind doing it, so he did. Sara got the package of ham out of the refrigerator, and took out some scallions as well.

"Chop chop here, chop chop there, and a couple of tra-la-las. That's how we laugh the day away in the Merry Old Land of Oz," sang Sara as she chopped the asparagus.

"Second verse, same as the first," sang Sara's father as he started chopping the scallions that Sara had put on a plate.

"We'll have to watch the Wizard again sometime," said Sara. "We haven't done that in a while."

Sara's father smiled and said, "I remember when I used to read the book to you."

Sara's mother laughed and said, "I remember the first time you read it to Sara. I couldn't believe that you changed Kansas to New Hampshire and changed Auntie Em and Uncle Henry to my Aunt Alice and Uncle Pete."

"Just tryin' to make the story local," said Sara's father.

"Well, local is nice for buyin fresh veggies," said Sara's mother, "but the next time we had a big thunderstorm, poor Sara was scared out of her wits that we would end up in Oz."

Sara's father smiled an impish grin and said, "Well, sometimes I do get a bit carried away."

While Sara was cooking the omelets, Sara's mother started setting the table. "Cereal, anyone" she asked?

"Ummm, no, thanks. I think I'll just have a piece of cinnamon raisin bread toast," said Sara.

"Sounds good. I'll have a piece myself as well," said Sara's mother.

"Cereal for me," said Sara's father as he looked in the cabinet. He took out a box of raisin bran and put it on the table. Then he put two pieces of cinnamon raisin bread in the toaster and started it.

"Thank you, my dear," said Sara's mother as she finished setting the table.

"You're very welcome, milady," replied Sara's father as he gave his wife a kiss before they sat down to wait for Sara to finish cooking brunch.

"We wanna eat. We wanna eat," said Sara's parents as they banged the ends of their knives and forks on the table.

Sara turned around from watching the last omelet cooking, rolled her eyes and said, "Now children, breakfast will be ready when breakfast is ready." Sara paused for a few seconds and said, "Breakfast is ready, except for the." Before Sara could finish her sentence, the bread popped out of the toaster. Sara's mother got up from the table and buttered the toast while Sara brought the omelets over to the table.

"Beverages?" asked Sara's father.

"Milk for me," said Sara.

"Apple cider, please," said Sara's mother. Sara's father brought the beverage containers to the table and handed the milk to Sara. Then he poured two glasses of cider, and started pouring cider on his cereal.

"Dad, what are you doing!" exclaimed Sara.

"Just thought I'd try something different," he replied. "You know, fruit on fruit. Raisins are fruit, and I just thought the cider would like to mix with a fellow fruit."

"You're a fruit alright," joked Sara.

"He certainly is," added Sara's mother with a smile. "But a very lovable one."

After Sara's father put the beverage containers back in the refrigerator, he came over to the table and sat down. They said grace, and ate breakfast. When they finished eating, Sara's father said, "Well, since Sara cooked breakfast, and my wonderful wife is going to make her scrumptious sweet potato pie, it looks like I'm stuck doing dishes again."

"Again," said Sara mockingly with a smile. "When was the last time you did dishes?"

"Well, I've been very busy lately," her father replied.

"Yeah, busy weaslin' out of doing housework," joked Sara's mother.

"Surrounded by assassins," sighed Sara's father as he got up and started clearing the table.

A few days later, Sara and her father were out checking their garden when Sara said, "Eggplant is coming along nicely. Two eggs about halfway ready and more on the way as well."

"Tomatoes are doing well, too," said her father.

Then Sara went over and checked the bean plants and said, "Uh oh. Looks like I'm gonna need some hot sauce here."

"Bugs?" asked her father.

"Yep," replied Sara as she walked toward the garage to get her bug juice.

When she got back to the garden, her father said, "Everything else looks fine. Only the beans need your special concoction."

"Good," said Sara. Her father went back in to the house while Sara sprayed the bean plants. After she finished spraying, Sara put her bug juice back in the garage and was about to go back in the house when she thought, *when was the last time we sprinkled Mom's favorite around the garden? Maybe I should do that now.* She took the rodent repellent and went back out to the garden. She had just started sprinkling the repellent when she felt what seemed like rain. Then it stopped, and Sara realized that someone had turned the sprinkler on. She dashed away from the garden just in time to miss the next wave from the sprinkler, and saw her father standing near the outdoor faucet with an impish grin on his face.

"Payback for sprinklin' hot pepper flakes on my banana split last week," said her father.

"But you love spicy food," teased Sara.

"Actually, it wasn't bad" said her father. "But I'm glad you didn't put too much on, and it did give it a nice little zing."

"Interesting," said Sara. "Maybe I'll try that myself sometime."

A week or two later, Sara went out to the garden on a Saturday morning to check her eggplant. When she came back in the house, her mother said, "You know, I'd like something different for supper tonight."

"How about fried eggs?" replied Sara.

"Fried eggs? Well, that is different, but I'll pass on that," said Sara's mother.

Sara laughed and said, "A different kind of eggs; eggplant eggs. They're finally ready. I'll fry them up, just like Naomi's mother showed me. It's a bit of a fuss, but very well worth it."

When Sara's father came out from the living room and saw the clock, he said, "Happy anniversary honey."

"Well thank you dear, and happy anniversary to you as well," replied Sara's mother.

Sara knew without looking at the clock that it was nine twenty six. September twenty sixth was her parent's anniversary, and whenever either of them noticed that the time was nine twenty six, whomever noticed it would say "happy anniversary" and the recipient would respond accordingly.

Then Sara's father said, "I heard we're having purple eggs for supper tonight; that'll be different. We haven't had ham in a while, and I could get some today while I'm grocery shopping. Should I add anything else to the list before I leave?"

"A loaf of sourdough bread. We can have toast to go with our ham and purple eggs," said Sara's mother.

"I'll add those things to the list," said Sara's father. "Then I'm off to see the grocer, the wonderful grocer of Oz."

"Ok Dad" said Sara. "But watch out for those lions and tigers and bears."

"And beware the Wicked Witch of the West as well," added Sara's mother.

Later that day, Sara and her mother decided to go for a walk. As they walked down the street, Sara's mother said, "I am so glad that you decided to go to Whispering Pines College. It's a great school with an excellent environmental engineering department, and it's close to home."

"Well, it was a difficult decision for all of us," said Sara. "Even with the scholarship money I'll be getting, I know it will be a financial strain for you and Dad."

"We'll manage," said Sara's mother. "Your education is very important to us, and if we have to make do with a little bit less, so be it." Then she added, "But I'm very happy that you'll be able to come home for weekends more often than if you were all the way across the country."

"Yes, I'll enjoy coming home as often as I can," replied Sara. "But education comes first, and I do have time commitments for ROTC as well."

"I know, but it just won't be the same at home without you," said Sara's mother.

Sara gave her mother a hug and said, "I know, but I can't be your little girl forever."

Sara's mother sighed and said, "Time; the older you get, the faster it seems to go."

"True, true," said Sara. "Even for me."

A little while later, Sara heard something and said, "Mom, are you crying?"

Her mother wiped her eyes and said, "I'm trying not to, but it's hard. I'm going to miss my little girl."

Sara chose her words of reply carefully, because she knew her mother was upset. "Yes, and your little girl is going to miss you as well," said Sara "But I won't be that far away and I promise I'll come home as often as I can."

"Cross your heart promise?" asked Sara's mother.

"Yes, cross my heart promise," replied Sara. They continued walking for a while, then decided to head back to the house.

When they got home, Sara's father was raking the front yard and said, "Uh oh, I just heard some grumblin'."

Sara looked up at the sky and said, "There's not a cloud in sight."

Then Sara's mother said, "That's your father hinting that he's hungry."

"When my stomach talks, I listen," said Sara's father. Then he added, "What can I do to help with the purple eggs?"

Sara looked at her watch and said, "Wow, later than I thought. Definitely time to start fryin'." They went in to the house and Sara's father helped Sara get things ready to fry the eggplant.

While they did that, Sara's mother said, "Let me know when the "eggs" are almost done, and I'll make the toast."

"Ok" said Sara's father. Then he added, "Oh yeah, I bought some sliced ham at the deli today, so that's all set. It's in the fridge, on the bottom shelf."

Sara had just about finished frying the eggplant when she remembered the toast. "Time for toast, Mom," said Sara.

Her mother came out from the living room and said, "How many slices for you Sara?"

"One's fine for me," said Sara.

"Two for me please," said Sara's father. Then he came out from the living room, set the table and took the ham out of the refrigerator.

"Thank you for helping with supper, dear," said Sara's mother.

"You're welcome, milady," replied Sara's father as he took her mother's hand and kissed the back of it.

"Silly lovebirds," said Sara with a smile. Then she remembered the time Mike Senecal had kissed her on the back of her hand and thought …..*Sara Senecal. It does have a nice ring to it*. She smiled again and thought *I might be falling in love. But what about college? Well, at least I'm not going too far away. Whispering Pines is less than a two hour drive from here, so maybe Mike can….*

"Earth to Sara; come in please," said Sara's father as he noticed the faraway look in Sara's eyes.

"Just thinkin' pleasant thoughts," said Sara. She finished frying the last of the eggplant and took it out of the skillet. Then she shut the skillet off and brought the fried eggplant over to the table.

Sara's mother finished making the toast and brought it over to the table. Then they sat down, said grace, and started eating. "Wow! This is not just good, it's scrumptily delicious," said Sara' mother after she had eaten a piece of eggplant.

"Best eggs I've ever tasted," said Sara's father.

"Thanks Dad, for helping me cook it," said Sara "And I'm glad you and Mom both like it. I'll be sure to let Naomi's mother know."

Throughout the summer and into fall, Sara and her parents enjoyed the bounty from their garden. Sara's father made pickles not only from cucumbers, but from beets as well. And of course, Sara's mother made her famous sweet potato pie. She always donated one to the Lafayette Old Home Day celebration in late September, and the raffle tickets for it were one of the best sellers at the fair. Sara and her parents also gave a variety of vegetables to their local food bank. They felt blessed to have such a bountiful garden, and wanted to share with others less fortunate than them.

"Wow. I can't believe it's almost time to carve my buddy here," said Sara as she and her friend Naomi looked at Sara's pumpkin plant one Saturday afternoon in early October. Sara had come home from college for the weekend, and her friend Naomi had come over to visit.

Every year, Sara grew a pumpkin plant so she would have a pumpkin to carve for Halloween. She usually got three or four pumpkins from the plant, and had told Naomi she could have one. "I'm presuming you're keeping the biggest one; that one over there," said Naomi as she pointed to a large pumpkin.

Sara laughed and said, "I grew, I choose, but you can have any other one you want."

"I'll take that one. It's almost as big, and I'm sure it will make a great jack-o'-lantern," said Naomi as she pointed to a pumpkin.

"Ok. I'll save that one for you, and bring the other two to the food bank," said Sara. "Or maybe I'll bring one over to Joe's house and help him carve it. Unfortunately, his arthritis won't let him carve it himself."

"Let me know when you go," said Naomi. "I'd like to meet Joe. He sounds like a cool dude."

"Will do," said Sara. Then she walked over to her eggplant and said, "Two left here. You can have them, and tell your mother thanks for gettin' me addicted……… to fried eggplant."

Naomi laughed and said, "You had me wonderin' for a second when you said addicted, but I know what you mean. I could eat fried eggplant all day."

A week later, Sara delivered the pumpkin to Naomi, stayed to visit for a while, and then came home to carve her pumpkin. She covered the kitchen table with newspaper, then went out to the garden, picked her pumpkin, and brought it in to the kitchen. After she cut the top and scraped out the seeds and string, she was trying to decide what to carve in her pumpkin when her father walked in from the living room.

"Come home from college to make a big mess, I see," said Sara's father.

Sara knew he was only kidding and said, "I need a little help here, Dad, I'm stumped. I don't know what to carve in my pumpkin."

"Well, carve a stump then. Or maybe you could carve your mother riding her new vehicle," said her father with a sly smile.

"I heard that," said Sara's mother as she came up the basement stairs. "You'd best be careful what you say or I'll turn you in to a pumpkin and carve you to pieces."

"Hmmm," said Sara as she thought. Then she said, "I've got it. Cinderella's carriage."

"Great idea," said Sara's father. "But I'd best be careful of what I say, or your mother will turn me into…"

"You bet I will," joked Sara's mother before her father could finish the sentence.

Saratoga

"Now children," admonished Sara as she went up to her bedroom to google "pictures of Cinderella's carriage" on her computer. She found an image she liked, printed it, and brought it downstairs to the kitchen. She took a fine point felt pen and drew an image of the carriage on her pumpkin. Then she carefully carved the pumpkin and removed the pieces as she cut them out. When she finished carving the pumpkin, she took a tea candle and put it on the flat spot she had scraped on the inside bottom of the pumpkin.

"Its show time," said Sara. By the time Sara had finished carving her pumpkin, it was dark outside. Sara's parents walked into the kitchen just as Sara lit the candle in the pumpkin.

Sara's mother shut off the kitchen light and said, "Nice job."

Sara's father was about to say something, then said, "Nope. Nope. I'd best be careful or I'll be turned in to a pumpkin. So I'll just say "great job Sara" and leave it at that."

"Thank you both," said Sara. Then Sara's father turned the kitchen light back on, and Sara took her pumpkin outside and put it on a tree stump near the front porch. Her parents came out of the house, and they walked down the driveway a bit before turning around to admire Sara's jack o' lantern. Then Sara took a selfie of her and the jack o' lantern and posted it on Facebook.

The End

Acknowledgments

First of all, I want to acknowledge my wonderful wife Brenda, and thank her for her patience while I wrote this book. There were many times when she wanted to do something with me, such as hiking, biking or kayaking, and I just had to say no, because I needed to work on the book. She was very understanding, and I appreciate that very much.

My mother-in-law Rita Lyon was very helpful with grammatical issues. She knows all the rules, and kindly pointed out errors to me.

My sister Chris helped me get through a difficult part in the very beginning of writing this book. She came up with some great suggestions on how to get things started.

Mike Goyette (Pete's Gun and Tackle, Hudson, NH) and Douglas M. Dack (NH Guns and Ammo, Londonderry, NH) were very helpful with the chapter on hunting. Scott Watson (one of my wife's co-workers) was also very helpful with this subject.

Although I ended up not having Sara actually join the ROTC in this book, Joseph LaPlante (University of NH ROTC) generously took the time to explain the program to me.

Claude Vezina, a hiking buddy of my wife and I, read the rough draft and gave many encouraging comments.

Mary Holland has an awesome blog, Naturally Curious. It is very interesting and informative, with a new post every day.

And last but definitely not least, Eric Van Der Hope was tremendously helpful in navigating the setup process for the softcover version of this book.